I0647393

POPULAR PUBLICATIONS

FACSIMILE EDITIONS

Terror Tales #2
(October 1934)

Starting in 1934, editor (and publisher) Harry Steeger unveiled *Terror Tales*: perhaps the flagship magazine in Popular Publications' so-called "Weird Menace" lineup of titles. Running for almost 50 issues, *Terror Tales* showcased some of the best suspense, mystery and terror stories to see print in the pulps. This facsimile of the October 1934 issue contains stories by Carl Jacobi, G.T. Fleming-Roberts, Wyatt Blassingame, and Hugh B. Cave, among others.

Authors:

Wyatt Blassingame, G.T. Fleming-Roberts, Carl Jacobi, Frances Bragg Middleton, Hugh B. Cave, James A. Goldthwaite

Illustrators:

John Newton Howitt, Amos Sewell

"THERE'S ONE MAN
WE'RE GOING TO KEEP"

"ED WILSON, there, is one of the most ambitious men in the plant. I notice he never fools away his spare time. He studies his International Correspondence Schools course every chance he gets.

"It's been the making of him too. He hasn't been here nearly so long as Tom Downey, who was laid off yesterday, but he knows ten times as much about this business.

"I'm going to give him Tom's job at a raise in salary. He's the kind of man we want."

How do you stand in your shop or office? Are you an Ed Wilson or a Tom Downey? Are you going up? *Or down?* No matter where you live, the International Correspondence Schools will come to you. No matter what your handicaps or how small your means, we have a plan to meet your circumstances. No matter how limited your previous education, the simply written, wonderfully illustrated I. C. S. textbooks make it easy to learn.

This is all we ask: Without cost, without obligating yourself in any way, put it up to us to prove how we can help you. Just mark and mail this coupon.

1

Volume One   October, 1934   **Number Two**

FEATURE-LENGTH MYSTERY NOVEL

THREE MYSTERY-TERROR NOVELETTES

SHORT TERROR TALES

— AND —

Cover Painting by John Howitt

Story Illustrations by Amos Sewell

Published every month by Popular Publications, Inc., 2256 Grove Street, Chicago, Illinois. Editorial and executive offices, 205 East Forty-second Street, New York City. Harry Steeger, President and Secretary, Harold S. Goldsmith, Vice President and Treasurer. Entry as second-class matter pending at the post office at Chicago, Ill., under the Act of March 3, 1879. Title registration pending at U. S. Patent Office. Copyright, 1934, by Popular Publications, Inc. Single copy price 10c. Yearly subscriptions in U. S. A. $1.00. For advertising rates address Sam J. Perry, 205 E. 42nd St., New York, N. Y. When submitting manuscripts kindly enclose stamped self-addressed envelope for their return if found unavailable. The publishers cannot accept responsibility for return of unsolicited manuscripts, although care will be exercised in handling them.

4

MOULDING A MIGHTY ARM

COMPLETE COURSE ON ARM BUILDING

MOULDING A MIGHTY ARM
By GEORGE F. JOWETT

THIS BOOK

SHOWS HOW TO BUILD A MIGHTY ARM AND A 16 INCH BICEP

ONLY 25¢

GET AN ARM of might with the power and grip to obey your physical desires. I have taken weaklings whose arms were scrawny pieces of skin and bone and in a very short time developed them into men of powerful proportions with bulging biceps and brawny forearms. He-men with strong, solid arms of power that are respected by men and admired by women! I don't mean just a 16-inch bicep but a 15-inch forearm and a powerful 8-inch wrist.

PROVEN, SCIENTIFIC TRAINING!

This course is specially planned to build every muscle in your arm! It has been scientifically worked out for that purpose. Many of my pupils have developed a pair of triceps shaped like a horseshoe, and just as strong, and a pair of biceps that show their double head formation. The sinewy cables between the biceps and elbow are deep and thick with wire cable-like ligaments. The forearm bellies with bulk, the great supinator lifting muscles become a column of power, and their wrists are alive and writhe with cordy sinew. Start now to build a he-man's arm!

THE SECRETS OF STRENGTH REVEALED

You can't make a mistake. The reputation of the strongest armed man in the world stands behind this course. I give you my secret methods of strength development illustrated and explained as you like them. Mail your order now while you can still get this course at my introductory price of only 25c.

I will not limit you to the arm. Try any one of my test courses listed below at 25c. Or, try all of them for only $1.00.

Rush the Coupon Today!

I will include a *FREE COPY of "NERVES OF STEEL, MUSCLES LIKE IRON"*. It is a priceless book to the strength fan and muscle builder. Full of pictures of marvelous bodied men who tell you decisively how you can build symmetry and strength the Jowett Way! Reach Out ... Grasp This Special Offer!

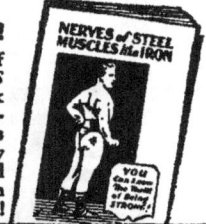

FREE BOOK WITH PHOTOS OF FAMOUS STRONG MEN

JOWETT INSTITUTE OF PHYSICAL CULTURE

Dept. 109Kc, 422 Poplar St., Scranton, Pa.

George F. Jowett: Send, by return mail, prepaid, the courses checked below for which I am enclosing———

- ☐ Moulding a Mighty Arm, 25c
- ☐ Moulding a Mighty Back, 25c
- ☐ Moulding a Mighty Grip, 25c
- ☐ Moulding a Mighty Chest, 25c
- ☐ Moulding Mighty Legs, 25c
- ☐ Strong Man Stunts Made Easy, 25c
- ☐ All 6 Books for $1.00.

GEORGE F. JOWETT
"Champion of Champions"
Winner of many contests for strength and physical perfection!

Name ——————————— Age———

Address ————————————————

5

VILLAGE of the DEAD

By Wyatt Blassingame
(Author of "Dead Man's Bride")

*Ann Meadows had come home .... But the quiet village she had known
was now a grim place where terror stalked—and death peered in with
hungry eyes on sleeping victims. Whence the townspeople had fled,
leaving those mindless creatures to roam at will through its
dusty streets and darkened houses, seeking—seeking with their
age-old lust for human flesh and blood.*

THE train pulled rapidly away
from the shack-like station.
Standing alone on the narrow
platform, Ann Meadows watched the
lighted windows glide past while a
feeling of distaste and loneliness
grew upon her. Then the train was
gone into the creeping, dusky twilight.

She should be happy, Ann
thought, not nervous and half afraid,
for she was coming home for the

Complete
Mystery-Terror Novel

first time in five years. But it wasn't the
sort of homecoming of which she had
dreamed. Tom wasn't with her, and her
sister's letter with its almost hysterical
note and the strange invitation to stay
away. . . .

Footsteps padded on the platform and
Ann turned quickly. A man in his middle fifties, his white hair almost a halo
above his round, kindly face, was coming
toward her, smiling. But as Ann ran
toward him, her hands outstretched, she
saw that his smile was tense, unnatural.

Bob Wilson's blue eyes twinkled as he looked at her, but there was a strained note in the cordiality of his greeting. "Gracious, child," he said, "when I saw you last you were seventeen and afraid to leave home. And now you come back prettier than ever with that red hair of yours. And a renowned pianist with a concert in Town Hall and all the New York papers raving about you. I was afraid you wouldn't speak to persons in the home town." He caught his words then, stopped short as if afraid of what he might say. Almost under his breath he added, "There aren't many persons left to speak to. . . ."

Ann's fingers tightened convulsively. "What—what's happening at home?" she demanded. "Marie's letter was so—so strange. Asking me not to come home, saying that everybody was leaving town. That's why I came so quickly. Is there—anything wrong? Is Dad . . .?"

Robert Wilson shook his white head. Ann had known him since she was a child, had gone to him with her troubles as everyone in the little town of Livingston had done. Now the old man's face was gray in the twilight. "I don't know what's wrong with the town," he said softly, "but nothing's happened to your father. Yet I wish you—you had done like Marie told you and stayed away."

Ann Meadows felt a weird, unreasoning fear crawl like a scaly thing along her slim legs and up her spine, as she watched the old man's face working, felt his fingers tremble against hers. He said, "Your sister told me you were coming on the train and asked me to meet you. She wants me to—to drive you over to York for the night, persuade you to go back to the city tomorrow. Won't you?" he finished with an eager, almost plaintive light in his eyes.

For a moment Ann stood looking at him and feeling that strange fear deep in her breast. Then she thought of her father, of his square, broad face and high brow. And of her sister Edith, who was two years older than Ann and who had been paralyzed since an accident five years before. That was one reason Ann had wanted to bring Tom Adams with her. He was a young doctor, but his reputation was growing, and Marie, Ann's younger sister, had written that the local doctor said it would mean death to move Edith at all.

"Won't you go over to York for the night?" the old banker asked again.

Ann squared her slim shoulders, raised her small, oval chin defiantly. "I don't know why all of you are trying to run me away, Mr. Bob, but I'm going home. I'm going to see what's the trouble."

The old man's hands quivered against hers. "I told Marie you'd say that. But we both hoped. . ." Fear was coming into his face, but he shook it off and tried to smile. "I'll get your bags," he said.

THE gravel road lay through flat, piney woods country. The noise of the motor, the whir of the tires on gravel, were the only sounds as they started the five-mile ride to Livingston. The banker drove slowly and Ann smiled as she remembered how cautious the old man had always been. A little suspicious of automobiles even yet, she thought.

"There've been strange things happening in Livingston for the past two weeks," Wilson said. "Perhaps you'll think I'm crazy. Maybe we're all crazy." He paused, added, "You remember those half-breeds that live along the edge of Crazy Man's Swamp?"

"Yes." Everyone in Livingston knew the stories, but few persons ever saw one of the swamp-dwellers. Ann didn't remember having seen but one. Years ago when she was squirrel hunting in Crazy

Man's Swamp with her father, she had heard something behind her and suddenly turning, gazed into the most hideous and abnormal face she had ever seen. It was a long, dark face with a twisted mouth. Close-set black eyes and black hair above an unbelievably narrow forehead. She had screamed and the man had vanished into the swamp the way a partridge can dive into brown sage and disappear.

Her father had told her about the people then. Two hundred years ago Spanish soldiers had deserted, married into a group of degenerate Creek Indians. Since then they had lived in the same swamp, doing a little farming around its edges, fishing, hunting. Countless intermarriages, malaria and other diseases had reduced the entire group to a large family of half-wits. A psychologist had come here once to study them, but he hadn't been able to learn much. They were a sullen, lonely people. Many persons in Livingston claimed that they murdered and scalped persons caught in the swamp as the Indians had done years ago. Others said they were harmless. There was a small wagon road that led to their village, but nobody ever went there, and they practically never came out of the swamp.

"What about them?" Ann asked.

The old man stirred restlessly in his seat and the car moved more slowly than ever. He said, "Well, about a month ago, some of them began to come to town. Persons saw them slipping around fences and down back streets. They never said anything to anybody, but they kept coming, more and more of them, slipping in and then out again. What they were after I don't know. And then—" The old man swallowed harshly—"then things started happening to the townspeople."

Ann was leaning toward him. Her hands were clenched in her lap and her eyes wide. "What things?" she asked.

"There were just rumors at first. Per-sons claiming they heard noises and saw things. Then one afternoon two weeks ago old John Perkins appeared suddenly in the middle of Main Street. He had blood all over his face and he was running, staggering like he was drunk. Everybody saw him, but he just kept running until he got right in front of Doctor Mc-Gruder's office. Then he pitched over on his face.

"I was at home, but Dan McGruder called me. He said Perkins had all his ribs cracked, but had died of poison of some kind. Dan said he was coming right out to see me. Several persons saw him leave his office. He—he—" The old man stopped.

"Yes." Again the girl whispered unconsciously.

"He never got to my house. He just disappeared. Old Mrs. Calloway claimed she saw him two nights later slipping along Jenkins Alley, but by that time everybody in town was seeing things. Two other persons had died. Ben Larkin is the town marshal now. He can't find anything. Those half-breeds kept showing up and everybody got to saying they were causing the trouble."

"But Mr. Bob. . ." Horror and incredulity were in the girl's voice. "Why—why don't they call out the National Guard or something?"

THE old man turned his face toward her for a moment, then looked back at the road. "Maybe you've forgotten how folks do things in this part of the country," he said. "We've always been able to take care of ourselves. I—I did suggest getting help but Ben Larkin jumped on me. Said as long as he was town marshal we didn't need any troops. Folks all seemed to think that way for awhile, but things kept getting worse. The half-breeds kept showing up and the idea that some kind of ghosts were at work got around. It sounds foolish, but—but just about everybody has left town."

Darkness had set in now and from far off to the right came the eerie chirping of crickets, the mournful cry of a whippoorwill. The white lights of the car jabbed through the night, touched on the decaying timbers of a short bridge. Beyond the bridge Ann could see a white blur, and knew it was the sign marking the Livingston town limits.

"I know it's absurd," the old man said. "But—but it happened. And everybody's running away now. There—"

The car rattled over the rickety bridge, drowning out his words. Ann was unconsciously reading the lettering on the town limits' marker.

They were across the bridge and abreast of the sign when the thing happened in one wild, terrifying second.

Ann Meadows saw the sign directly beside the car and in the same instant heard the blasting, rending explosion, felt the car shiver under the impact. Flame leaped. Window and windshield smashed in a shower of flying glass. The car staggered, reeled toward the shallow ditch on the right, plunged into it. Ann was flung forward, her head cracking against the instrument panel. The world spun in a blaze of light and darkness. . . .

The laughter sounded far away and detached. A dark, reeling blindness gripped Ann's eyes and brain. Then she heard the laughter again, closer and hideous with evil and ugly hunger. She fought to steady her spinning brain. Her eyes came open, slowly, slowly, with lights and round, dark spots dancing before them.

The laughter rumbled in her ears and sent terror surging through her. She tried to scream, but the muscles of her throat were contracted and there was no sound.

The dashlight on the car was still burning. Ann's head was hanging forward, almost touching the dashboard. She realized these things dimly, but objects still swam before her eyes. Then into the swimming circle came a dirty, clawlike hand holding a piece of jagged, knife-edged glass. The hand moved toward her throat, reaching underneath her chin, the glass gripped, ready to slash.

In a wild surge of terror, a cry broke from Ann's throat. She flung herself back against the seat, her scream a furious thing leaping into the night.

The seat stopped her backward movement. She saw not only the hand, but the wrist and forearm now as they moved the glass toward her throat.

A white light burst soundlessly, flooding the car with brilliance for one second. Ann Meadows crumpled in a faint.

SOMETHING wet and slimy striking Ann's face brought wild fear and consciousness surging through her brain. She heard herself scream, heard the sound beat like wings against her ears. She tried to spring erect and run, but something held her, pushed her back.

"That's all right, Miss Meadows," a voice said. "Jest take it easy, take it easy. You ain't hurt much."

Ann's eyes flew open then, but unconscious terror was still jerking at her limbs, fluttering her eyelids. In the darkness she did not recognize the man leaning through the window of the car, holding his hands on her shoulders. He said again, "Now jest take it easy, Miss Meadows."

Then she recognized the lean, sallow face, the blond eyebrows and colorless eyes of Ben Larkin, the town marshal. She remembered him as a man of about thirty, but now the dashlight showed deep wrinkles in his sallow skin and there were dark lines under his eyes.

The wild terror had gone out of Ann now, but her body felt weak. Her knees trembled and her voice quivered when she asked, "Who—who was that laughing—that reached for me with the glass?"

The wrinkles deepened in Larkin's face and the lines under his eyes seemed to tighten. He opened his mouth, shut it. After a moment he said, "Musta been that idiot Lem Prune I seen running away from here when I drove up. One of them half-breeds from down in Crazy Man's Swamp. But you jest set still while I look at old man Wilson."

Ann remembered Bob Wilson now and turning saw him leaning forward over the steering wheel, his face twisted toward her. From a bruise on his forehead a narrow stream of blood was running down into his left eyebrow.

She caught his shoulders, pulled him back against the seat. "Mr. Bob," she whispered. "Mr. Bob."

The old man stirred. His eyes blinked open but did not focus. He put a shaking hand up to his blood-stained forehead.

Larkin asked, "You hurt bad, Mr. Wilson?"

The banker moved his head slowly, blinked again. At last he said, "Hello Larkin." He twisted in the seat, saw Ann. "Child," he asked anxiously, "are you hurt?"

Abruptly Ann realized that she had a headache from the blow against the dashboard, but she said, "No, sir. How're you?" She opened the car door and stepped out into the ditch. Her knees quivered and she had to grip the door to keep from falling.

Larkin helped the old man out, made sure there were no broken bones. Strength was returning to Ann's legs now, but her head still ached. Larkin asked, "What happened? How come you-all run in the ditch?"

Wilson shook his white head. "I don't know. We had just come across the bridge when something seemed to blow up. My head must have hit the windshield and I don't remember anything else."

Ann heard her voice saying in a hushed, frightened whisper which she could not believe was hers, "It happened just as we passed the city limits sign. It was like something had been waiting there, just inside the town, to keep us from entering."

Both men stared at her for a moment. Larkin said, "I'll take you-all on into town in my car, since a wheel's broke on yores, Mr. Wilson. I reckon Miss Meadows will be wanting to see her folks."

Few lights showed as they rode down the main street. There was a dull glow from behind the door of the big white home where Wilson had lived alone since the death of his wife several years before. One or two other lights showed, but most of the houses were dark and deserted.

"I reckon after the folks hear about this," Larkin said, "there won't be *nobody* left round here."

The old banker's voice was brittle when he answered, "I'll be here, alive or dead. I been running this bank for fifteen years and the only time it shut down was when Roosevelt closed all of them. Every other bank in the country failed, but I kept mine open. And I don't mean to shut it now."

CHAPTER TWO

Death's Footsteps

THERE were two beds in the large, high-ceilinged room. On the one nearest the windows, her face white as the pillows on which she rested, was a girl. Her hair was long and chestnut-colored and lay in a soft mass about her face.

Ann Meadows felt a queer tightening of her throat as she came into the room and looked at her invalid sister. She said, "Edith, dear!" and ran toward the bed.

Edith Meadows turned her head slightly and her pale lips smiled. But under the cover her body was as motionless as wood. Then Ann was kissing her and kneeling beside the bed. "I heard you in the front hall," Edith said, "and thought you'd never come in here."

Ann said, "We were telling Mr. Bob Wilson good night. He brought me home."

"I know," Edith said. "Dad is—is—"

Ann pushed away from the bed, gripping the cover with taut fingers. "Where —where is he?" She turned to look at her younger sister standing in the middle of the room.

Marie Meadows said, "Aw, he's just out for a little while. He'll be in here soon. He should be back now." Marie was a tall girl, well built, with hair the soft auburn color of Ann's. She was pretty, but her face had a harder look than Ann's and her mouth was straight and thin.

Beyond Marie stood Dorothy Harkins. She was small, plump, with a round face, round eyes, and close-cropped brown hair around her small head. Before Edith Meadows had been injured, she and Dorothy had been close college friends. When Dorothy's father had lost his fortune in the 1929 crash and committed suicide, the girl had come to live with the Meadows. Now she said, "Mr. Meadows told me he would be back for dinner." She looked at Ann, smiled slightly. "You know there aren't any servants any more. All the Negroes have left town."

"*All* of them?"

"Every darn one," Marie said. "Been gone two weeks now."

Ann felt the cool touch of Edith's fingers and turned to look at the girl on the bed. "Didn't Marie write you not to come?" Edith asked. "She promised me she would."

The cold, empty hollow formed in Ann's breast again, but she said, "You shouldn't try to keep me away when there's trouble. I want to be with the family."

"But you shouldn't be here now. None of you should." Edith put her fingers against Ann's lips when her sister tried to interrupt. Her pale face was deadly serious and in the brown eyes a fire was burning. Her voice was scarcely above a whisper, but vibrant, heavy with emotion. "Marie and Dorothy thought I was foolish at first. They still try to pretend. But they know I'm right. Just lying here all day a person *feels* things that other human beings don't. And I *know* you can't stop what's happening here. You can't! It'll kill you all if you don't go. Please. Leave me, there's—"

"Hush! Hush!" Ann said. She put her hand on her sister's mouth. "Don't talk like that. We're going to have you well soon. Tom Adams, you know, the boy I wrote you about, the one I'm going to marry, will be down tomorrow if not tonight. I came as soon as I got Marie's letter, but I left a note for Tom."

The girl on the bed tightened her fingers about Ann's. "Listen," she said. "You're in love. You've got everything to live for. Please leave. Go back to Tom. If you don't—" She stopped, her head half raised from the pillow, her face taut, listening. There was a dead silence in the room, through which Ann could hear the ticking of the little radium-faced alarm-clock on the dresser.

Edith said, "That must be Marie's friend coming up the walk. He's staggering like he was drunk."

"If I could hear as well as you—" Marie began. The expression on Edith's face stopped her. "What is it?" she asked.

"That's not a drunk. It's—It's—"

They all heard the sound then. Two quick bumps on the front steps. Silence. A dragging foot.

Every person in the room was facing the door into the hallway. Dorothy Harkins moved deeper into the room and stood close beside Marie.

THE sounds came again. The person was on the porch now, crossing it. The steps were irregular, jerky. A heavy *bump, bump.* A long pause. The sounds took on an eerie, unreasoning significance. They hammered at Ann's ears, at her brain. She found herself leaning forward, waiting for each new step, her heart beating and pausing with the sounds.

There was a scratching sound at the front door. A wavering, scraping noise that ceased abruptly. The lock on the door clicked.

Then the steps were coming down the hall, weaving, irregular, dragging along the floor. Twice the unseen person fell heavily against the wall, dragged himself erect again and came on. Almost unconsciously Ann stood close against the bed, between her invalid sister and the door. She could feel Edith's thin, cold fingers gripping her left hand. She heard her own breathing, harsh under her eardrums. Her eyes were straining in their sockets, swelling, staring at the dark frame of the doorway.

The steps thudded. Stopped. Came on again.

Dorothy Harkins screamed, a high, flat cry. Marie Meadows choked, "Oh God!" Ann staggered back against the bed, almost fell, and stood there wavering. Her eyes were aching in sheer disbelief. Her heart was a cold lump of horror deep in her stomach.

Framed in the light of the doorway was her father. He was a big man, and his shoulders, swaying low in front of him like those of an ape, almost touched the sills. His broad, square face was a mass of blood and torn flesh out of which his eyes showed like dulled lights. His big jaw hung crazily to one side, pulling his mouth open. Ann saw that his big hands were bloody and in that long, horrible moment one drop slid from his forefinger with infinite reluctance, to fall with a dull thud upon the floor.

Then Ann was running toward him, pushing her sister out of the way, crying aloud, "Dad! Dad!"

She stopped two feet distant, unable to fight herself closer to the hideous thing that had been her father. Behind her she heard Dorothy Harkins sobbing hysterically.

The big man's face moved, contorted itself behind its bloody mask. The jaw wagged slightly and from the blood-filled mouth came an unintelligible mumbling.

Ann jerked herself a half step closer. She put her hands on his coat. "Dad!" It was the only word she could say.

The big jaw wagged again and the face twisted in torture. Ann rocked, clinging to her father, all but fainting. She knew that he was trying to talk and that his broken jaw and blood-filled mouth made words impossible. She managed to say, "Come over here; sit down." Marie was beside her now, reaching out for her father's arm.

Light flared in the man's eyes. Ann realized that her father *had* to speak, had to tell them what had happened to him— to warn them.

For now *he* knew the thing which terrified the village!

He leaned forward, opened his mouth and spilled bloody saliva on the floor. He raised his head but the words were still muffled on his tongue. Twice he tried, his face twisting in agony. *"Gewu buer. . ."* The sound trailed off into nothing.

The man seemed to draw himself together, collect every muscle in his great body. The light in his eyes flamed.

Pulling himself away from the hands of his daughters he turned toward the writing desk. His bloody right hand pawed in front of him. He took two steps, stopped. For a moment he wavered, then fell over on his face.

FOR the next half hour Ann Meadows moved in a dream. Her body felt cold from the sheer horror of her father's death, and a chilling fear enveloped her like a fog. This whole thing was incredible, fantastic. It sounded like some weird folk-tale that had been handed down from generation to generation, growing more monstrous with each repetition. It was unbelievable—yet it was happening before her very eyes.

She hardly heard her voice as she called Old Bob Wilson and Larkin, the marshal. Larkin had just come back from inspecting the place where the wreck had occurred, and had found nothing suspicious. He told her this before she was able to tell about her father. Then she had gone back into the room where her father lay and had sat on the bed with Edith while Marie called Sam Mason, the undertaker.

She thought dimly, sitting there holding her sister's frail hands in hers, that at last Sam Mason would come inside their home. But her father wouldn't know it now. For years Marie and Sam had been in love. Wayne Meadows had opposed them both because Mason was ten years older than Marie and because he drank too heavily.

Edith Meadow's cool hands quivered as they gripped her sister's. She whispered, "Ann, you and Marie and Dorothy must leave here. You'll die if you stay here! I've been lying here, thinking about this thing. Invalids get to know things, just lying and thinking. And I know it'll kill us all, one at a time. One—"

"Hush," Ann said. "We'll be—" She stopped, thinking about her father and unable to say the last word. But she wasn't going to leave her sister here to die, trapped by some monster that nobody knew. When Tom Adams came. . . .

But suppose he—suppose the same thing that had happened to her father. . . "Oh God!" she said aloud.

Steps sounded on the front porch, in the hall. She sat there, mouth half open, face bloodless and drawn as the men came into the room. There was Bob Wilson, his round, old face full of fear and determination and sorrow. The sleepless lines in Larkins' sallow face were deeper than ever.

And then Sam Mason came into the room and Marie went to him quickly. Mason was a short, heavily built and dark-haired man. He had a full, pleasant face that was drawn now with deep lines about the mouth and eyes. His nose seemed swollen and red and there were red lines in the whites of his eyes. He wavered slightly as he walked, and the odor of liquor came into the room with him. He was carrying a folding stretcher and Ann thought dully that all his assistants must have fled the town, leaving the terrible work of the last few days to him alone.

Dully through the mist of pain and grief, Ann heard Mason ask if the body should be buried or changed to ashes in the crematory. He framed the question so that it favored cremation, and when Marie turned toward her, Ann nodded dully. She thought it was odd that so small a town should have a crematory. It hadn't before. . . .

Wilson crossed the room, his head twisted slightly to one side. His thin white hands reached out, caught the hands of Ann and her sister. Ann heard the old man's cracked, kindly voice and the sound was comforting though she was too dazed to heed the words. She kept her face turned from the thing on the floor, not wanting to see her father's body removed.

And then, without warning, laughter struck like a foul knife at Ann's eardrums, jarred at her brain!

For a moment she could not move, but sat frozen in terror, cold sweat oozing from her body, muscles jerking but helpless to answer the call of her brain. Then her head moved, slowly. Even before her eyes reached the window she knew what she was going to see. Every sound inside the room except the laughter had died; even the ticking of the clock, it seemed to Ann, had ceased and there was no movement in all the world but the slow turning of her head and no sound but the horrible, cackling laughter.

The same laughter she had heard after the wreck.

HER eyes found the window. Beyond it she saw the hideous face, leering at her. Black straggly hair hung over a narrow forehead. Close-set eyes glared madly, and below them was a twisted red mouth. She had seen such a face once before. She had been a child, squirrel hunting with her father, and—

Dorothy Harkins screamed shrilly.

Behind her Ben Larkin's voice boomed, "It's Lem Prune!" Larkin's shoes banged as he raced down the hall toward the front door and Sam Mason's steps beat an unsteady chorus.

The man beyond the window was standing with his head flung back, mouth open, laughing the wild, maniacal laughter of the insane. The sound flung high, clicked short. The face seemed to fade back into the darkness of the night—and vanish.

In the stillness that followed Edith's voice sounded loud. "You'll leave, Ann. You and Dorothy and Marie. You'll die —you'll *have* to die if you stay here."

Wilson said, "I—I think she's right. The three of you take my car tonight and drive to York. I'll take care of Edith." He tried to smile, but his thin lips quivered. "I bounced her on my knee twenty years ago; so I ought to be able to look after her now."

Ann hesitated. Marie and Dorothy Harkins watched her. Their lives, her life, might depend on what she said. Then

she saw the bloody body of her father stretched on the floor. She turned to the old banker.

"No. I'm going to stay with Edith. Father—" Her voice caught. "Father wouldn't have left, and I'm going to stay, find out. . ." Her voice trailed off and she swallowed hard. "Let Marie and Dorothy take the car," she said. "No need we should all stay."

Marie said flatly, "If you stay, I'm staying."

Ann could hear the quiver in Dorothy's voice though the girl fought to keep it steady. "After all these years with you, if you think I'm going to run away when you're in trouble. . ." She began to sob, and Ann heard the clip of her heels as she turned away.

From outside the window came the sound of voices. Three minutes later Mason and Larkin came back into the room. "We couldn't find him," Mason said.

The town marshal's voice was gaunt. "By God! I'll get him if I have to chase him through—" He glanced at the girls, caught himself and said—"through hell and high water."

IT WAS ten minutes after eleven. The three men had all promised to come by again early in the morning. Dorothy and Marie were sleeping in the next room. Ann, her silk pajamas molding themselves around the soft, full curves of her body, stood straight and slim, looking down at her invalid sister. She felt cold and hollow and sick with grief. There was fear also, a gnawing and unmentionable fear of this thing that struck without warning and that left in its wake no track but death. She tried to shrug off the fear and leaning down kissed her sister's thin, pale lips.

Straightening, she cut off the light. Soft moonlight glimmered through the screened window to touch on Edith's bed. Her own bed was a white blur farther back in the shadows. She went to it, eased her slim body under the covers. Beneath the pillow she could feel the lump formed by the tiny automatic Tom had given her a year ago.

The soft ticking of the clock filled the room with a murmuring current of sound. She thought of her father, as he had been five years ago. Kind, smiling, understanding. . . A sob choked in her throat.

There was a low wind blowing. She could hear it in the sweet-gum tree outside and in the flutter of the curtains at the window. Once, years ago, she had climbed that tree and couldn't get down. Her father . . . she rolled over, buried her face in the pillow and began to cry quietly.

The covers quivered over her body, but gradually their motion ceased. Ann's breathing became more regular, less labored. The clock on the dresser kept beating out its little double-noted tune. The three-quarters moon was swinging downward and the light slid from Edith's bed to huddle in a milky pool near the screened window.

Somewhere, off toward Crazy Man's Swamp, an owl hooted. On the outskirts of the village a dog began to bay at the moon. . . .

Ann realized suddenly that she was wide awake. She was lying on her side, her eyes straining open, staring into darkness. There was the chanting of the clock's endless ticking and her eyes, moving slowly, fearfully, found its face. The radium dial showed spectral in the darkness.

It was exactly midnight.

As suddenly as she had awakened Ann knew that she was afraid, horribly afraid. There was no sound except the ticking of the clock, but there was *feeling*. In an uncanny, inexplicable way Ann *felt* the

eyes staring into the room before she turned her head, before she heard the tearing sound against the window-sill.

Near the edge of the village the dog began to howl again, and in that moment of bone-chilling terror, when she lay stiff and unable to move, she remembered the stories that Negroes told of a dog howling at the moon. A sign of death.

The tearing sound came from the window-sill again, a bare whisper of noise, yet in the stillness she heard it. She was turning her head when she heard Edith's breathing. It was a harsh, catchy sound.

The girl was awake, and frightened.

Ann's eyes found the window as her right hand started groping toward the pillow and the small automatic beneath it. Then her hand jerked, her body turned to ice, a sob burst in her throat.

In the pool of moonlight beyond the open window was a man. His face was slightly turned, twisted sideways in an awkward position when Ann first saw him. He was sliding his hand and the long knife which it held through a hole cut in the screen. And less than two feet from the window, unable to move on her bed, was Edith Meadows.

As the sob burst involuntarily from Ann's throat the man jerked his head about, stared into the darkness of the room. Ann saw his face then. It was full, square, with deep lines about the eyes and mouth. The nose was large, swollen.

In that first shocked moment Ann could not remember where she had seen this face before. . . Then she knew that it was Dr. McGregor, the man who had disappeared. Yet it wasn't his face—or it was changed.

Breath whistled from her nostrils. McGregor and Sam Mason had always looked alike. . . .

CHAPTER THREE

Madmen Play

ANN'S hand flashed under the pillow, came out holding the automatic. She saw the man beyond the window swing the knife high. Her finger tightened on the trigger and the little gun made a blasting sound.

The man leaped backward, jerked his hand out through the screen. Ann knew she had missed. Tom had always joked about her shooting.

She flung back the cover, struck the floor with her bare feet. Twisting around her sister's bed, she reached the window. Dark in the moonlight, a man was racing across the lawn toward the distant, serrated wall of trees that marked Crazy Man's Swamp.

She stabbed the gun through the hole in the screen, fired twice. The man kept running. There was a cornfield beyond the lawn. The man raced into the corn and vanished.

"What—what's happened?" It was Marie crying frantically from the next room.

Ann did not answer. She was down on her knees beside her sister's bed, whispering, terrified, "Edith, Edith! Are you all right?"

Edith Meadows' eyes were wide, almost glazed. Her lips were parted and her breathing harsh. After a moment she said, "Yes. I—he frightened me, but I'm all right."

The door of the room swung open and against the light from the other room Ann saw Marie and Dorothy Harkins framed in the sill, holding tightly to each other. "Nobody's hurt," Ann said. "Come on in." She heard Edith's breathing under the sound of her words and a wild idea flashed in her mind. Ann said huskily, "Edith—you saw the man before I did. Why didn't you scream?"

Edith Meadows turned her head away. There were tears on her cheeks. Ann could scarcely speak when she asked, "You —you wanted him to kill you?"

Edith whispered, "I thought then you would leave, save yourself. I'm going to die anyway."

"Oh God!" Ann dropped on the bed beside her sister, arms holding her tight.

Marie and Dorothy had come close to the bed. Without warning Dorothy cried, "Look! Look!" She jabbed a finger toward the window.

Ann came to her feet, spun to face the window, still gripping the automatic. At first she saw nothing but the empty window, the torn screen with the moonlight white beyond. "Look!" Dorothy cried again. "Near the corn!"

A man was racing across the lawn toward the house. He was squat, heavy set, and carried something big in his hand. The thing seemed heavy, and he wavered a bit as he sprinted.

Ann pulled up the gun, waiting, her heart hammering high in her throat, fear shaking at the muscles of her arm. She mustn't miss this time! The man came running head on. Ann's finger began to tighten about the trigger.

Something struck at the gun, knocking it to one side. Ann swung, saw that Marie was gripping her wrist. She cried, "Don't! Don't! That's Sam!"

The man had swerved and was running toward the front of the house. Marie threw up the screen, called, "Sam! This way."

Sam Mason jerked to a halt, spun and came back to the window. He was carrying a gun in his right hand, a gallon jug in his left. He asked between heavy, panting breaths, "What's happened? I heard —shots. Came running."

Ann explained, but as she talked she stared into the face of Sam Mason. It wasn't the same face which had showed in the window, but there was a resemblance. It must have been McGregor, she thought. She turned to Edith. "Did you know who it was?" she asked.

The girl on the bed hesitated. "It—it looked like Dr. McGregor. But there was something didn't look like him. I reckon it was, though. I was too frightened to see clearly."

Mason said, "I been down in the swamp getting a little liquor. They're still bootlegging in this state you know, Ann. I— I need quite a bit to keep going like I have been these—"

Ann thought of her father and her teeth closed on her lower lip. Mason saw her and clipped his words short. He stood there, spraddle-legged, holding the jug and gun. His broad face turned slowly to look squarely into Marie's eyes as she leaned across the window-sill toward him. He said, "I'll be up all night, and'll come by here every now and then . . . make sure there's no more trouble. But tomorrow we're leaving here, you and I. There's no need that everybody should be killed. . . ."

He turned on his heel and went toward the front of the house.

DR. THOMAS ADAMS sent his big coupe bounding over the narrow, bumpy road. His headlights spotted dark mud-holes, a wagon-track, and farther ahead where the lights widened they touched on dark trees parked close on either side. Giant oak and cypress towering overhead made the road a narrow chasm of blackness. A myriad lightning bugs glimmered white and gold, vanishing and reappearing among the trees. Far off in the swamp a bullfrog hoarsed and another answered in basso. Somewhere an owl hooted.

Adams' wide, pleasant mouth was pulled hard across white teeth. His wide-set brown eyes, looking oddly dark under his blond hair, kept steady on the road ahead. His long, slender surgeon's fingers held the wheel easily despite the pull of the mud-holes, the jerk of the ruts.

He had been driving all day and the muscles in his back and shoulders ached. Now, within thirty miles of Ann Meadows' home, he'd lost his way, got on this confounded swamp track. It was just a little after midnight now. He'd be seeing Ann soon, find out what she meant by that note. Thinking of the girl and her copper-colored hair, he smiled. Lord! He loved that woman.

Ahead of him a light wavered dully, like a fire built near the road. Then he saw another beyond the first. There was an opening in the trees, and through it he saw figures moving about the fires. Whoever it was, he'd stop, find out how far it was to Livingston and if this mud track went there. . . .

He was within a hundred yards of the fires when he saw a number of small wooden shacks built back from the road on a high knoll in the swamp. "Well, I'll be damned," he said aloud. Why would anybody want to live out here? Perhaps these were the persons Ann had told him about once. Half-breeds, half-wits or something. He'd like to see these people. A worthwhile psychology study. If they had any white blood it was a wonder malaria hadn't killed them.

Then he heard the chanting. It came through the night, drowning the low song of his motor, drowning the croak of the bullfrogs. Several fires burned in the small yards before the shacks and about one of the fires a crowd was gathered. They were chanting, a weird, eerie, singsong cry that rose and fell like the chirping of crickets. But in it there was one note, hideous, continuous, filling the whole chant to overflowing, throbbing.

The horrible, age-old sound of unreasoning fear.

Dr. Adams stopped his car and got out. The houses were more than a hundred feet away, and every person in the group had his back to the road. Men, women, children, clustering about something in one thick, terrified knot.

Adams reached back, took the heavy Colt automatic from the pocket of the car. Foolish to think that he might need it—yet there was something about that chant, something about those persons. He hesitated, wondering if he should drive on without asking the way. But they must be the inbred half-wits and he wanted a close look at them. Not often would a doctor find people like these. He started picking his way toward the group.

It must have been a person on the far side who saw Adams. He was within thirty feet when there was one high, shrill cry, a word he did not understand. The whole group spun like puppets on a string and he stopped dead in his tracks, staring into faces the like of which he had never seen before.

His first impression was that he had wandered into another Jukes or Kallikak family, one of the groups that psychologists study to prove how insanity and feeble-mindedness may be inherited. But there was more than feeble-mindedness in the snarling, half savage faces which he saw. There was lust, and hate, and a primitive, unnamable fear.

The firelight blazed clear on the black hair, and close-set eyes of one of the men and Adams noted the little muscle jerking under the right eye, the way the bony hands kept twitching. A dope addict. And in the same moment he wondered how these poverty-stricken people got dope. Perhaps something they manufactured from swamp herbs. He sniffed. "Smells like an autopsy room," he thought.

Adams was surprised at the harshness of his voice when he asked, "Can you tell me how far to Livingston? I got lost

and—" The words clogged in his throat and he went back a half step as he saw the thing on the ground beyond the fringe of men and women.

He checked himself, went forward at a half run. "I'm a doctor," he said, pushing one of the men out of the way.

But there was no need to kneel beside the man on the ground. One glimpse showed him the fellow was dead, had been for more than a week. He lay sprawled beside the fire, face up. And his half decayed face was still marked with purplish, coagulated blood as though he had died of a hemorrhage. His hands were bloody, fingers bent clawlike, and his chest had a flat, deflated look as though some gigantic arms had crushed his ribs. The body was smeared with blood and dirt, had evidently been dragged around the yard. From it arose a nauseous, sickening stench.

ADAMS looked up and saw that half the crowd had vanished like shadows. There had been no sound and yet only half a dozen men remained. One of them was twitching nervously at his trouser top and Adams saw the gleam of a bone-handled knife.

"What happened to this fellow?" Adams asked.

The men were silent, some of them backing away, the others sidling closer. They were beginning to circle him and he took one long step toward the road. One of the men said, "He . . . he's dead."

The doctor's head jerked, stopped. No need to get angry. The man was only a half-wit and death would mean nothing to him. Adams turned toward another, repeated his question. The man stared back at him, sullenly, blankly.

Adams looked at the body on the ground again. Judging by what was left of his clothes the fellow had not been one of these morons. Perhaps he had been murdered. It would do little good to report to the police in the next town. By that time these idiots might have hidden the body, destroyed it altogether. Best to take it with him he decided.

He raised his eyes to one of the men, said, "I'm a doctor and I'm taking this body with me." He bent broad shoulders, clutched the collar of the dead man's coat.

The little group broke like a sudden clap of thunder. Adams heard a man snarl, spun as two of them launched at him. A knife gleamed red in the firelight. Adams leaped away from the man with the knife, squarely into the other. His left fist jarred on the man's chin, flinging him backwards. His right hand came from his coat pocket, holding the automatic.

A body crashed into the middle of his back, driving him forward, straight down at the fire. He twisted sharply to his right, caught one sucking breath as the fire rushed up at him, as he struck at the very edge of it. He heard the crackling of the wood and flame, saw red sparks leap and whirl. The man who had dived against him had fallen squarely into the fire!

With a furious, howling shriek the man leaped to his feet, smoke and flame streaming from his ragged clothes. Like a bull of Hannibal, trailing fire he tore through the group, hurling them right and left. An odor of burning flesh and cloth hung thick in the air behind him.

During the moment when the other half-breeds stared spellbound at their burning fellow, Tom Adams rolled away from the fire and came to his feet holding the automatic. The muzzle centered on the five men still clustered near the body.

"Listen, damn you. . ." he said harshly. "I'm taking this dead man away with me. To the police."

Two of the men began to back away. Two stood hesitantly, mouths open, faces blank, dazed. The other made a whimpering, insane noise in his throat, took one quick step forward and dived straight at the automatic.

Tom Adams went back a step before the madman's rush. His finger was tense about the trigger, but he did not pull. He wasn't the police and to shoot a man, even a crazy man, was murder. The idiot was almost on him when he swung the gun out to the right, then hard against the half-wit's temple. But he had struck too late and the man's shoulder crashed into his knees, pitching him forward.

Like a pack of hounds the others came at him, snarling, crying, shouting. Knives glowed red and yellow in the firelight.

Adams saw a hand swing up, then down. A knife-blade plunged at him. He swung his gun, heard the clang of steel on steel. Fire ripped across the flesh of his left arm. He lashed out with his feet, felt them thud hard against shinbones. Then three men crashed down and he was buried under a wave of bodies.

A gun roared twice, close at hand. One of the men above Adams seemed to jump straight into the air. A voice roared, "Goddam it! Stand up and then don't move!" There was the crack of a fist on bone.

Adams flung the last man from him, rolled to his knees, stared squarely into the black muzzle of a .45 revolver and into the sallow, lined face of the man behind it. "Drop yore gun," the man said.

Adams let the gun slide from his fingers, got slowly to his feet. The moron he had hit with his automatic, and another, lay unconscious. The others stood cowering in the firelight.

The man with the gun turned his slow glance from Adams to the body on the ground. Abruptly he stiffened. His sallow face drained of blood, leaving the dark circles under his eyes like lines painted on a mask.

"Great God!" he said aloud. "That's old John Perkins! He was burned in the crematory a week ago!"

CHAPTER FOUR

Lem Prune Calls

THE moon had gone down beyond the dark line of trees that marked the edge of Crazy Man's Swamp, and the room where Ann Meadows and her invalid sister slept was a pool of black shadows. With the approach of dawn the wind had freshened and grown cool. It rustled the drying leaves of the sweetgum, jarred gently against the window which Ann had closed against a return of the midnight visitor.

In the room where the sisters slept the sound of a dog howling was muted by the closed windows. On the dresser the small alarm-clock ticked its monotonous song. The breathing of the girls was hushed, slow. The bed made a tiny, creaking sound as Ann turned slightly.

Through the silence came noise marching in heavy, ominous beats. *Boom. Boom. Boom.* The sound struck through the thin mist of sleep which held the girls, brought Ann erect and quivering in her bed, snapped open the pale eyelids of her sister. In the next room Dorothy Harkins made a short, frightened cry.

Boom. Boom. Boom.

Ann whispered, "It's somebody at the door."

Lights snapped on in the next room and she saw Dorothy and Marie coming toward her. "Who is it?" they asked.

Ann reached up, turned on the light over her bed. Edith lay with her pale face turned toward Ann, her large dark eyes open and staring. To comfort her sister Ann said with a diffidence she didn't feel, "How do I know who it is? I'll go see."

Boom. Boom. Boom. Heavy and un-hurried, the sound struck through the house again.

"Take your gun," Edith whispered.

Ann slid from the bed, stuck her feet into a pair of purple mules. Reaching under the pillow she pulled out the small gun and turned toward the hall. Her slippers made clacking sounds in the stillness.

In the hall Ann turned on the light. It was probably that drunken undertaker, she thought, wanting to make certain they were all right and frightening them to death in doing it. But she mustn't be afraid of a knocking at the door. This was no time to be pulling any Lady Macbeth stuff.

She reached the front door and without unlocking it called out, "Who is it?" There was something tight and hard in her breast.

"Ben Larkin, ma'am. The marshal."

Some of the fright went out of her at the sound of the voice. But why. . . ? "Oh, all right, Ben," she said, and turned the key in the lock.

The light from the house spilled out in a bright rectangle across the porch. There were two men, one back near the shadows, one just outside the door. She saw the blond hair, the lean, good-natured face.

"Oh, Tom!" The tight thing in her breast broke and the words leaped from her lips. With them she threw herself into the man's arms. "I'm so glad. So glad!"

Tom Adams gently pushed her head from his chest, leaned down and kissed her. She could feel his hand cool against the flesh of her back, the roughness of his coat against the tops of her breasts. For the first time she remembered that she was wearing only a pair of silk pajamas. But she didn't care. It was good to have Tom here at last, someone on whose shoulder she could cry, someone to share the responsibility with her.

WITH his arm still around her, Adams turned toward the man on the porch. "Well Larkin," he smiled, "you'll believe now that I'm Miss Meadows' fiance?" Ann liked the way he smiled, the bare glimpse of even white teeth showing below his full upper lip.

Larkin said, "Yes sir. I—"

Ann looked up to the lean, sallow-faced marshal. "Why Ben," she said. "What—?"

Larkin grinned a taut, nervous smile. "Well ma'am, I told you I'd catch that prowlin' half-breed Lem Prune, the one we seen lookin' in yore window. So I went out to Swamp Town and I found Mr. Adams—I mean Dr. Adams." He tried to smile again but there was no humor in the faded, heavy-lidded eyes. "He was havin' a fight with a bunch of them half-breeds, and—well. . . I didn't know who he was, and. . . ."

Adams said, "Oh forget it. I don't blame you for picking me up. I owe you a lot of gratitude. They'd probably have killed me if you hadn't come."

Ann could feel the hard thing in her breast growing again. The terrible strain. The weird menace. This thing that killed and left no track. Had she gotten Tom into it? Was he too going to be murdered like her father? Wasn't there anything. . . ? She said aloud, "Oh God! No! No!"

The doctor spun to face her. "What do you mean, Ann? What's the trouble?"

Ann buried her face against his chest. "Nothing," she whispered. "But you'll leave town—now? Get in your car *now*. You can't stay here. *You mustn't.*"

He pushed her away from him, looked hard into her face. "Keep quiet," he said harshly. "You know I'm not going to

leave you now. I've got to stick—as your doctor," he added smiling.

Larkin shifted restlessly in the light. He looked down at his feet and when he raised his face it was grayer than ever.

"At that town," he said, "was old John Perkins. He was one of the first to die. Sam Mason burned him in the new crematory a week ago."

Adams kept his arm about Ann, turned his head towards Larkin. "I suggest, Marshal, that you get some sleep. That's professional advice. You need it. You look as if you hadn't slept in two weeks and your nerves are going to crack if you don't get some rest."

Strength came into Larkin's drawn face. He said, "Thanks, Doc. But I'm the marshal here and long as this stuff is goin' on I ain't got time for sleep." He turned and stalked across the porch into darkness.

For a moment Ann stood there, her head close against Adam's chest, feeling his hand against her back, the pressure of his coat against her breasts. She said, "Come on, Tom. You've got to meet my sisters, and Dorothy."

"At this time of the night?"

"We—we haven't slept much. They're awake now."

Adams' arm tightened about her shoulders. "You poor kid," he said. "Larkin told me."

MORNING sunlight lay with the warm gold of autumn along the dusty street. Tom Adams, up for an early walk after a sleepless night, turned left, toward what appeared to be the center of the little village. The houses on both sides of the street were closed, shutters pulled tight. The day was usually well started in towns this size by eight o'clock, but now there was no sight of human life in Livingston. On one of the porches a dog was standing, his head cocked to one side, puzzled. Off to the right an unmilked cow mooed in pain.

After two blocks Adams reached the six stores of the village. Their doors were closed. Beyond them was what appeared to be a small bank. The doctor went toward it, stopped in surprise.

The bank doors were wide open, and from the inside came the sound of voices.

He reached the bank, went in. Morning sunlight flooded through the open door. Inside were two men. One was a cherubic-faced old man with white hair and kindly blue eyes. In those eyes now was a worried, frightened look as he turned toward Adams.

The other was a squat, powerfully built man with a red nose and red lines spider-webbed in his eyes. He had evidently had a great deal of liquor and little sleep. He raised a pint bottle toward Adams as he came in, said, "Welcome to the Village of the Dead, stranger. It's a great town for undertakers."

Adams introduced himself. Both men had heard of him from the Meadows. "Ann told me last night you were coming," the banker said.

Adams looked at the old man, said, "It seems funny to see your bank open when nothing else in town is."

Mason took a pull from his bottle, offered it to Adams. "Oh yes, something else is," he said. "My undertaking shop. I'm doing a damn sight more work than the bank."

Adams said nothing but his mind was racing. Ann had told him of Dr. McGregor looking into her window last night, told him of the doctor's resemblance to Mason. He wanted to recognize McGregor if he saw him.

Wilson was saying slowly, "You are Miss Ann's fiance and should have some influence with her. Somebody tried to kill her sister Edith last night. Maybe he would have killed all the others. But I

wish you'd get the girls to leave. If Edith can't be moved, I'd be glad to look after her. But the others. . . There's no need. . ." He paused, half embarrassed.

"But why—what's back of this?" Adams asked. "What can anybody gain by it?"

The banker shook his white head, said miserably, "I don't know."

"I'll see that the girls leave," Adams said. "But I'm going to stay here with Edith. I examined her last night—to move her now would kill her. The recent shocks have weakened her. She needs a doctor, but—I'll see that the others leave."

He went out then, strode back toward the Meadows home.

SOME time later, Adams was forced to admit to himself that the task of convincing the Meadows girls was more difficult than he had expected. Ann wanted the others to go, but refused to leave Edith herself. Marie would not go without Ann.

In the meantime, while he had been away, Dorothy Harkins had gone out to find the undertaker or the banker, to get one of them to milk a cow before lunch. Hours had passed now and the girl had not returned. Tension was growing in the house. The strain showed in the face of every person; it crept into the very atmosphere, like a bow stretching until it must break.

Adams had searched the town for Dorothy. There was no sign of her. The marshal too had disappeared. Neither Wilson nor Mason had seen the girl.

Now Adams sat facing the three sisters, taking up the old argument again. Edith joined with him. Her voice was low but steady. "Dorothy's gone, disappeared," she said. "She wouldn't run away. The thing has her. It'll get you all if you stay. I wish—"

She stopped when the sound of knocking on the back door jarred through the room.

Adams stood up. "I'll see who it is," he said, and went out of the room.

He pushed open the back door, and stopped. His right hand jumped toward his coat pocket. His breath made a whistling sound through his teeth as he looked into the evil, half-witted face of the man before him. For a moment he thought it was one of the group he had seen last night, then knew differently. But it was the face that Ann had described to him— that of Lem Prune, the man for whom Larkin was searching.

The idiot was babbling in a broken, half-Indian dialect. "You come, come with me." He stabbed out nervous fingers, plucked at Adams' coat. The doctor noted the twitching of the man's mouth and hands. Another dope addict.

"You come. You come," Prune kept saying. He began to tug on Adams' coat.

Adams said, "All right." If he could keep this man in sight, he could turn him over to the town marshal. Perhaps then the mystery behind these horrors would be cleared. The whole thing sounded mad, insane. He had known insane men to be monstrously clever in ways. And yet. . . .

The idiot kept saying, "You come. Come with me." He had Adams by the hand now, leading him across the wide back yard, past the garage. There was a rickety fence separating this lot and the yard of the deserted house which faced the only other street in the small town. They climbed the fence and went toward the empty house.

The idiot went straight ahead, bent on reaching some unknown point. He kept pulling on the doctor's hand, hurrying him. Adams could feel his heart hammering under his ribs. There was something satanic, something monstrous about the half-wit and about the way he drove forward, head lowered, shoulders sway-

ing. Adams began to hold back, to look about him nervously. "Where are we going?" he asked.

"You come," Prune said. They had reached the back of the house and began to walk beside it toward the front. They were a step short of the front corner when Prune said again, "You come." He turned suddenly, caught Adams' hand in both of his, and jerked.

The doctor was snatched forward, almost off his feet. "What the hell?" he snapped.

From behind the corner of the house a dark figure surged forward abruptly. Adams, spinning, caught one glimpse of a falling hand, a blackjack, a square, masklike face with a large nose. He flung himself sideways, jerking the gun from his pocket. In the split instant the name, "Dr. McGregor," burst in his brain. Then the blackjack landed.

The face was wiped out by a blanket of darkness. Dully Adams felt the thud of his body striking the ground. . . .

CHAPTER FIVE

Out of the Swamp

THROUGH a fiercely revolving sea of blackness Tom Adams felt his body go swinging. Then after a while it began to move more slowly, and in the distance red and white lights began to glitter. Even before he was completely conscious his professional brain told him that he was coming out from under the influence of chloroform.

The red died out of the glittering lights and the white began to grow steady, driving away the darkness. He felt a little sick at his stomach and once he thought he was going to vomit. After a time he began to see things around him, and to hear.

He was in a small, shack-like room, bare

of furniture. He lay flat on the floor, hands tied behind him, ankles bound together. His gun, of course, was gone. There was one small, paneless window in the room and through it he could see sunlight and the tops of pine and cypress trees. One of the planks on the sill had been torn loose at one end and hung swaying. He decided he must be somewhere in the swamp.

Lem Prune was sitting on the floor near Adams' feet. His red mouth was curled in an ugly smile and when he saw that the doctor's eyes were open he began to laugh. He leaned toward Adams, thrusting his face within inches of the doctor's—and Adams could smell the sweet, sickly odor of dope.

"You're goin' to die. Die, die, die." Prune began to chant the word, laughing constantly.

As Adams' brain cleared fear began to take hold of his body. Who was the man who had knocked him on the head? The missing doctor? And why had he done it? Did he mean to. . . He remembered the way the week-old corpse had looked with blood still smeared on its rotting features. Sickness struck at him, adding to the nausea of the chloroform.

The idiot began to laugh more loudly.

"You're goin' to die," he chanted. "You're goin' to burn, burn, burn."

Adams rolled over, struggled to a half sitting position. Sweat was breaking out on his forehead and there was a cold lump in his chest. "Burn?" he husked.

The idiot chanted, "Burn. You're goin' to burn." As he talked his mouth kept twitching and he rocked back and forth, eyes half closed. The dope had fingers deep in his system, Adams noted, but was beginning to wear off. In another hour, unless he got more, there was little telling what the man might do. Adams had seen dope addicts go completely insane. Some sat and cried like babies. He had seen one stamp the life from another with his feet.

Adams forced his voice to be steady. "How am I going to be burned? Why?"

The idiot ran a tongue over his dirty lips, said, "He'll burn you. Ashes. Nothin' but ashes. That's what you'll be." He began to laugh again.

Adams felt the muscles jerk along his back. "He? Who's he?"

The idiot kept laughing.

For a moment Adams lay there, breathing harshly through clenched teeth. How could he be burned into ashes, or was that merely the gibberish of a madman? In a crematorium. . . But why had he been brought here? To wait until dark so that he could be slipped into the funeral home?

Adams flung the thought from his mind. The thing to do now was to get free. Questioning Prune gained nothing. Evidently the madman did not intend to tell who his master was, if he himself knew. The missing doctor? How otherwise did these people who couldn't buy food get dope?

Tom Adams began to try his bonds, straining slowly against them and keeping his eyes on Prune. The ropes held firm, biting into his wrists when he tugged. He felt sick in his chest, hopeless. He'd never pull loose from these things. The twitching of Prune's mouth was growing and the swaying of his body became broken, jerky. He'd have to have another shot soon, the doctor knew. . . .

ADAMS looked out of the window again. The sun was white and gold on the tree-tops, but around the window were heavy shadows. It must be late afternoon. Whoever was holding him here would probably return soon after dark. He had to get free now, or. . . His teeth made a grating sound as he clenched them, braced himself and strained at the ropes.

Lem Prune snarled and lunged forward.

His open right hand struck Adams' face with a sound like gunfire, popping the doctor's head to one side. "Loose, huh? Loose!" Prune shrilled.

The half-wit's right hand drove to his belt on the left side, came back holding a big, bone-handled knife. The point stabbed at Adams' side in a rough gesture, went through the coat and into flesh. Adams rolled away, feeling a slow trickle of blood along his ribs.

Prune squatted, staring at Adams with squinted, fiery eyes. The doctor lay, breathing heavily, mind racing, fear cold along his back. It would be death to keep trying to free himself. If the half-wit stabbed that hard in warning he would kill at the next effort. And the dope was dying out of the man, leaving him angry, insane, and with a knife in his hand.

Adams swallowed twice at the hard lump in his throat. He said, keeping his voice steady, "You want more dope? Powder?" He sniffed, as if taking the white opiate.

Prune's body jerked taut. His eyes were wide and red and his mouth hung open. He grunted, "Huh? Huh?"

"Dope," Adams said, and sniffed again. "I'm a doctor. I've got plenty."

The red eyes flamed. The maniac began to edge toward him, still squatting, his left hand touching the floor, right hand holding the knife. "Gimme," he whined. "I want it. Gimme."

"Not here," Adams said. "I haven't got it here. Turn me loose and I'll get it." He jerked at his wrists, nodded toward his ankles.

The sagging mouth of the maniac drew tight. Lust, fury and wild desire were in the red eyes. "Now," he said. "Gimme now." His right wrist was hooked, muscles hard. The blade of the knife touched the floor as he moved, making a low scraping sound.

Adams knew that he had made the wrong attempt. The idiot would never believe he didn't have the dope with him. Instead of turning him loose, the madman would kill him while he was tied, then try to find the powder on him.

Sweat was cracking from his body. His lungs ached and his eyes bulged as he watched the madman edge toward him. Adams tried once more, but the muscles of his throat all but choked back his voice. "It's not here. Turn me loose and I'll go get it."

Lem Prune's voice had changed from a whine to a snarl. "No," he said. "I take it now." The forearm began to bend, the knife to rise from the floor. He was squatting now, his knees almost against Adams' hips.

The doctor sucked one long breath through hard lips. There was just one chance. A poor one, but a chance. . . "All right," he said. "It's in my pocket. This one. . ." He jerked his head toward the side away from the idiot. "Reach in and get it."

Prune grinned. He was panting like a dog and his eyes were asquint again. He leaned forward, reaching out with his left hand across the doctor's body. His shoulders, then his waist, were over Adams as his hand curved toward the pocket.

Tom Adams flung his back against the floor, hard. Both knees came up with a rush. There was a thudding sound and Prune's breath wheezed from his mouth as the knees drove deep into his groin. The blow lifted him from the floor, flung him over on his back. The knife skidded harshly across the room. Prune's breath was an agonized gasp.

TOM ADAMS rolled furiously to his knees, but his hands were bound behind him and he went over on his head. He swirled, pivoted on his left hip while his eyes flashed about the room for the knife. He saw it, six feet to the right, wriggled to his knees and dived. He heard his trousers rip on the jagged floor, felt the skin tear from his knees, but the knife was close by. He squirmed, twisting his back to the blade, caught it up with his hands.

Prune was lying balled in a knot ten feet away, groaning, his hands wrapped around his belly. But even as Adams fumbled with the knife the half-breed began to straighten his body, twisting until he faced the doctor. Then the pain in his face gave way to an immense and terrible rage. Whimpering, he lunged to his feet, staggered and clutched at his belly again.

Adams had twisted his wrists until the bones seemed ready to snap. The blade of the knife was against the ropes, but when he tried to work it back and forth he could not keep the steel pressed down. Prune was erect now, glaring around the room. His eyes reached the window-sill where the plank hung loose at one end. He dived for it.

Adams could feel the rope giving now, twitching along his wrists as he sawed. The muscles in his arms ached, the bones in his hands seemed to be breaking. Sweat stood in cold beads all over his body. His eyes bulged from his head as he watched the maniac swing around, hands gripping the plank he had ripped from the window.

The madman took one step forward, swung the plank back. It made a swishing sound in the air. He held it there for one long moment, his red eyes glaring. Adams balanced himself on his knees, waiting. The hands clutching the knife were motionless now. No time to saw at the ropes.

The board swung.

Adams flung himself backwards and to the right. Wind whipped his face and his eyes blinked as the heavy plank ripped past, less than an inch above his nose. He hit rolling, came to his knees. His wrists were arched furiously again, sawing at the ropes.

The swing had carried Prune off balance, spun him half around. He caught himself, turned back to face Adams. At the same moment the ropes around the doctor's wrists parted.

Prune flung the board up, whipped it down hard. Adams was off balance and his roll to the right was slow. He barely had time to jerk up his left shoulder before the blow landed.

It caught him full on the shoulder, bowling him over, smashing paralyzing pain through his left arm. But he clung to the knife with his right hand. He hit the floor on his right side, knees doubled under him. One sweep of the knife slashed the rope about his ankles.

Prune had swung back the board again, straight over his head now to smash it down on Adams' skull. He rocked back on his heels, balancing, muscles bulging in his arms. He started the board down, fast.

Adams was on his knees. He saw the board start, saw there was no time to dodge right or left. He went straight forward, under the sweeping plank.

His shoulder struck Prune's shins, knocking them from under him like ninepins. Both men came to the floor with a crash. The plank tore loose from Prune's hands. The idiot made a snarling sound, sprang half erect, then launched himself like a mad dog at Adams' throat.

For a man who, three years before, had been intercollegiate light heavyweight boxing champion, the rest was simple. Adams dropped the knife, brought up his right fist in a short uppercut. The blow cracked when it landed and it turned Lem Prune over backward. He hit the floor and lay still.

For ten seconds Adams stood breathing heavily. He took off his coat, examined his shoulder. It was a bad bruise, but nothing else. There was a welt across his biceps where a knife had grazed him the night before. The place on his ribs where Prune had pricked him in warning had already stopped bleeding. Adams grinned wryly. Close shaves, all of them. That luck couldn't hold out forever.

Taking off his tie and belt he bound Prune, gagged him with a handkerchief. He took the knife and stuck it under his trousers, stepped to the door of the hut and pushed it open.

The shack was on a heavily wooded knoll which sloped down to boggy swampland. Through the swamp a wagon-trail wound from knoll to knoll. A wagon and a pair of moth-eaten mules stood nearby. The trees shut out the direct rays of the sun, making semi-twilight in the place. Nearly sundown, Adams decided.

For three full minutes he stood there, thinking. After dark the person back of this whole foul business would probably return. If Adams stayed, he might capture the fellow, solve all the mysteries of who and why and how. But the man would probably be armed. He might bring more of these dope-eating half-wits with him. And Adams had only the bone-handled knife.

Ann Meadows, where was she all this time? With no one there to look after her, what might have happened? Adams sucked a deep breath through parted lips. It couldn't be far to the town. He should be able to make it, see that Ann was safe, and be back here before dark. He wondered if Dorothy Harkins had been found. . . .

IT WAS farther than he had thought. At times his feet sank up to the ankles in bog that sucked at him, tired him with every step he took. There was still a slight pain in his head from the blow and his stomach was weak from the chloroform they had given him.

It took someone who knew his business to administer chloroform: too much

would easily kill a man. Adams thought again of the missing doctor, grinned crookedly. Whoever had given him that crack on the head hadn't cared whether he was killed or not. It had been only a matter of a few hours anyway.

Muscles corded along Tom Adams' jaw and his chin pushed forward. He'd find what lay back of this now—and by God! he'd settle it. Even if he and Ann and her sisters were to escape from the thing now, they'd never be able to have peace and happiness while this mystery, this dread of the unknown, hung over them. It *had* to be settled, and, damn it! he meant to do the settling.

It was sundown when he finally came out of the swamp and saw the house-tops of the village half a mile away. His muscles ached with fatigue and his feet felt heavy. His eyes sagged from lack of sleep, but his lips were hard, his jaw thrust forward.

He returned to Ann Meadows' home by slipping across the deserted back street and up to the back door. He meant to leave again without seeing anyone but Ann. He didn't know the monster who had originated this reign of terror, and until he did know he trusted no one.

He went across the back porch quietly, moving on the balls of his feet. He tugged on the door, found it locked. The windows also were locked. He whistled the soft, three-noted whistle that Ann knew.

A moment later the door burst open and she had her arms around him. Her brown eyes were wide with relief. "Where have you been?" she cried softly.

He pulled her inside the kitchen, kissed her. He outlined briefly what had happened. "I'm going back there," he said, "and I don't want anybody to know I've been here."

"Mr. Bob Wilson is here now," she said. "We called him when you didn't come back because we were afraid. Oh, Tom!" She pulled him close to her again.

"I'll be all right," he said, and patted her shoulder reassuringly. He added, "If there's another gun in the house beside that little one I gave you, I'd like to borrow it."

"There's a twenty-two rifle upstairs, and a shotgun."

"Get me the rifle. It'll shoot more times and farther."

"All right." She paused. There was fear in her eyes when she said, "Tom, why do you suppose Dr. McGregor is doing this?"

"Are you sure it's McGregor?"

"I—I don't know. The man in the window last night looked like him. But —he looked like Mason, too, and it couldn't have been Sam. Didn't you say it was McGregor who struck you?"

Tom Adams shook his head. "No," he said. "I've never seen McGregor and I didn't get to see much of the fellow who bumped me. Just a glimpse. He looked like what you had told me of the doctor—but he looked like he had on make-up, or some disguise."

"His face did look . . . painted!" Her voice went slow, hesitant. "Do you suppose it might have been—Sam, made up to look like McGregor?" Then she shook her head, harshly. "No! It couldn't. Why would he do this?"

"Your father didn't like him?"

"No-o-o. But—" Her words cut short. A wild, throat-tearing shriek had sounded from the bedroom! A cry in which terror and despair and surprise conglomerated in one high, flat wail. There was the soft, rapid tattoo of bare feet in the hall.

Both Ann Meadows and Adams swung to face the kitchen door. With his left hand Adams pushed the girl behind him, while his right hand dug the knife from his trouser-top. He held it, waiting, eyes

fastened on the door. His heart and lungs seemed suspended.

The sound of the feet came with a surging rush. The kitchen door burst open. There, framed in the long hallway, was Edith Meadows, who had not taken a step for five years!

CHAPTER SIX

Terror Kills

"OH, GOD!" Ann sobbed.

The girl in the doorway started toward them. Her face was as white as porcelain, save for two vivid spots of red in her cheeks and the dark pools of her eyes. Her lips were open and all but transparent over her teeth. She whispered, terror shaking her voice, "Oh, I know. His head twists. . . ." She swayed, caught herself.

Tom Adams leaped forward, dropping the knife to clatter on the floor. Before he reached her the girl said, "I know. It's—" The words choked in her throat. She pitched headlong.

Adams caught her, went down on his knees, holding her cradled in his right arm. He snapped at Ann, "Get my bag! Quick! The adrenalin!" His left hand went in the throat of the girl's lace nightgown, down to her small left breast. Before Ann returned with the bag he knew he had no use for it. The girl was dead.

Footsteps sounded in the hall. Adams looked up to see Wilson's white head showing above the auburn hair of Marie Meadows as both stared at him, wide eyed, open mouthed. Marie began suddenly to cry. She came forward, swaying, and dropped beside her sister. "Edith . . . Edith. . . ." she whispered.

Adams lay the girl gently on the floor, stood up. There was a hard question in his eyes when he looked at the old banker. Wilson said huskily, "I was standing by the window, talking to both of them. Suddenly she looked past me and screamed."

"What was outside?"

"I don't know. I turned to her when she screamed, and then I saw her jump out of bed. It surprised me so that I followed her to the door without looking."

"Damn!" Adams said. He ducked, scooped the knife from the floor, turned and went out of the door on the run. There was nothing in the back yard and he cut to the left, his tousled blond hair blowing as he sprinted.

There was a wide, empty lawn on this side, the tall sweet-gum tree just outside the bedroom window. A brown, autumn-tinged leaf swirled down from it as Adams raced toward the front of the house.

He went around the corner, running fast. And stopped. A squat, heavy-built man was staggering up the front steps. Adams' hand tightened on the knife and he leaped forward as he recognized Sam Mason.

The undertaker heard him, turned and stood swaying on the top step. His hand moved clumsily but quickly to his coat pocket, came out holding a gun. Amazement and surprise flashed on his face.

"Stay where you are," he said. The words were thick from liquor but the hand was steady on the gun.

Adams stopped. A knife wasn't much good against a gun, not at this range. His body was tensed forward, weight on his toes.

"You just come from around the side of the house?" he asked.

Mason didn't answer, but a puzzled look was growing on his face. "Who're you?" he said. "I meet you somewhere?"

Adams grinned crookedly. "At the bank this morning. I'm Ann Meadows' fiance."

"Oh, yeah. My future brother-in-law, huh?" He put the gun back in his pocket, said apologetically, "I've been drinking pretty heavy these days. Lot of work for an undertaker, you know, and my memory's not so good."

Adams went toward him, the knife seemingly forgotten in his hand. "Did you come from around the corner of the house?" he asked again. "Or see anybody?"

The drunk said, "You."

Adams cursed under his breath. Was Mason the person Edith Meadows had seen outside the window? If not, who was it? Where had he gone? He couldn't have vanished . . . but if it wasn't Mason then he *had* vanished.

Adams took the undertaker by the arm, held him while he explained what had happened, watching his face at every word. Surprise, sorrow, a tinge of fear crossed the man's face. That was all. Acting? Perhaps. . . . What could Mason or any man hope to gain by spreading wholesale murder and terror? . . .

Inside the house again, Adams once more examined the dead girl. He had known cases before where a great nervous shock had cured paralysis, sometimes permanently. But in this case the shock and the exertion had been too great and had killed instead of cured. He stood up, went back into the bedroom where the others were gathered.

Mason was holding Marie Meadows by the wrist, saying, "You've got to leave now. I'm taking you to York. I'll come back then, and—" He stopped. Looking at Ann, he said, "You come with us if you want."

Ann hesitated. She saw Adams in the door and went toward him, hands out, her face a mask of grief. Near the window, Bob Wilson stood with his white head bowed. Two tears had slipped from his faded blue eyes.

Adams stood flat-footed, hands gripping each side of the door. His lips were thin, nostrils distended with heavy breathing. If Mason was the fiend behind this, Ann certainly wasn't driving away with him. If Mason were innocent, it would be best to have him take her to safety. Personally, he was staying and fighting this matter through to the end. There had to be a reason, and by God! he meant to find it.

Ann settled the matter for him. "I'm going to stay here," she said huskily, "until. . . .".

Abruptly the thought came to Adams. If Mason were guilty, there might be evidence at his home—or more likely, at the funeral home. It was empty now. And while he'd be gone, it wasn't likely that Mason would try anything here, with three persons to watch him.

Adams said aloud, "I think I know where to find Dorothy Harkins. If you will all wait here a little while, I'll be back." To Ann he said, "Will you get me that rifle now?"

Ann held to him. "Where are you going . . . ?"

Adams gently pulled free. "I'll be back," he said.

THE Mason funeral home was an oblong, stucco building with the sedate, solid front of most funeral houses. A lighter-colored extension at the rear showed where the crematorium had recently been added.

The front door swung open at Adams' touch and he went in without pausing. He crossed the thick-carpeted reception room, the chapel where services were held. He was at the door of the long corridor leading to the offices and working rooms at the rear, when he heard the sound. It tied him motionless, head pushed forward and cocked to one side, listening. The butt of the rifle was tucked into his right armpit.

The sound came again. The rasp of a drawer being pulled open, a man's grunt of satisfaction.

Adams started forward, quietly. He kept the rifle at ready, finger on the trigger. The sound had come from the rear of the building, where the crematorium and the new offices were cut off by a curtain.

He pushed past the curtain, saw light spilling across the gloomy hallway from a doorway on his right. He heard papers rustle, the sound of footsteps. Adams kept close to the left side of the hall until he reached a point where he could see inside the room. It was the crematory room. On the left wall he could see the end of the plant, the square door through which the caskets might be shoved to the heat.

He took another step, saw a table and chair in the middle of the room. Against the far wall was a low, rubber-wheeled carrier for coffins. The man was evidently working near the door on the right, out of Adams' sight.

The doctor took one more step forward. It brought him full into the yellow rectangle of light.

Inside the room Ben Larkin, the town marshal, was bending over a small office-desk. The top was littered with papers and Larkin was shuffling through them awkwardly, his sallow, lined face held close. He did not see the man outside and in the quiet Adams could hear the rustle of the papers as Larkin moved them.

Adams lowered the rifle, took one step into the room, letting his heels thud. "Hello, Marshal," he said.

Larkin leaped like a frightened cat. His right hand dropped a long envelope, flashed to his hip, swung up the big forty-five. His shoulders swooped low; his lips parted.

"How the hell—?" There was a dazed, surprised look on his face that faded quickly. "Whatta you want?" he asked.

Adams hesitated. He was a stranger in this town and country folk were suspicious of strangers. And why was Larkin so surprised to see him? Had he believed him to be tied up in the swamp? Adams lied, "I saw you come over not so long ago and followed. I wanted to see you."

"Yeah?" Larkin said. "What about?"

"About these damn killings, this whole horrible mess." He began to pace the floor as though nervous, his eyes darting about. He wanted to see as much as he could.

"What about 'em?" Larkin asked. He tried to make the words sound harsh, but Adams caught the strain in the man's voice. His nerves were cracking. Born in the lower middle class, the constable had been raised on stories of Negro superstition, though as a white man, he denied their truth. Now a combination of eerie happenings, a lack of sleep, and a constant fear for his own life was breaking down the man's resistance. He'd go to pieces soon.

Adams was near the desk now. He stooped, carelessly picked up a sheet of paper from the floor. His eyes flicked over the page. The second sheet, evidently, of a government report. He saw the words, "oil on sandy land is—"

Larkin jumped forward, snatched the paper from Adams. His face was purple with anger. "Why the hell you lookin' at other folks' mail?" he snapped.

Adams' lips curled back and words rose to his throat, but he stopped them. If he angered Larkin now, it might cause trouble, serious trouble. And a new idea had come to him. Unless the missing doctor was the man back of all this killing and terror, the criminal would not return to the shack in the swamp. Every other person in the town had learned that Adams had escaped. But why not bring Lem Prune to the criminal, let him identify the man who gave him dope?

He said to Larkin, "I was just picking it up," and tossed the paper on the desk. "I think I'll go on back to the Meadows'." The rifle cradled under his arm, he went out. Larkin glared after him. . . .

CHAPTER SEVEN

The Girl in the Swamp

THE three-quarters moon had swung up into the sky, but a tinge of sunlight remained in the west. Tom Adams set out on a long-legged trot for the point where he had left Crazy Man's Swamp. As he ran, the last faint sunset glow died and darkness came out of the swamp to meet and mingle with the pale moonlight.

He pushed steadily through the swamp, flicking occasional bushes out of the way with the rifle butt. The knife stuck in his trousers handicapped his movements slightly and he shifted its position, kept going. Already the lightning-bugs were out in myriads, weaving webs of silver and gold light that twinkled and vanished.

When first he heard the voices ahead he thought it was some night-sound of the swamp, but then it came again, and he paused, listening. Abruptly the hideous, jarring laughter of the idiot Lem Prune struck at his ears. The sound came from directly ahead—from the shack. But he had left Prune gagged.

The idiot laughed again, someone else joining with him this time. And then a woman's voice whimpered through the darkness in a soft, hopeless cry of pleading and despair.

Tom Adams sucked a wild, agonized

breath into his lungs? Ann. . . . ? He shook his head, cursed through clenched teeth. He plunged forward, rifle ready.

The voices came clearer as he started up the low knoll to the shack. From the window came a dull, flickering light. He heard the girl whimpering now, a low, almost continuous moaning. Laughter and jabbering, insane voices. The unceasing, confused babble of half-wits.

Adams reached the open window, moving with long, cautious strides. His knuckles were white about the rifle, his fingers curled hard around the trigger. He could feel his breath move like a hard, frosted thing from his lungs to his nostrils. He stopped it, held it soundless while he peered in the window.

The breath wheezed from him, a sigh of mingled relief and furious anger.

The room was a lurid flickering of yellow and red and black from the smoky pine torch stuck in the window-sill. There were two men in the room: Lem Prune and another half-breed whose face and even the ragged overalls he wore resembled Prune's. On her knees near the far wall was Dorothy Harkins.

Her short black hair was in wild confusion about her face, in which fear and pain and horror had mingled to wipe out all coherent expression; so that now she crouched on hands and knees, moaning like an animal. The clothing had been ripped from her body and bits of it were scattered about the shack. Adams could see the lurid glow of firelight on the flesh of her throat and breast. Something had scratched her right cheek, leaving a narrow thread of blood. Two large welts showed red upon her shoulders.

Hatred flamed through Adams then, a hatred as bitter and intense as if he had at last found the murderer of Ann's father. Both Prune and the other half-breed had their backs to the door, looking at the girl and laughing. In his hand

Prune held the belt which Adams had used to bind him, and as the doctor watched he swung the belt high, whacked it across the girl's back! A bloody streak showed where the blow fell. The girl moaned softly, but did not try to move. There was utter helplessness and despair in her position.

Adams went forward with a rush, but before he could reach the door the second half-breed had moved. Laughing insanely, he leaned down, caught Dorothy's bobbed hair and jerked her head erect. The firelight glowed on the girl's round breasts, on the curved flatness of her stomach. Prune lashed out with the belt again, full across her breasts. The girl cried out in agony.

Adams burst through the door shouting, "Damn it! Take your hands off that girl and keep 'em up! Both of you!"

THE two men whirled like frightened cats. Prune flung the belt away as he spun. A mad hatred blazed in his eyes, turned to fear when he saw the gun. Both began to cringe backward, simpering.

The girl kept sobbing, her head sunk on her breasts again. All hope of escape had long since gone from her and she knelt there, her mind drowned by the horror of what had happened, thinking only that this was another half-breed come to molest her.

Adams was breathing heavily, his finger twitching against the trigger. For the moment a wild impulse to kill these beasts burned him. He shook his head fiercely. He had to take Prune back to the village, use him to help solve this mystery. He'd take the other also. Much better to let the law settle with them. His eyes flickered to the girl and he said gently, "Dorothy. Dorothy Harkins."

The girl quit whimpering but did not raise her head. Adams could see the muscles in her shoulders and in her plump legs tightening, as though the words had stirred some memory in her and she was fighting to understand. "Dorothy," he said. "I'm Tom Adams. Ann's friend. I'm going to take you home."

She raised her head then, her eyes big and wild in her face. For a moment she stared uncomprehending. Then suddenly she swayed forward, buried her face in her arms and began to sob. Adams nodded grimly. Crying was good for her.

The two half-breeds were crouched in the corner. Their eyes caught the light of the burning pine torch and glowed like the eyes of wolves. Their faces seemed to twist and weave in the smoky light. Adams could see the bone handle of a knife above the second one's belt.

"Pull that knife out," he said, "and slide it along the floor, over this way. Easy." The muzzle of the rifle swung to cover the man's chest. The half-breed did as Adams told him, and the doctor picked the knife from the floor, stuck it beside the other one.

The girl's sobs were quieter now. "Can you walk?" he asked her. "We've got to take these fellows with us, so I can't carry you."

She raised her head and the tears in her eyes glittered in the firelight. "Yes," she whispered. "I—I can walk." She got to her feet weakly, holding against the wall.

Adams said, "Slip on that dress. It's not too badly torn." And when she had finished, he added, "We've got to tie these fellows' wrists so they'll be a little safer, and we'll halter them together so they can't run away." His eyes found the belt and tie with which he had bound Prune. He nodded toward them, told Dorothy, "Pick those up and tie them while I keep 'em covered." He looked at Prune, jerked his head. "Come out in the middle of the room."

The girl picked up the bits of clothing while Prune edged forward. His mouth was open and there were white flecks of foam about the corners of his lips. His face was dirty, his black hair tangled. He looked like a dog gone mad as he came, half crouched, his breath making a whistling sound. He paused in the middle of the floor.

The girl had started toward him, but her eyes were on Adams in the doorway. Tears were still trickling down her face and the torn dress had fallen from her right shoulder. Then, in the tear-dimmed eyes, light flamed abruptly, terror. She screamed, flung both hands up, pointing toward Adams.

The doctor whirled, leaping inside the room. The movement was not fast enough. A man struck him full in the back. Their legs tangled and they smashed to the floor. Adams caught a glimpse of a snarling idiot's face, of a knife-blade glittering. He released the rifle, stabbed up his right hand, felt the thud of the wrist bringing the knife down.

Even before the other two men had crossed the room to bury him under a rolling, tossing mass of flesh, he knew what had happened. As silently as the animals they lived with, another half-breed had slipped upon him. Only the girl's warning had saved him from a knife in the back. Now, as he struggled furiously, his right hand gripping the other's wrist, he shouted, "Run, Dorothy! Get out of here!"

HE FELT knees driving against his legs, bruising him. A fist crashed into the top of his head. In their fury the three men were handicapping one another. But the knife-blade was three inches from Adams' cheek, bearing down. Every muscle in his body ached as he tried to hold it off. His body creaked from the strain and sweat leaped from his pores. The wrist began to grow slippery in his fingers. He fought frantically to hold it.

A knee jarred into Adams' hip. His feet beat the floor as he tried to roll, but legs were tangled with his own. Fists hammered at his ribs, at the side of his face. If the men had not been fools, he thought wildly, they would have picked up the rifle and killed him. But in their half-witted anger they thought only of their hands and knives.

One of the knives in his trousers sliced at Adams' stomach as he tried to roll, but he managed to get his left hand under the man on top, grip a bone handle. He jerked the weapon out, slashed wildly. A man screamed.

At the same instant the wrist slipped from his right hand. He snapped his head to one side, felt fire rip across his cheek. Warm blood spewed over his face.

Adams struck with the knife again and a man howled, jumped from the doctor's legs. The half-breed's knife flashed high again, paused for the downward stroke. A hand tightened on Adams' left wrist.

With one terrific movement the doctor got his feet under him, heaved. His body went skidding across the floor. The idiot's knife came down, missed. Then Adams was struggling to his feet, back against the wall, blood pouring from his sliced cheek.

Prune and the late-comer were facing him, between him and the door. The other half-breed was on his knees, both blood-stained hands gripping his ribs low on the left side. Dorothy Harkins had gone.

Adams' eyes flickered. If he could get the rifle. . . . But it lay at Prune's feet, and as the idiot took a half step forward, his toe kicked it. He looked down now, yelled in joy, and ducked for it.

It was Adams' last chance and he didn't hesitate. He launched his body straight at the idiot with the knife and the open door beyond. His right arm was as stiff as the blade he held in front of him, driving like a halfback ready to stiff-arm.

The idiot's arm flashed up. His knife was blood-smeared and foul in the shifting light. But Adams came straight on and the breed's nerve broke. He flung himself to one side, snarling. Adams went out the door and into darkness like a rock from a catapult.

He twisted to the right, away from the trail. If Dorothy had gone that way he didn't want them to catch her. The moon had come higher and the house and the tops of the knoll were washed in light. Forty feet away were the dank swamp and the black shadows of the trees. Adams raced for them.

Behind him he heard the idiots shouting. The rifle cracked and a bullet whined past his ear. He flung himself sideways in midstride. His foot caught in a trailing vine and he pitched ten feet through the air, struck rolling. The idiots shouted and came pounding after him, thinking the bullet had struck home.

Then Adams was on his feet, driving into the darkness of the swamp. Mud had sucked at his feet, slowed him down. Prune screamed in fury and the rifle cracked twice; but Adams was blotted out by the shadows and the bullets went wide. The half-breeds came racing after him.

He turned sharply to the right, trying to move silently. He slipped, fell with a splash into slimy, inch-deep water. But Prune and his companion were plunging into the swamp and did not hear.

Adams kept heading toward the rising moon, but without the wagon-trail the going was hard. Time and again he sank in mud above his ankles and once plunged waist-deep into stinking water and slime.

IT TOOK him more than an hour to get out of the swamp. He had lost his coat. His shirt and trousers were mud-caked and tattered. Blood and slime had made his face into a mask of horror. Weariness was like a drug in his muscles and his feet dragged as he moved them forward.

He came out of the cornfield and started across the wide lawn of Ann's house. Lights showed from several windows, but the house was as quiet as death. He could see the dark shadow of the sweet-gum tree like a blot of ink against the white.

Even when he reached the tree and turned toward the front of the house, he heard no sound except the wet sloshing of his shoes, the scraping of the muddy trousers as he walked. There would naturally be quiet, he thought. This was not a time for laughter and talking.

Then he noticed that Mason's automobile was no longer parked in front of the house. He paused for a moment, swaying on weary legs. Had the undertaker persuaded Marie to leave town with him? Had he taken Ann?

Abruptly fear thrust its cold fingers into his chest. The mud cracked on his lids as his eyes grew wide. The utter silence of the house took on a new and terrible meaning. The quiet seemed to grow, to take on weight and crowd about him, thrusting at his eardrums. Slowly, his breath heavy in his nostrils, he went toward the steps and up them to the front door.

The door was open and beyond the hall showed brightly lighted—and empty.

Tom Adams' nerves broke for a moment and he went down the corridor with a rush. "Ann!" he shouted. "Ann!" The words boomed through the house, drowning the thud of his mud-coated shoes, echoing along the hall and up the dark stair-well.

He reached the bedroom and stood there, gripping the doorsill with blood-coated hands, staring at the empty room. "Ann," he whispered. The word stirred tiny waves of sound that lapped out into stillness, and faded.

He turned and went rushing from room to room, shouting. In the kitchen where she had fallen, lay the dead girl. He and the corpse of Edith Meadows were alone.

Two persons had died in this house—Edith Meadows and her father. Now Ann had disappeared. If she, too. . . . All his efforts, all his fighting and wounds had amounted to nothing. This monster, this demon had won in the end.

He didn't *know*, of course, that this Thing had carried Ann away. And yet. . . . "It's nerves," Adams said harshly. "If I were one of my patients, I'd say take a rest." But his laugh was without humor.

He went back to the bedroom, staggering with fear and the weariness which had descended on him again. There was not even a note. But against the right wall was an overturned chair. And on one leg of the chair was a small blood-stain. He leaned closer, staring, his breath frozen.

The blood was fresh.

The silence of the house came like thick-packed, black cotton about his ears, about his body, holding him motionless, as still as the corpse two rooms beyond. Across his muddy forehead one slow drop of sweat trickled, growing bigger, mud-colored.

It was a strain to raise his hand to wipe away the perspiration. As the bloody fingers moved upward he saw that they were quivering. He stopped the hand, chest high, tried to force it to steadiness. The fingers kept quivering and he cursed aloud.

So—he had lost. The monster had won, and this was Ann's blood upon the chair. She had been killed. He would go next. Another victim to the creature that could kill and vanish. Well, if Ann was dead, he didn't care. . . .

Then . . . he had turned and was running toward the front of the house before the thought had become clearly conscious in his mind. He never took time to put it into words, even mentally. Before his eyes had flashed a vision of Ann; and his right hand had suddenly felt warm as though he was touching that crematory door. . . .

The three or four street lights which the town boasted were not burning tonight but the moonlight made a dull white river of the dusty street. Once he thought it was odd that this street should be so dusty and that little white clouds should flutter around his feet as he ran, when only a mile away Crazy Man's Swamp was full of water and muck. Then he had rounded the corner into the rear street of the village and was racing down it toward the Mason Funeral Home. It was less than a block away.

Two men came from a house on the right, shouting. One of them was pointing wildly, the other raising a rifle. Tom Adams whirled toward the trees lining the left side of the street, the house beyond the narrow walk. He leaped sideways, running, twisting, dodging. Breath was like a hot iron in his nostrils. He wondered how well the idiot could shoot.

He heard the whine of the bullet so close that he jerked his head even as he heard the report of the gun. Then he was into the shadows, hurtling for the protection of the deserted house beyond. The gun cracked three times, fast. A bullet glanced from one of the trees, went wailing out into the night.

CHAPTER EIGHT

Into the Crematory

AS ADAMS raced toward the back of the house, he heard the half-breeds start after him, still shouting. He reached the rear, cut to the right. Thirty yards ahead was the dull tan outline of the funeral home.

No light showed from the windows of the funeral parlors and evidently the building had no rear door. Behind, the idiots were still searching for him. His lungs felt swollen as thought they would burst against his ribs, and the race had started blood flowing from his cheek again. He could feel it dripping onto his shoulder. He was too weak to fight now. If the half-breeds caught him it would mean death. And if he entered this home of death, unarmed except for a knife— if the monster behind these killings, the man who had doped and bribed the half-witted village were here—what then. . . ?

He stood there while the jaws of hell closed on him from both directions.

Abruptly he heard Prune scream, and knew that the man had seen him. He leaped along the side of the funeral home toward the front, crouching low, hidden now by the shadows. He heard the swish of grass as the breeds came rushing toward him.

Adams saw that he couldn't make the front without being seen. Three feet ahead was an open window, shoulder high. He leaped for it, slapped his bloody hands on the sill, and throwing the last ounce of his strength into the effort, flung himself up. His knees hooked on the sill and he balanced there for one second, staring into the darkened room.

Behind him, Prune shouted again. A rifle cracked and the bullet struck like a hot pin in Adams' left arm. He swayed forward.

Across the room and corridor beyond a door burst open. Light fell out into the hallway, almost to the open door of the room into which Adams was crawling. He saw the dark figure of a man framed in the doorway, saw the gun in his hand. And he saw the lighted room beyond the man—the crematory room!

In that room Ann Meadows, her clothes half torn from her body, her long auburn hair wild about her face, was tied to a chair!

Then the man saw him framed in the window of the darkened room, swung up the gun.

Tom Adams dived forward and to his right. He heard the pistol thunder, the smack of a rifle-bullet striking the window-sill while he was still in the air. He hit the floor with a boom, rolled farther to the right, out of range of the hall and window.

For a moment he knelt there, regaining his breath, eyes jerking from doorway to window. Evidently the fire from inside had frightened the breeds, for they made no sound. The doorway remained empty and Tom Adams grinned a blood-caked, crooked smile. Whoever had tied Ann didn't know whether or not he had a gun and was afraid to come in the room after him. Adams began to crawl toward the doorway, silently.

Outside in the hall he could hear the man's expectant breathing—like some animal waiting at the mouth of his lair.

He was near the door when he heard the first move. The soft *tup tup* of stealthy walking. Then came the clunk of wood on wood from the room across the hall, and what might have been a muffled cry.

His face flat against the floor so that a man watching would look over him, Tom Adams peered around the door-sill. His jaw sagged open at what he saw.

IN THE room directly across the hall old Bob Wilson, his white hair tousled over his head, a gun in his right hand, was trying to drag Ann from her chair. He was keeping his eyes on the doorway, and, using only one hand, seemed unable to move the girl. She jerked away and half fell from the chair.

"All right!" the old man snapped the words aloud. "You're going in the fire unconscious." He swung the gun up over her head.

Tom Adams never heard the curse that broke from his lips. He came to his feet in a surge, but had to round the door and stumbled. His wounded left arm struck the sill. Then he was leaping across the hall at the banker, shoulders low, head forward.

Wilson heard him strike the door, swung the gun around. Adams saw the black muzzle straight in front, but there was no chance to dodge. He dived. Flame leaped. The gun roared.

A star-shell exploded on Adams' skull and the world was a blaze of light that went out suddenly.

He never felt himself strike the floor, though he never totally lost consciousness. Through the blackness where lights sparkled came strange words. "Well, you've seen *him* die. Right through the head. Now both of you in the crematory and there'll be no trace of you." Then there was another sound: footsteps beating. More voices, cursing, shouting.

Finally Tom Adams fought his eyes open, fought the blackness from under his skull. Wilson, the gun still gripped in his hand, was standing before Ann Meadows. The girl's head was flung back, her eyes wide and rolling. To one side of her were the two half-breeds.

Wilson was gesturing toward the open door of the crematory. "Throw those two in," he snapped. "Then we'll talk."

Lem Prune shook his head. "Not the girl. Want her."

"Uh-huh," his companion said. "Other girl got 'way. Want this one." He took one step toward Ann, punched her in the breast with his forefinger and began to laugh. The girl tried to jump away from him and as she tottered on the edge of the chair, the breed put his arm around her, pulled her back.

Wilson caught him by the shoulder, snatched him around. "You can't have her!" he yelled. He pointed at the crematorium with the gun, said, "Throw her in there."

The breed kept his arm around Ann. His hand began to feel along the flesh of her throat, downward. His breathing was harsh. Prune asked, "Throw 'em in there, you give more powder?"

"Damn you," Wilson snapped. "I haven't got any more. I told you that."

The words seemed to strike the half-wit's brain slowly, soaking in. His eyes began to glitter; his mouth was open and Adams could see his tongue licking at his lips.

The other man was still holding the girl, laughing at her struggles, his right hand crawling down her breast. He kept gloating eyes on Ann, but his words were for Wilson. "Want the girl. We keep her, throw in the man for you."

Wilson swung the gun toward him. "Damn it! You'll throw them both in, or—" He stopped, staring at the expression on the half-breed's face.

The man had taken his hand from Ann's breast. He was half crouched, glaring at the old banker. Saliva drooled from his snarling mouth. "Gona keep the girl," he husked. "Maybe kill you, but keep her."

Wilson went a step backward before the threat of the madman's eyes. His finger twitched at the trigger of the gun as he hesitated. Lem Prune was moving toward him, slowly.

"All right," Wilson said. "You can have her. But throw in this fellow." He nodded at Adams lying helpless on the floor, his face a mass of blood.

With a quick cry the half-wit jumped back to the girl. Ann screamed against her gag as he began to paw at her, running his filthy hands over her body. Adams fought his weakened muscles, tried to crawl erect, but his legs barely twitched.

Wilson was saying to Lem Prune, "Throw the man in that door. Quick!"

"You gimme powder then?" The idiot was breathing rapidly. His tongue licked across dry lips.

"Throw him in," Wilson said.

THE half-wit moved slowly. He bent, put the rifle on the floor. He slid his arms under Adams' neck and knees. The doctor struck at the man's face, cursing hoarsely. The blow was feeble and Prune laughed shortly. He picked Adams from the floor, took one step toward the crematory door.

Despair, fury, terror, surged like a black wave through Adams' body. Three seconds to live. And then, Oh God! to burn. . . . He tried to fight, but the idiot held him like a baby.

Then a desperation-born idea came to him as in a dream. He heard his voice without knowing the words it was going to speak. "Wilson's not going to give you any more dope—more powder. He hasn't any more. I have it all."

Prune stopped. Still holding Adams in his arms, he turned toward Wilson. "You got powder? Show me."

Wilson's face flushed red with anger under his white hair. "Damn it!" he snapped. "I told you there was no more. Now or ever!"

The whole thing broke like thunder.

Before Wilson could swing his gun, Lem Prune had dropped Adams, launched his body straight at the banker. He smashed into the old man, driving him back toward the crematory, battering at his face.

Adams struck the floor not more than five feet from the rifle. His head spun dizzily, and he was conscious that his left arm worked slowly, painfully. He heard the roar of Wilson's gun, but did not turn. Every fiber in his body was bent on reaching the rifle. He lunged, rolled, fought toward it.

The half-breed who held the girl heard him, whirled. His dark hand whipped to his waist, came up holding his knife. He jerked it high, dived at Adams.

Adams made one last roll, caught up the rifle. The twenty-two spat once, twice. Two small holes popped in the breed's shirt, but the small slugs did not slow his rush. The knife drawn back, he came down at the prostrate doctor.

There was no chance to fire again. Still lying on his side, Adams jabbed with the rifle, stuck the muzzle full into the falling man's throat.

Behind him he heard Wilson's gun blast again. Heard the banker scream furiously, a wild, horrible cry of terror.

The breed above Tom Adams swayed on the rifle muzzle. Adams squeezed the trigger of the gun again. The report was muffled, softer than the thud of the body striking the floor. . . .

He saw the girl's wide eyes staring beyond him, and turned. It was a slow, agonized movement. He kept waiting to hear Wilson's gun once more, to feel the bullet crash into him. His body seemed to move like a slow-motion picture, endlessly.

The banker screamed again. His gun roared.

Adams stopped his movement. "Great God!" he whispered.

The banker's head and shoulders were inside the crematory and the half-breed Prune was shoving, cramming in his body. It seemed incredible that Wilson could have missed his shots at that range, but even in the long second that Adams watched, Prune made one last heave. The banker cried again, a cry that turned Adams' stomach and that suddenly burned short. The body slid out of sight inside the square door.

Slowly Lem Prune turned. Adams tried to bring up the gun but it was heavy . . . heavy. The room was spinning. He saw Prune take one step toward him. Adams tried to center the rifle but the muzzle wouldn't move.

The room kept spinning and Prune seemed to waver with it. The rifle muzzle wouldn't follow him. The half-breed was almost on Adams now. Too late to use the gun. The man was pitching down at him. Down. . . .

For a long while Adams lay staring, dazed, at the man beside him, at the blood oozing from Prune's chest and belly.

Bob Wilson had not missed his last shots. . . .

THE things that followed seemed to Adams as though they were happening in a dream. He somehow forced himself to his knees, crawled and cut the ropes from Ann Meadows. He remembered the abrupt appearance of Sam Mason, and heard the faraway sound of the man's voice as he explained that he had just returned from driving Marie to York. Later, Dorothy Harkins had entered.

Next, he remembered Ann telling him to be quiet as they drove toward a hospital. She was explaining that she had recognized Wilson as the man outside her window by the way he held his head. "Edith must have recognized him, too," Ann said. "That's what frightened her. Maybe he wouldn't have hurt me if I hadn't recognized him. He only wanted me to leave town."

"I know," Adams whispered. "All the property around this town has oil. I saw the government report. But the townspeople didn't know about the oil. Wilson's bank must have had mortgages on nearly all the property, but the government is making it difficult to foreclose. He figured if he could make everybody leave town, they'd all be glad to get what they could, stay—"

"Hush!" Ann said. She cradled his bloody head in her left arm. Put her right hand to his lips.

It was the next day before Adams learned what had happened to Ben Larkin and to Dorothy Harkins. Larkin, too, had recognized Wilson, Ann said. Then Wilson had killed him, cremated the body. Dorothy had been kidnaped during the morning, held prisoner in the swamp village until she was carried to the shack where her captor found and released Prune.

"Wilson told me about the explosion that happened when we were first coming here," Ann said. "He had fixed it up, had the idiot set it off. Then he ran his car into the shallow ditch on purpose. If Larkin hadn't come by they would have killed me then."

"What about Dr. McGregor?" Adams asked. "Was that a mask?"

"Yes. He told me he'd killed McGregor because the doctor suspected him. He drugged Mason's liquor, slipped McGregor's body into the crematory instead of old John Perkins'. He threw Perkins' body into the half-breed village where you found it, thinking that would throw suspicion on Sam, who claimed he'd burned the body. He made the mask using the doctor's actual face after he'd killed him." Ann shuddered.

Adams raised a hand to his bandaged cheek. "They nearly made a mask of me," he said. "And a damn ugly one."

Ann leaned forward, stopped. "I can't kiss you, there're so many bandages."

"Take 'em off," Adams said. "No need to save my life if I can't use it."

THE END

THE HOUSE WHERE HORROR DWELT

By G. T. Fleming-Roberts

(Author of "Blood Magic")

Fleeing the death that had reached for them from out the storm, they lived to wish that they had died before entering that bloated, cliff-perched house of evil hospitality.

LOOKING straight down from the rocky promontory on which he stood, Bill Tethwick could see little more than the foamy sea fog that rose like steam from the bubbling waters below. He ought to have been thankful he was safe, but it was hard knowing that, down there beneath the mist, pounding waves and jagged crags were grinding the *Darling* to matchwood. The *Darling,* a sixty-foot gas cruiser, had been a present to his wife a year before. Tethwick had considered himself quite a sailor until tonight. Gail, his wife, stood beside him, salt water molding her once natty sport suit close to her body.

"Swell way to end our vacation," he said. It was an apology to Gail.

"If it were only the end," she murmured fearfully. "Bill, have you *any* idea where we are?"

He knew they were somewhere along the Maine coast, but that covered a pretty ragged stretch of territory. "Somewhere near Folly Point," he hazarded. "You're not worried, darling?"

"Not worried!" Gentle chiding there. "Perhaps hundreds of miles from home, shipwrecked, standing here on this lump of rock like a pair of—of—"

"Not scared?" Tethwick had yet to learn the meaning of the word fear.

"Yes. The sea frightens me when it's like this. Land seems so small, such a precious thing besides the ocean. So hungry, the sea; so eager to swallow the very rocks we stand on." She hugged her cold, wet shoulders.

He stamped his foot to convince her of the solidity of the rocks. Then he saw that she was cold, grunted, and began peeling off his jacket. "We're mighty lucky," he spoke seriously. "We got all the breaks —every one." He wrapped his chamois jacket around his wife and pulled up the zipper-fastener.

A huge wave dashed its tons of water against the rocks, snarled in defeat, and fell back into the clammy mist. Gail clung closer to him, making them both warmer. "Bill," she said huskily, "we can't stay here. I've read of people dying of exposure."

"We're not going to," he assured her; "not stay here, I mean—and the other, too. I've got the flashlight, if the water hasn't ruined it." He fumbled in his pocket, learned he had spoken too soon. He'd lost the light some way.

For another minute they stood there shivering. He wondered when Gail would ask why he didn't turn the flashlight on. The full moon was pushing aside its mottled veil and revealing sinister shadows among the crags. Tethwick looked around. "Think there's a sort of path winding up that way. We'll try it. Want to stick here while I reconnoiter?"

For an answer, she clung a little closer to his arm.

It was a path—a narrow, irregular trough ambling upwards through the rocks. Moonlight wasn't very dependable. They groped their way for a hundred feet or so.

"I might try shouting," he said, knowing that if she didn't say "yes, do!" he would try no such thing. There wasn't a chance of anyone being near a God-forsaken spot like this at midnight.

"Try it," Gail urged.

Tethwick sucked a deep lungful of salt air and bellowed, "Halloo there! Help!"

Then they walked on. Echoes, following up the twisting natural corridor, whispered back eerie, phantasmal mutterings. He didn't try any more shouting.

A sharp turn in the path, and Tethwick felt the sudden pressure of his wife's hand on his arm. Almost as soon as she, he saw a light bobbing towards them— a lantern of some sort, its glare mellowed by the mist. Gail hung back. "Who do you suppose it is?" she whispered.

"It's luck, honey. We get all the breaks. That's a man, and we can't be far from shelter."

The gaunt shadow came on at a rolling gait, lantern swinging like a pendulum.

"Ahoy, strangers!" the man called.

"Bill, I don't like his voice," Gail insisted.

TETHWICK had noticed it, too. An odd, chuckling voice, yet it was hardly cheerful. Perhaps mist dampened it. He could see now that the strange man carried a lantern that sent out a dozen miniature star rays from its black shield. He was tall. Hard work or over-indolence had humped his shoulders. His forehead was narrow and plastered with a handful of red hairs. His jaws were broad, powerful; lips thin and cruelly humorous. One of his eyes was patched with a black cloth.

"Know why you came here, Mister?" asked the stranger.

"Not from choice, I assure you," Bill replied.

"Guess not, guess not!" laughed the man. "Oughta steered t'other side of the reef, but I guess you didn't know there was a reef there."

"Any place my wife and I can get shelter for tonight?"

"Sure. Ain't that what I'm here for? Sure it is. You can stay up here tonight," he chuckled again. "House big enough for a dozen."

"Good." Bill sounded enthusiastic. "I'll pay you for your trouble, Mister—"

"Jus' call me Ole—Ole One-Eye, it is, count of that's how I am. Runnin' your own boat? A skiff, maybe?"

"Sixty-foot gas outfit," replied Bill, in spite of the warning tweak Gail gave his arm.

"Well, that's tough, Mister." Again the unpleasant giggle. Then One-Eye turned and beckoned them up the path. "The sea's bad," he mumbled as they continued the ascent. "There's bad men on the land, but there's more in the sea. Howsomever, they're dead, most of 'em. My old gent went down. Where he's at, they ain't no good."

The narrow way twisted sharply to the left at the same time presenting a flight of stairs cut in the stone. Tethwick became suddenly aware that the sky above them had been shut out by a towering, crooked building that, rooted among the scraggy rocks, seemed more of a natural growth than a work of man. More to

blemish than to beautify the ugly face of the house, small round windows were dotted here and there and glowed faintly with yellow light. A little gable jutted over the doorway and was covered with time-curled shingles. There, moss had got a foothold and tufted a portion of the roof with velvet green.

Ole One-Eye thrust an iron key into the eye of the lock and pushed back the door. Gloom was thick inside the hall. Bill Tethwick, in the doubt of a moment, looked backwards into the night, saw a full moon, wind-smeared clouds, mammoth crags, and below—the hungry maw of the sea. Nothing cheerful outside, certainly! He watched the vista narrow and disappear entirely as Ole closed the door, locked it.

One-Eye blew down into his lantern, puffing out its flame. He crossed the hall and opened a low door. Silently, he nodded towards the next room. Bill and Gail entered hesitatingly. A depressingly low ceiling with sagging beams, ridge-worn pine flooring, a Dutch oven cluttered with dull copper pots, a scattering of battered furniture. There, a woman was having trouble lounging in a broken-backed chair. She was young, though hideous as compared with Gail's wholesome beauty. Her sallow skin was pock-marked; rat-nested hair straggled over her eyes; heavy, brass ear-rings, habitually worn, had elongated the lobes of her ears. She started from a threatening doze. "More of 'em, Ole?" Her voice had an edge.

"Shut!" Ole stage-whispered. "These here is—what'd you say your name was, Mister?"

Bill told him.

"Yeah. She—" he thumbed at the ear-ringed woman, "my woman, Sadie." He clucked with his tongue and winked presumptuously at Gail. "We'll just fix up you two for the night. Got a room on the north end snug enough if you don't go for walks in your sleep. What I mean, it wouldn't do to lean too far out the window."

"Ole, you ain't goin' to put 'em next to *him?*" the woman asked.

One-Eye lifted the chimney of the lamp and flamed a wax dip. "Sure. Best bed in the house. My old woman ticked it out herself. You two're goin' to like it, and *he* won't bother—much !"

"Oh, any place will do," said Tethwick with his usual optimism. "Of course we'll pay."

"Sure," said Ole.

"Sure," echoed Ole's wife.

OLE lead off through a side door, candle guttering and spewing hot wax on his huge, red-bristled hands.

"Bill, I don't think we ought to stay here," Gail whispered. But they were already following up narrow, creaking steps. Tethwick pressed her hand and said, "They're queer folk, but decent enough."

The room in which they were to pass the night was too large to be snug. A small fireplace heaped with glowing coals tinted the place a dull red. Ole One-Eye dropped wax on a marble-topped table and anchored the candle there. He rolled back to the door and paused, one eye blinking. "Goodnight, folks—and we'll talk about pay later." He closed the door, and they could hear his footsteps receding down the corridor.

"Oh," suddenly from Gail's lips. She had left Tethwick's side and was doing miracles with her disordered hair.

"What's the matter?"

"Just the mist, dear." She laughed uneasily. "It comes up through the floor. I saw it in the mirror. Positively wraith-like !"

"The place *smells.*" Tethwick made a wry face. "Something rotten." He listened to the drumming of the sea. It sounded from below like the rhythmic beating of a giant heart buried beneath the floor.

"Bill, why wasn't there a buoy or light or something to warn us of that reef ?"

"Maybe there was. Ought to be." He was wondering how the room could be located so that the sound of the sea might come up from beneath their very feet. He was still wondering when his wife said: "Bill, listen !"

"Eh-what ?" He turned around. Gail had gone to the west wall and was listening intently.

"There's someone in the next room," she said. "Someone or *something*. Listen !"

It was the sound of some heavy body dragging across the floor of the next room, accompanied by breathing that resembled the sobs of a sick child.

Very quietly Gail said, "I don't want to stay here. I'd rather take chances on finding someplace else. I don't like that thing in the next room."

"I'll see if I can't find a better room in the house, anyway," said Tethwick. He went to the door, put his hand on the knob and turned it. Slowly, his fingers peeled from the knob. He turned helplessly towards his wife.

"I knew it would be," she said. "We're locked in here, aren't we? We're prisoners !"

Tethwick didn't hear her. He was staring at the center of the floor where a large crack extended from beneath a rag rug. From the crack clouds of mist were rising ceilingward, towering above them. He crossed the room and kicked back the rug. An iron ring was imbedded in the floor. He stooped, seized it, and pulled upwards. The trap opened. A cloud of fog puffed into the room and separated his wife from him.

"What are you going to do?" Gail asked.

"Look around a bit. There's a stairway going down. Got to see where it goes." He went to the wall, took a candle from a sconce, and lighted it from the candle on the table. "You stay here. I'll just run down to the bottom of the steps. Get into bed and pull the covers over your head if you see any spooks." His humor wasn't very funny.

He started down the steps, shielding the the candle from the draught. He knew where the smell was coming from! Air was bringing it up from this basement or whatever it was. The stairs were damned shaky. If somebody didn't break a neck one of these days—

He stopped, holding the candle high above his head. The stair rail had ended and in its place jagged rock walls crowded against the wood stair-treads. Ten more steps and he came to a smooth, stone floor. He was in a natural cavern apparently without any other entrance than the stairs from the room above. It was centered with a pool of water that throbbed with every wave that hurled itself against the rocks outside. Perhaps at low tide it would be possible to get to the open sea from this rock room. But what made the stench? Certainly, it wasn't the smell of the water.

Then he saw at the edge of the pool that which turned his blood to ice water. It was a puffy white thing like—he stepped closer to make sure—it was a human hand! Once Tethwick had found a dead rat in their basement-drain. It had been swollen all out of shape like that human hand.

He took a short step backward, gasped involuntarily as his foot touched something. He looked down. At his feet lay the body of a woman. From head to toes, the corpse was strangely twisted. Decay had bloated her face until it was a thing of horror; but even time, the action of mist and water had not erased the look of terror on those set features.

God! What hell had she been dragged through!

SUDDEN realization staggered him. Seeking refuge from the sea, he and Gail had stepped into far graver danger. He remembered the words of Ole One-Eye's wife: "More of 'em?"

Then he and Gail? . . . Like these others . . .?

With a sharp cry of dismay, he spun on his toes and leaped for the stairway. He paid for his haste with a snuffed-out candle. He reached for matches, remembered that they were water soaked, and hurried up the trembling steps as best he could in the dark. Why couldn't he see a light from the room above? He continued his mad ascent, head turned back, neck craned. Something struck his forehead a smashing blow. He staggered down a step, grasping for support that wasn't there. He regained his balance and groped with his hands above him. The trap had been closed. Surely Gail would never have done that. He pounded on the door with the flat of his hands. He shouted insane things.

Then came the sound which drove panic from his mind. It was a half-smothered scream that choked, rattled, became thin, and tapered into silence. Bill lowered his head, took another step backwards, and heaved with all the strength in his back. The trap yielded. Some heavy piece of furniture had been placed on top of it and had crashed over as he catapulted into the room. He glanced around. "Gail!" he called huskily, though his eyes told him she was not there. The door into the passageway was wide open. He ran into the hall. There, he froze like a rabbit.

In those two seconds in which he was unable to move, he experienced more horror than generally comes in an entire lifetime. Moonlight—a round, oblique column of it—passed through one of the circular windows and clearly illuminated the head and throat of a young woman. And striping her throat were pulsing shadows.

Shadows? Impossible! Fingers gripped that woman's throat—fingers that were sinewy, cruel and blunt.

But the woman wasn't Gail!

Tethwick launched a blow that started from the toes of his right foot and put the whole weight of his body behind his flying fist. He struck flesh that was hard and unyielding with an impact that sent dull pain up his arm. He saw the woman's face drop into blackness, heard the thud of her body striking the floor. A thick arm flung around Bill's waist. A great, moist palm crashed into his jaw and strained his body slowly backwards. Tethwick rained blows into a broad, beastial chest. The terrific pressure never relaxed. His spine crackled. Inches more, and he knew his back would break.

Suddenly from behind him came an odd scuffing sound accompanied by short, sobbing gasps—the same sound that Gail had noticed coming from the room next to theirs. The hideous, unseen beast that held Tethwick in deadly embrace uttered a hoarse cry. With a suddenness that shocked, Bill felt his enemy's grip relax. He pitched backwards, his head pounding onto the floor. There was a confusion of sounds—guttural cries of fear, stumbling feet, and the strange shuffling as if a heavy body dragged along the floor. Tethwick rolled over, got to his knees—but no farther.

At first, he thought it was some wraithlike cloud of mist floating along close to the floor. Mist would have moved noiselessly. This *thing* uttered little sobbing cries as it squirmed along the corridor. Striking the patch of moonlight, the writhing horror presented itself fully to Tethwick's frozen stare. It was as long as a man, yet all gleaming white like a grubworm. A misshapen hairy head was pegged on at an odd angle. It snaked along by means of stiff, white forelimbs that supported it like flippers support a seal.

Then it was gone, leaving the walls of the corridor the echo of its sobbing breath to play with. Tethwick picked himself up. His anxiety for Gail made him forget the pains that were shooting through his back. He returned to the room for the candle, went back into the hall. There were signs of neither the feverish giant who had attacked him nor the white, crawling horror that had saved his life by its opportune appearance.

He found the woman as the strangler had left her, blackened tongue lolling out between blue lips. Tethwick knew she was dead. He was about to turn away when he saw a scrap of paper gripped in her small, clenched fist. Tethwick peeled back the stiffening fingers and examined the paper. It was a note printed in smudgy penciled characters:

"Get oot of heer! Thay aint humans. Just wants to ring money oot of yer."

Tethwick stared down at the body. The features had been marred by savage brutality, but they were still delicate. Her clothes, what remained of them, were fine material. This woman hadn't written the cruel warning note! Who had?

HE CRUSHED the paper into the palm of his hand and raced down the hall towards the stairs, his wife's name sobbing in his tight throat. At the bottom of the steps he saw a huddled shadow, heard mumbling voices. The shadow became two shadows—one that moved and the other that crouched motionless. Tethwick's candle flame caught the sheen of plastered red hair. It was Ole One-Eye huddled on the steps. Sadie, his wife, was bending over him mumbling nervously: "I told you, Ole, there weren't no sense to gettin' Big Joe here. He's gone nuts, like I said he would. Women makes him like that. He got his hooks on the Carter woman. No money in straight killin'."

Ole didn't move. His wife kicked his legs savagely. "Get up! You can't have Big Joe runnin' loose over the house. You know how he is with women. He'll be after me next."

Ole didn't move. Suddenly, Sadie noticed Tethwick standing on the stairs looking down at her. Her eyes stared; her jaw dropped. When she had found her tongue, "Lord! You give me a turn! Somebody's knocked Ole on the head. Musta been Joe. Ole's bleedin'."

Tethwick could see that. Crooked lines of blood traced down Ole's forehead and trickled beneath the black cloth that patched his blind eye. "He'll get worse than that when I'm through with him," he thought grimly. But he knew he would have to keep somewhere near the good side of Sadie if he was to find Gail. Aloud, he said: "I don't give a damn about Ole. What's become of my wife?"

"Your wife? The pretty lady? How'd I know? We ain't touched her."

"What's that revolting monster that tramps around upstairs?" he asked.

'That's Big Joe. He's on the rampage. I told Ole he oughtn't to bring a half-witted maniac into a game like this."

"What kind of a game, sister?" Tethwick snarled at her.

Sadie sneered. "You'll find out!" She leered up at him viciously.

Tethwick's eyes narrowed. He leaped the remaining steps, seized the woman by the arm, and twisted it down cruelly. She shrieked, with pain and fright.

"Where's my wife, damn you? I know your dirty game. You silenced the bell-buoy that's supposed to keep the boats off the reef. You're wreckers, that's what you are. You pick up the people who get smashed on the reef, and hold them for ransom if they look like they had money. After the money's come, you kill them because you're afraid they'll squeal.

Then you throw them through that trap into the sea-cave below the house."

He shook her until she choked.

"One mistake you've been making right along—when the tide comes in, it floats the bodies so far up into the cave they can't get through to the open sea. They get caught on the rocks. You thought the bodies would be carried away, didn't you? Well, every bit of ghastly evidence —enough to hang you a dozen times—is right down in that cave. Corpses of the people you've killed! You show me where Gail is or I won't even wait for a jury to decide you deserve the death penalty!"

The woman looked frightened. "I tell you I don't know where she is. I ain't touched her. Maybe Ole or Big Joe—" she stopped, listening intently.

Tethwick heard it, too—the shuffling noise and the short, painful breathing. The white crawling thing was upstairs moving along the hall. "What's that—*thing?*" he whispered.

"That's Bubb, my brother," the woman breathed back. "He's got loose. Ole swore he'd kill him if he ever come out of his room again. Bubb's sick—has fits. You've got to help me get him back in his room. Ole hates him. He'll kill him!"

"To hell with your brother! Ole won't be hurting anyone in a long time. I've got to—"

A woman's scream, terror-laden and wavering on the pinnacle of hysteria. Gail! Tethwick's head jerked around as he tried to locate the source of the cry. It came again, fainter now. Tethwick flung Ole's wife aside and sprang through the door leading to the west side of the house. He ran across the room to a door opening upon a twisting passage. Dead ahead, he could hear huge clumsy feet pounding the floor and Gail's half-muffled screams. Somewhere, a door slammed.

Tethwick turned a corner, ran squarely into a locked door. He toed around. They could have gone no other way; there was no other door. He backed, hunched his shoulders, and drove hard against the panel. It cracked but did not give. He backed again. Now, harder! The lock was torn from its moorings. The door broke open. Tethwick tried to check himself, failed, and fell—not to the floor—into empty space. Damp wind hummed in his ears. His head was whirling. His own fear-filled voice screamed like a siren as he whirled down, down into seemingly endless darkness. A burst of yellow flame, and again the terrible dark. . . . .

GLEEFUL words were the first thing that met Tethwick's ears when he returned to consciousness. They were spoken with a bubbly, idiotic accent.

". . . An' I'm goin' to have all the fun myself, pretty lady. Usual, about the first little twist, they all hollers out they'll pay anything, and Ole makes me stop twistin'. But Ole ain't goin' to boss this show again. I'm the head man. I busted Ole's head open! That'll shut his big mouth for him!"

At first, Bill couldn't remember how he happened to be where he was. It was evidently a lofty-ceilinged room in the basement. In front of him, shutting off his view of the greater part of the room, was a scaffold staircase on heavy rollers. Then he remembered. Some great beast-man had taken Gail. He himself had followed through the door. He realized now that the basement stairs could be rolled away in order to prevent interference from the outside. But Bill hadn't waited, after smashing the door in, to find out that the stairs had been removed. He had fallen. Sharp pains twisted the length of his back. He could hardly repress a groan as he hauled himself to his feet. Beyond that movable staircase the monster was mumbling in a low voice to someone. Perhaps it was Gail. He tiptoed to one of the

wooden supports and peered around it. The hideous giant was standing facing a rusty iron fly-wheel perhaps four feet in diameter. Tethwick had never seen such a brute. He was all of seven feet tall, stripped to the waist; his great back was a mound of solid flesh and muscle. This was Big Joe.

The big man moved to one side of the fly-wheel, his thick fingers smoothing the flanged rim affectionately. Then, Bill could see the whole hellish machine. The wheel had evidently been salvaged from some wrecked steam-engine. It was mounted on an axle so that it would turn easily once its counterbalance had been thrown off dead-center. Lashed to the spokes of the wheel were two trim ankles. Gail! Good God, his wife! Her body was supported by a narrow plank; her arms and shoulders were strapped to a framework against the wall. This black fiend had only to give the fly-wheel a push and it would turn—twisting his wife's body slowly—producing a torture that would result in death.

A hoarse, mad cry was torn from Tethwick's throat. He ran from behind the movable stairway, leaped upon the back of the man-mountain. Immediately, he felt his own impotence. He might just as well have vaulted onto the back of a rhinoceros! With a snarl, Big Joe shook him off and whirled around. His great square teeth champed together like the jaws of a steel trap. His protruding eyes rolled idiotically, flamed with rage. He advanced slowly towards Tethwick, his thick arms swinging in front of him. Tethwick didn't wait. He knew what would happen if those great arms encircled him! He charged, arms swinging, but when still two yards away from the huge maniac, he changed his tactics and tackled the giant's knees like a football player. Big Joe crashed to the floor, fairly shaking the house. Tethwick released his grip, scrambled up to get astride the massive heaving chest. Big Joe rolled suddenly, pulling Bill over with him, smothering him beneath his great weight. Tethwick felt thick fingers dig into his throat. He had already seen what those great hands could do! He beat his fists wildly against the ugly, beastial features. The room was taking on a reddish glow—swirling. Tethwick felt the drumming of his heart in the arteries at his temples. Another moment and—

"Joe, you damn' fool!" A voice rang out, reverberating throughout the cellar. The half-wit's fingers stiffened. His great bulk rolled from Bill Tethwick. Red mist cleared from Bill's eyes. He looked up at the door high in the wall. Ole One-Eye was standing there, his face bespattered with blood from the wound on his head. In his hand, he swung a steel-barbed leather lash. "Joe, you fool!" he shouted. "Damn you, these people are worth money. They'll pay plenty to get out of a mess like this! You crazy, murdering devil!"

A new figure appeared in the doorway. It was Ole's wife, Sadie. In her hand, she carried a coil of rope which she dropped down into the cellar. "Get down there, Ole!" she ordered. "That slobberin' idiot will ruin our game with his killin'!"

Ole One-Eye crouched at the door sill, feeling for the rope that hung over the edge. Big Joe stood there, blood-shot eyes afire, his shoulders heaving from the exertion of his struggle with Tethwick. He seemed unable to comprehend Ole's movements. Of one thing Bill was certain—the maniac had felt Ole's lash—feared it as a lion fears the whip of its trainer. Tethwick picked himself up and turned to the fly-wheel where his wife was bound. He was surprised how quickly his nerve-shaken fingers untied the rope, released her ankles. Next he squirmed around the wheel and removed the straps that held her shoulders rigid against the frame.

Gail's timorous gaze left his face, strained towards the other end of the room and filled suddenly with horror. The room was filled abruptly with a roar of pain and fury. Tethwick turned. The giant imbecile had flung all his weight against the movable stairway, had pushed it back into place, pinning Ole like a fly against the wall as the red-haired man commenced to descend the rope. Ole's arms beat out madly, frantically, from behind the stair supports. From his throat shriek after shriek was wrenched as Big Joe pushed mightily—*pushed* until Ole's cries were crushed within his racked mangled body.

THEN another figure was framed in the high doorway above Tethwick's head—a slight slender figure of a man in a cotton night-gown. A small rifle wavered in his nervous fingers. He shouted in a thin, shaky voice. "This time I'll get you, you dirty—" His gun started cracking—wild shots that spanged against the cellar walls. And with every shot, he came down a step towards the big negro.

A savage oath exploded from Big Joe. With a blurred motion of his right arm, he jerked a vicious-looking knife from his belt, lunged up the steps at his diminutive foeman. Once, a bullet thudded into him, stopped him, but only for a moment; then he was moving on, facing the hail of lead, his left hand clawing clumsily at his blood-splashed chest. The knife commenced its ghastly work. One swift, upward blow, and the little man in white uttered a surprised gasp, toppled over the edge of the stairs, and sprawled disjointedly to the floor below.

With a bellowing roar of triumph, Big Joe lunged through the door at the head of the stairs and disappeared.

Bill released his fear-stricken wife

hastily, crossed to the little man in white. The latter was bleeding profusely from a slash in his chest, like a steer in a slaughter-house. Tethwick knelt, raised the frail man gently. He opened his eyes—muttered low words, smiling a little. "Guess I got him, stranger. Big Joe was always plaguing me. But he always was scared when I got one of my fits and crawled along the floor—"

This, then, was Bubb, the epileptic brother of Sadie. He went on weakly. "It was a bad game, stranger. Sadie wasn't to blame. It was Ole. He's a wrecker . . . held people for ransom . . . tortured them when they wouldn't pay. And when they *did* pay . . . he killed 'em. To keep 'em mum. The last one, that Carter woman, they took off a wreck—Big Joe and Ole did. I tried to warn her . . . wrote her a note . . . Ole kept me locked up most of the time—"

A paroxysm of coughing seized him, ended only when a terrified scream sounded from some place in the upper part of the house. Bubb's eyes blazed. "That's Sadie, my sis. Help her, for God's—" Then Death gave Bubb a final twinge, and he became limp and still.

Bill released his hold on the man's shoulders. His eyes turned to Gail. His glance asked, "Shall I?" After all, Sadie was a criminal too.

"Bill!" Gail cried. "That big half-wit. He's got that poor woman—!"

Tethwick bounded up the stairs, guided by the woman's screaming to the front of the house. The front-door was open and he could see a faint rosy glow off in the eastern sky. A muffled choking sound somewhere was nearby. Tethwick peered to the left from where the sound had seemed to come. Nothing. Nothing but a pile of small rocks, but from behind the rocks came the sound of struggle! Tethwick hurriedly skirted the pile, saw Big Joe walking in his curious rolling gait toward the east. Sadie lay across his arms, kicking helplessly, terrorized. Tethwick broke into a run. He had tackled Big Joe once before and he could do it again! He lunged, arms wide-spread to encircle the maniac's knees. Something struck his toe, twisted his leg. He felt himself roll sideways. His hand and arms thrust out to save him. He lurched into Big Joe's body with his shoulders, fell flat against the rocks—head and shoulders out *over the precipice!*

He saw then what he had done! A spinning bundle of arms and legs was hurtling down the face of the cliff to meet the sea. A hoarse diminishing whimper of animal fear was coupled with the thin, fearful screams of the woman. In falling, he had thrown the giant off balance just as he was about to hurl the woman into the sea. They had gone together instead. Perhaps, Big Joe's arms still crushed against Sadie's body down there under the floating mist, deep under the water.

As Tethwick lay there, thinking of the narrow margin by which he had escaped death, he became conscious of someone standing beside him. He turned his head. It was Gail. Terror had left its mark on her face, but she was beautiful in spite of the lines of fear and fatigue.

"It's over, Bill," she said softly. "Let's get away from here. We can't be far from somebody—"

Tethwick got to his feet shakily. "Or *something* . . ." he amended. He put his arm around her waist, and they turned westward, walking together out of a night of terror.

S A T A N ' S

By
Carl Jacobi

A crushed body and a grinning death's-head led Stephen Benedict to a night of horror in a house of

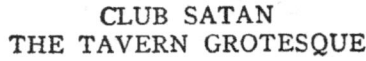

CLUB SATAN
THE TAVERN GROTESQUE

TWO signs shimmered in the glare of the idling roadster's headlights, one on the right, one on the left shoulder of the rain-drenched highway. The larger said officially:

NEW ORLEANS 32 MILES

The other, marking the entrance to a black side-road that snaked down into the dripping swamp underbrush, was a hundred times more sinister. It was a skull, a sheet-iron likeness of a white, grinning death's-head with vacant eye-sockets and low-hanging jaw. Above in blood-colored letters were the words:

Below, a painted skeleton hand pointed in the direction of the side-road.

52

ROADHOUSE

**Terror
Novelette**

*hell — where hanging corpses
looked with sightless eyes upon
such scenes as would have driven
living men insane!*

Hugh Milden dug a pipe out of his pocket and pushed tobacco into it slowly. "Damn horrible, some people's idea of entertainment," he said to his companion at the wheel. "Me, I hate night clubs. Let's get going."

For a moment Stephen Benedict made no answer. The private detective drew himself lower into the folds of his worn trench coat and stared through the drooling windshield, mouth slowly turning in a frown.

"I think, Milden," he said finally, "we'll give the place a look-over. A roadhouse usually means a blues-singer. And blues-singing is the one clue we've got to find old Clermont's daughter. There's always a chance, you know."

Milden sighed. It was just three weeks

ago tonight that hawk-faced, grim-eyed Louis Clermont had burst into their apartment in New York, tossed a check-book on the table and stated tersely: "My name's Clermont of the Clermont-Lannon Shipping Yards. You're Stephen Benedict, the man who solved the Kilburn hatchet murder case over in Brooklyn. Benedict, I want you to find my daughter."

And Benedict, sitting there in his old tweed smoking jacket with his habitual Rosa Trofero cigar jammed between his teeth, had smiled a quiet smile, waved the millionaire to a chair and demanded details.

The facts were simple. Ann Clermont, beautiful daughter of the shipbuilder, society debutante, club-woman, had disappeared. Disappeared completely and without a single trace. On Saturday evening a week previous she had gone to the opening night performance of Broadway's latest horror play, *Death Mask*, accompanied by her mother. At the conclusion of the second act she had suddenly left their box and walked out to the foyer. Her mother had suspected nothing, though she had noticed that the girl was strangely nervous all evening.

Ann Clermont had not returned.

"The police are bungling fools," Louis Clermont had snarled. "There's something devilish about this. Oh, I know girls disappear every day in New York. But Ann had been acting peculiar for days. She seemed to be walking in her sleep. Walking in her sleep, do you understand? I want action and action damned fast. Bring back my daughter, and you can name your own price."

The description and photograph he had left behind were of a young woman, twenty-five years old, blonde, with a striking intelligent face. The one outstanding detail, curiously enough, was her addiction to blues singing. She was said to have an attractive, throaty voice and had sung in costume at several Junior League benefits. The police were inclined to believe she had lapsed into a spell of amnesia and and was blindly utilizing her singing somewhere as a means of support.

With a last glance at the grinning skull sign, Benedict slid the gear-shift into low and wheeled the roadster into the muddy entrance of the roadhouse lane. Overhead thunder snarled in a pitch-black sky.

"Looks like that clue that brough us clear down to New Orleans was no good," he said to Milden over the scream of the wind. "But I hate to go back to New York and start all over again from scratch. I'm positive Ann Clermont is somewhere in this vicinity."

The road narrowed abruptly to two ruts coiling like fat snakes through the tall swamp grass. A second skull sign, announcing the roadhouse, rose up, leered at them and swirled by.

And then suddenly Benedict slammed down hard on the brakes, jerked the car to a halt and leaped out. With Milden close at his heels, he ran forward into the circle of headlight brilliance and bent over a mud-covered figure that lay sprawled face downward in the long rip grass. Slowly the detective bent down, seized the inert form and turned it over.

"Good God!" cried Milden.

AN OLD negro, dressed in tattered workman's clothes, gaped up at them. The man was dead. But it was his face that had caused Milden's horror-striken out-burst and held Benedict there in the pouring rain like a wooden image.

Mouth open, lips pulled far back over toothless gums, eyes bulging like two swollen balls of dried paste, the black man's face was twisted into an expression of stark terror. The flesh was colored a deep purple.

Blood and sticky clumps of mud encrusted the body from head to foot. And now they saw that the torso above the hips was caved in like a broken drum— as if a band of steel had been fastened around the waist and submitted to terrific pressure!

"Good God!" Milden repeated hoarsely. "Now who the hell . . . ?"

Benedict's gray eyes tightened. His jaw grew hard. He turned to the wall of reeds at the side, drew a flashlight from his pocket and pushed into the tangled growth. For twenty yards a blood-spattered trail led them inward. Then two gaunt cypress trees loomed up in the glare of the flash, and between them they saw a shallow, shovel-made depression in the boggy soil. It was a hole half-filled with rain-water—an empty grave!

For an instant Benedict stood there motionless, lips white, fingers trembling. Then he clenched his fists and whirled savagely.

"Somebody killed that poor darky," he growled, "lugged him out here and buried him before he was completely dead. They were in a hell of a hurry too because they barely covered him with dirt. The negro came to again and in a last dying move stumbled back to the road. But in heaven's name, what could have crushed him like that . . . ?"

Milden's black fedora was dripping water like a sponge. His face was ashen. He offered no answer.

They fought their way back to the road and the lights of the car. Once again Benedict bent over the body, this time to make a careful search of the victim's pockets. The overalls and ragged coat revealed nothing, but in the breast pocket of the shirt the detective's hand touched something firm, drew forth a small object.

It was an ordinary pill-box with tight-fitting cover. Inside, lying on a bit of red cloth, was an acorn, the center of which had been hollowed out by some sharp instrument. In the little opening, held in place by a tab of glue, was a tuft of human hair. Four holes pierced the acorn's sides and drawn through these to form a rude cross were two chicken feathers.

Bendict turned the thing over and over in his hand. His eyes glittered. "Odd," he said. "Damned odd."

He returned the acorn to its box, pocketed it, and stood up.

"We'll move the body off the road and mark the spot. The thing must be reported to the local authorities; but first I'm anxious to have a look at that Club Satan."

CHAPTER TWO

Murder at Table

SECONDS later the roadster was advancing down the road again. For a quarter mile the twin ruts twisted drunkenly. Then the lane widened, and the roadhouse appeared like a dead face in a fog.

In times long past it had been a private home. Now it shrank back despondently from a line of murky lanterns suspended on a wire before the entrance, a huge vault-like structure whose frowning walls seemed to sway with each onslaught of the wind. From within came the wail of a jazz orchestra.

Bendict slid the roadster into a parking stall and climbed out.

"Evil-looking place," Milden muttered. "Listen."

The orchestra had dwindled to an accompaniment now, and over the sobbing cry of a muted trumpet the words of a strange song sung in a feminine voice came to their ears.

> Eh! eh! Bomba, hen hen
> Canga bafio te
> Canga moune de le,
> Canga do ki la
> Canga li.

The voice rose and fell like a litany. Abruptly it died, and the raucous music swelled into a crescendo. The two men paced forward through the rain to the entrance. At the doorway a huge Negro, clad in evening clothes, glared at them, nodded, and led them inside. Across a corridor and through a second doorway they passed. Stephen Benedict drew out one of his long cigars and squinted about him.

"Since when," he said slowly, "have undertakers gone in for interior decorating?"

A single long room stretched before them, crowded with tables and chairs. Black velvet drapes covered the four walls and ceiling. Across those drapes, embroidered in crimson, was a crawling network of snakes—small snakes, large snakes, crossed and interwoven to form an endless horror-filled tapestry. In the center stood a fountain and basin of carved basalt, the figure-piece a hideously carved gargoyle, half-beast, half man. Illumination came from a single chandelier. Giving off an unnatural bluish light, it was fashioned into a three-dimensional counterpart of the sign on the highway —an enormous leering skull.

The orchestra occupied a raised platform at the extreme front. The musicians were all Negroes, black, sullen-faced men, dressed in costumes of scarlet silk. Not all the tables were occupied, but those that were bespoke clearly the calibre of the clientele. Mostly women, members of the upper social strata, they were richly dressed in expensive evening clothes.

A breath of evil hung like a fog over the place. Both men sensed it, knew instinctively that it had as its source something more than the weird furnishings.

To a corner table Benedict led the way, eyes roving about him while he sucked on his cigar.

"Always knew the American public was crazy," Milden muttered through his teeth. "But this is the worst yet. Club Satan. . . . I'm damned if I see what makes you connect a place like this with Ann Clermont."

They sat across from each other, ordered drinks from a Negro waiter who approached. And then abruptly leaned forward and touched Milden's arm.

"I think we're going to have company," he said.

A tall, stoop-shouldered individual with carrot hair and a broad forehead was pacing across the room toward them. Reaching the table, the man stood quiet a moment, then kicked back a chair and lowered himself into it.

"Act as if you weren't surprised," he said quietly. "Act casual. And for God's sake, don't turn around."

A gleam shot into Benedict's eyes. His brows jerked upward in recognition. "Jimmy Lodge!" he breathed. "What the devil are you doing this far from home?"

The newcomer poured water from the carafe, sipped a mouthful and spread both hands flat on the table before him.

"Listen," he said, "and don't ask questions. We're being watched. One false move, and there's hell to pay. Now laugh as if this were idle conversation."

MILDEN forced a mirthless smile while he knocked the ashes from his pipe. "Sounds like the beginning of a dime novel," he muttered. "What is all this?"

"The *Tribune* gave me two weeks' vacation," Lodge explained. "I left New York and came down here to my old home town. Four days ago I blundered into this place. And man, believe me, it's the biggest scoop of the age. It's the most damnable, horrible story I've ever stumbled on in my ten year's newspaper experience."

"Murder?" asked Benedict softly. The detective was slowly chewing his cigar.

"Murder and everything else. It's a story, I tell you. But I can't run it down alone. You've got to help me. I think they suspect already that I'm not a regular patron. Turn around slow and flash a glance at the end table nearest the orchestra."

With a casual movement Benedict turned in his chair, looked over his shoulder at the point directed. He saw a lone figure sitting, profile turned toward them, at a separated table. The man's features were half Caucasion, half Negroid. He was tall and bulking, dressed in a suit of white linen with a black ascot tie. Even at that distance and in the diffused glow of the blue skull chandelier, the detective noted the sinister expression of animal brutality that hung like a mask over the face.

"That's Fabre Leveau," Lodge said. "He runs this place. House was in ruins till a couple of months ago. He fixed it up, called it Club Satan. Now it's the social hangout for all New Orleans. In the back room—"

A bell sounded somewhere, interrupting the reporter. Up on the platform the drummer began pounding the bass drum in slow, intermittent beats. The light in the blue chandelier dimmed.

"Tell you the rest later," Lodge said. "The floor show starts in a minute. It's different every night. Watch it, and you'll be partially prepared for what I've got to say."

The light in the skull chandelier flickered and went out. Thick blackness engulfed the interior of the roadhouse. The pounding drum grew louder. Then suddenly a red glow sprang into existence in the center of the room, and Benedict stiffened in his chair.

Moving slowly, halfway between ceiling and floor, floating with no apparent support, an object of stark horror appeared ten feet from their table. It was a human head, a man's head severed high up on the neck, resting on a white platter filled with blood! The pupils of the eyes were swollen five times their normal size as if from an overdose of belladonna. The damp hair was clawed wildly over the forehead. Acid apparently had been poured on the jaw, and the lips hung away from the mouth, a featureless mass of gray flesh.

From one end of the room to the other the head floated, the red light following. As the intervening distance increased, it seemed to grow in size until it was a fat bulbous thing, the cranium protruding as with encephalitis. Then abruptly, like a darkened picture, it disappeared.

Lodge leaned over and spoke in a whisper. "Trick stuff," he said. "I don't know how the hell they do it, but it sure looks real. And the customers eat it up."

Two more drums had joined the steady *boom boom* on the platform, and now the orchestra began a low, wailing strain. The reddish glow changed to purple and back to red again.

Milden's teeth clamped down hard on his pipestem. "Good Lord," he said hoarsely. "Look!"

AT THE point where the decapitated head had disappeared two new shapes were beginning to take form, two skeletons of incredible height with bones gleaming like polished brass, black eye-sockets and enameled teeth. To the rhythm of the drums they moved in unison, gyrating their legs and arms, holding their heads stiffly erect. Knives were in their hands. Whirling, they faced each other and began hacking with jerking, mechanical strokes.

Then once again the scene changed. A girl moved into the foreground, a white girl with long streaming black hair and a chalk-white face. She stood naked save for a narrow sash of red silk. In her right hand she gripped a leather thong, at the far end of which was fastened a cluster of rude shell castanets.

With a scream of the trumpet the music swelled into a pounding roar, and the girl began to leap and sway like a puppet controled by wires. At each revolution she whipped the leather thong about her. Horribly, like sharp razors, the rough edges of the shells cut into her white flesh, and thick drops of blood began falling to the floor. Her legs and body rapidly were colored crimson.

As she danced, the girl mouthed the same song Benedict and Milden had heard when they first entered the roadhouse:

> Eh! eh! Bomba, hen hen
> Canga bafio te
> Canga moune de le,
> Canga do ki la'
> Canga li.

Over and over she repeated the words until they seemed to fill the room with a thousand echoes. Round and round she whirled, lashing herself with the shell castanets.

Then somewhere in the background, hollow and muffled by the intervening walls, that bell sounded again, and the girl dropped exhausted to the floor. The red light gave way to blackness. A moment passed. The light in the skull chandelier returned to its blue glow, revealing the chamber as it was before. The orchestra ceased.

Benedict drew his cigar from his mouth and frowned. "Damned clever stage effects," he said. "Now, Lodge, what's the story?"

No answer came to the question. The detective drummed his fingers erratically on the table.

"Tell us," he urged. "If there's some-thing doing here, maybe we can join forces. That girl. . . ."

Benedict shot a startled look across the table. An instant he stared. Then with a hoarse intake of breath he lurched to his feet. Beside him a water glass slipped from Hugh Milden's hand and crashed to the floor.

Across the table sat Jimmy Lodge, star-reporter for the New York *Star-Tribune*. The fingers of his right hand still held a lighted cigarette, its smoke coiling lazily ceilingward. His eyes were wide open, staring blankly into space. But there was something else, something that held Benedict as in a vise, that glittered mockingly in the cold blue light.

Protruding from the center of the newspaperman's throat was a knife. The blade had been driven to the hilt, and a bubbling stream of blood was slowly running down the gray-flannel suit to the floor.

"He's . . . he's dead!" Milden cried hoarsely. "He's been murdered!"

WITH a snarl Benedict kicked back his chair and stepped to Lodge's side. A quick feel of the pulse told him death had been instantaneous. A look into the ghastly face showed a twisted expression of surprise and excruciating pain. The mouth hung open. The head lolled drunkenly to one side. The blood oozed forth like thick syrup. And the knife-handle, a fantastic wooden thing, representing a diminutive carved face, leered back at him with tiny gargoyle features and agate eyes.

As Benedict bent forward in examination, he was vaguely aware of a woman's shriek of horror at an adjoining table, of a sudden breathless hush descending like a pall over that black chamber. Then glasses rattled, chairs screamed on the floor, and the crowd surged forward.

Swiftly, hardly knowing why, Benedict passed his hand from the pulseless wrist to the reporter's pockets. He dumped articles, one after another, on the blood-stained table—fountain pen, pencil, pocketbook, keys—and a box.

It was the same type of box they had found on the dead Negro's person back on the swamp lane, a small, gray-colored pill-box. And inside, reposing innocently on its red cloth, lay that same meaningless object they had seen accompanying death once before—an acorn with a tuft of human hair and two chicken feathers in the form of a rude cross!

The crowd about the table was ten deep now. White faces peered over shoulders. Women clutched at escorts. Men coughed deep in their throats.

Benedict stood up, lips tight, eyes glittering under crescent lids. He pushed his way through the gathering, paced down the narrow aisle between the deserted tables and stepped slowly, deliberately to the figure clad in white that sat alone by the orchestra platform. Reaching the man's side, the detective gripped him by the shoulder, jerked him to his feet.

"You run this joint?"

The man's eyes smoldered with hatred. His lips parted, shut. He shrugged.

"Answer, damn you, or I'll—"

"My name is Fabre Leveau. This is my establishment, yes. Is there something wrong?"

The words came flatly, without emotion, in a deep guttural voice strained with a foreign accent. A suggestion of a smile moved across the mulatto face, and the right hand casually flicked the ash from a cigarette.

"There's been a murder." Benedict's own voice was coldly quiet now as he steeled his emotion. "Murder, you understand? On your property. The police will be informed and—"

"I am well acquainted with the police. They will not bother me. If there has been an accident, I am sorry." Leveau

glanced through an opening in the crowd at the far end of the room. He clapped his hands, and a Negro waiter appeared from nowhere. "Mamba, a clean cloth for Table Five. Quickly."

For an instant Benedict stood there, fists clenched, a strong desire to crush that yellow face sweeping over him. He controlled the impulse. He pulled a fresh cigar from his vest pocket, bit off the end.

"Leveau," he said, "you stay where you are. No one leaves here until a thorough search has been made. Milden there will guard the door. I'm going to search this rat-hole from top to bottom."

CHAPTER THREE

Death Warning

SLANTING rain from a leaden sky pounded New Orleans' streets. Stephen Benedict, still in his worn trench coat and battered gray hat, strode westward along West Haven Street. It was a narrow, cheerless thoroughfare, flanked on both sides by red brick apartment houses set flush with the sidewalk.

"Helluva way for a private dick to spend his time," he muttered to himself. "I come down here looking for a millionaire's daughter with a fat check waiting for me when I find her, and what do I do? Run into a couple of roadhouse murders, drop everything and butt into an affair that's a matter for the local police."

He felt far back in a corner of his brain, nevertheless, that in some indefinable way a relationship existed between the two cases. The girl he had seen perform the weird blood dance under the glare of the red light could not be Ann Clermont. Black-haired, taller, with coarse features, there was no similarity between the roadhouse performer and the girl on the photograph in his pocket. And yet on the tavern floor, lying too carelessly it seemed, Milden had found a woman's handkerchief bearing the embroidered initial "A." Coincidence? Benedict could not say. But Lodge, the ill-fated newspaperman, had discovered something of grim significance at Club Satan, something that sealed his lips forever, something apparently that would have been of great interest to the reading public back in New York. It was toward Lodge's apartment that the detective was heading now.

He found the place presently, a slightly newer building occupying the corner lot. Benedict passed through the entrance, paced up three flights of stairs and halted before a dark mahogany door bearing the tin figures: 356. His hand slipped in his pocket, pulled out the set of keys he had taken from the dead reporter's person, chose one and inserted it in the lock.

Seconds later he was inside, looking about him. It was an ordinary overnight apartment, a small sitting room equipped with table, chairs, a cogswell and a couple of lamps. Beyond, partially hidden by a curtained doorway, was the bed-chamber.

Benedict slipped off his trench coat, drew forth a Rosa Trofero, and lighted it carefully. At his feet, where it had been pushed under the door by an obliging landlord, lay the latest edition of a New Orleans' daily.

The headlines screamed foreign affairs, faraway threats of war. A picture of a divorced movie star covered two columns center. But down in the lower right corner was an article headed:

CITY VISITOR MEETS
MYSTERIOUS DEATH
AT WAYSIDE TAVERN

Benedict dropped into a chair, propped the paper up before him and read slowly. The running story told him nothing new. It referred to Club Satan simply as a "new roadhouse." And it stated that police as yet had made no arrests in the killing. The death of the aged Negro was attributed to an automobile accident!

Frowning, Benedict sat smoking in silence while the ornate clock on the wall ticked off the passing seconds. Up until now his activities toward either an explanation of Jimmy Lodge's death or the more remote whereabouts of Ann Clermont had run up against a blank wall. Fabre Leveau had even aided them in their search of the roadhouse, had escorted them upstairs into the cobweb gloom of the building's abandoned second floor, down into the cellar and sub-cellar and out into the adjacent swamp grounds. Yet other than the handkerchief, neither he nor Milden had discovered a single clue.

There was a spinet desk in the far corner of Lodge's room. The top was open, papers and writing material spilled out carelessly. Benedict rose from the chair, moved across to it. A telephone stood on a shelf bracketed to the near wall. The detective glanced at it, and with sudden decision, lifted the receiver and dialed a number.

"Milden?" he said at length when his own hotel room had been connected. "Milden, I've got work for you. Yes, I'm here now. But listen. Go out and dig up all the information you can about this Fabre Leveau. Start at the real estate agent who leased the property for Club Satan. Locate the interior decorators who fixed up the inside. See who made those roadside signs. I want all angles. Got it? Then put a long distance call through to New York to old man Clermont. Find out if his daughter ever had a record made of her voice. If she did, tell him to take it to WXKY and make arrangements for them to broadcast it at a certain time today. Meet me in the hotel lobby at three."

HE HUNG up and turned to the array of material on the desk before him. For some time he waded through personal papers and letters of the reporter, all of them without interest. Then he found a small loose-leaf notebook filled with notations. The first page seized his attention:

June 1st. Stumbled into an odd place on the north highway today, roadhouse called Club Satan. Cheap joint with fantastic horror appeal, yet for some strange reason it seems to get the best of New Orleans' social crowd.

June 2nd. Club Satan again. Some irresistible attraction about it. Manager's name is Fabre Leveau. Seem to have seen him somewhere before. Orchestra has a theme song with a peculiar savage strain; words sung by a black-haired girl in an unknown language. Can't help feeling there's something wrong here, something foul, evil, something which shouldn't be. Looks like a story in the background.

June 4th. Decided not to return to New York just yet. Wandered out to Club Satan, and there *is* a story, the most damnable impossible story. Can't believe I'm right in my suspicions. It's too horrible to be true. Hired an old Negro by the name of Lem Thomas to look around the outside of the tavern and see what he can find. He's so simple-looking no one will suspect him. I mean to work this out to an end.

June 5th. Good God! I didn't think such things existed in present day civilization. Fabre Leveau is a fiend. And now somebody suspects my movements. Today I received the first warning—an acorn hollowed out in the center containing a tuft of hair and two chicken feathers. I lived long enough in the South in my younger days to know what that means!

June 6th. The realization of what the whole thing means is terrifying. Sometimes I think I'm going mad in my suspicions. Club Satan is a house of hell! I shall go there every night until I have the entire story. God help me if Leveau suspects my purpose.

The writing ended here. Face a mask, Benedict turned back to the first page and read the notation over again. The innuendoes were potent, but of revealing facts, there was only one. That the aged Negro they had found murdered, crushed to death, had been employed by Lodge to help him in his investigations. It was a single piece of the puzzle fitted into its slot. Benedict slipped the book into his pocket and rummaged through the rest of the papers on the desk. He drew then from a blank manilla envelope a familiar object.

It was a gray-colored pill-box, the third of its kind that he had seen in the last twenty-four hours. He knew without opening it what would be inside—that same meaningless acorn and the two chicken feathers arranged to form a cross. For a moment Benedict stared down upon the box curiously. Then he pressed his cigar ash into a tray and lifted the cover.

His hand jerked rigid, and he stiffened in his chair. The acorn and its cryptic adornment was inside as he had expected. Like its two predecessors it rested on a strip of red cloth. But there was something else, something that held the detective's eyes hypnotically while his right hand moved slowly under his coat and groped for his service revolver.

A tiny strip of paper was glued to the acorn. Upon it in strangely stilted letters were ten printed words. They were addressed to him—yet he had entered this room but moments ago! Ten words which seemed to scream their death message into the ringing silence:

STEPHEN BENEDICT, IN ONE MINUTE YOU ARE GOING TO DIE.

SECONDS snailed by, marked evenly by the thundering ticks of the clock on the wall. A drop of cold sweat oozed out on the detective's forehead. More seconds, and still he sat there, staring fascinated at the paper in the box. Then slowly he replaced the cover, shoved the box into his pocket and stood up.

The dismal furnishings of the room stood before him like a clean photograph. Outside, far away, a street-car clanged its bell for a crossing. An automobile roared its exhaust.

Benedict stepped to the door, ripped it open and peered out. The hallway and the end stairs as far up and down as he could see were empty. Yet it seemed wiser to remain than to flee. He shut the door, locked it, moved across to the twin street windows. Scattered traffic hurried by the intersection below. A man pushing a baby carriage sauntered along the sidewalk, whistling as he walked.

Scowling, the detective tested the two window locks, found them both secured and returned to the desk. He slumped into the chair, drummed his fingers on the walnut. More seconds ticked by.

Then impulsively he jerked down the telephone, lifted the receiver to his ear and thumped the hook up and down. There was no click, no answering hum! The line was dead. He replaced the receiver. Revolver in hand, heart pounding, he waited. . .

It came like a vision out of hell! A sudden scraping sound attracted his attention to the right window. Benedict turned and felt his body suddenly jerk taut. Nausea welled through his vitals. A cold piece of ice shot up and down his spine. He lurched to his feet.

Framed in the soot-smeared window, leering at him with huge pupil-less eyes, was the face of a monster! It was utterly hideous, a semi-human, semi-anthropoid horror face, bloated five times out of proportion, covered with black, matted hair. The mouth was a gaping hole, crowded with yellow fanglike teeth. The skin gleamed a leprous slate-gray. From the nostrils protruded a sharpened piece of bone. Draped around the swollen head was the body of a dead snake.

Straight into the room the thing peered.

The jaw moved up and down, flabby flesh without muscular control. From the throat came a soughing, rasping gurgle. Yellow saliva dribbled from the misshapen lips.

For a split second the thing remained there, motionless. Then a hairy hand shot upward, struck at the window. The glass crashed and fell inward. The hand penetrated the opening, jerked forward and hurled something into the room, something that hit the carpet with a soft thud and then popped like a pricked balloon.

Benedict stood there, propped against the desk, staring ahead of him, unable to shift his gaze. The horror held him powerless to move, riveted to the floor. A hypnotic will blanketed his own, gripped him like iron to a lodestone.

On the floor, ten feet away, a thin coil of yellowish smoke was slowly rising from a liquid blot on the carpet. Ever thickening, that smoke spread across the entire room, filling the air from wall to wall with a fulvous, swirling miasma. As it did so, those walls, the furniture, the monster itself seemed to waver, to glimmer uncertainly as a scene viewed through water. Objects close to the detective grew remote and far away. The ceiling pressed downward.

WITH a choking cry, Benedict shot his hands upward and clawed wildly at his throat. That yellow smoke, diffused now, covering everything, was surging over his head like a sea of varnish. It entered his mouth and nostrils and closed off his breathing passages.

Gasping, Benedict tore free his tie and collar, wrenched his eyes from the monster and stumbled drunkenly to the door. Hand on the latch, he shot the bolt, twisted and pulled frantically. The door was locked on the other side! And from somewhere in the outer corridor came a hoarse, mocking laugh!

He whirled, heart racing. Across the room the leering gargoyle face in the broken window watched him in fiendish satisfaction. Five steps, ten steps Benedict staggered toward it. Then red spinning lights swirled up before his eyes; his legs buckled beneath him, and he fell headlong to the floor. Face turning a slow purple, he tore at his throat, coughed, sucked wildly for air.

And vaguely as he lay there, the detective saw the horror face move inward, saw a tall, hulking body with apelike arms enter the room. With the stealthiness of a jungle cat it approached, slid nearer, until it crouched at his side, foul face looking down. A thick gibbering sound issued from its mouth.

Benedict's throat was on fire. His temples pounded as from the blows of a bludgeon. He tried to rise, fell back.

The monster drew forth a long, hooked knife, flourished it, moved the glinting blade slowly downward. Inch by inch it came on while the detective dug his fingers into the plush of the carpet and an invisible heaviness pressed upon him, holding him down.

And then suddenly, like the peal of a tocsin, the clock on the farther wall struck the hour. The plangent sounds rolled into the room with the roar of surf, seeped into Benedict's fogged brain and brought a sharp sense of mundane reality. Something snapped in his brain. He set his teeth, gathered his strength and heaved upward.

As in a dream he felt his hands reach out, clutch the knife and wrench it to the floor. He clawed at the hideous face, fastened his fingers about the neck and pressed inward. Pressed while thunder roared in his head, and his lungs pounded at the bursting point.

The monster fought like a caged animal. Back and forth, from one side of the room to the other, they stumbled. A table over-

turned, spilled its contents. A floor lamp fell, broke its shade and bulb with a pistol report. Then momentarily the thing freed itself and sent a fist crashing straight into the detective's jaw.

Benedict stumbled backward, spitting blood. The monster whirled, leaped like a spider to the window and hurled its body through the jagged opening. On the fire escape without, it turned and looked back, eyes smoldering with hatred. A jangling cry of defiance belched from its throat. Then it ducked downward and disappeared. . . .

CHAPTER FOUR

A Woman's Scream

HUGH MILDEN, still pajama clad, turned away from the telephone in his hotel room and swore good-naturedly while he cast a longing look at the table. On that table there was a steaming cup of coffee, untouched, as well as a well-packed pipe. At this time of day he liked to puff that pipe in leisure. Yet Benedict had just ordered him to leave these pleasantries and embark once again upon an errand of investigation. It had been that way for almost three years, he reflected morosely. Ever since his law practice had dwindled to nothing and his small fortune had disappeared in bad stocks. Ever since he had entered into partnership with the detective. True, that partnership had plunged him into a list of fascinating adventures, which in his earlier days he had never dreamed were possible. But this man, Benedict, whom even now he did not fully understand, was a most ambitious, restless person with no sense of peace or relaxation at all. At times it was damned annoying.

The ex-lawyer dressed, seized his hat and coat and strode out, muttering. A cold, drizzling rain was falling when he reached the street. He yanked up his coat collar, stood there a moment in indecision and then turned north.

During the next two hours Milden worked hard. He may have possessed no unusual sleuthing abilities, but he was persistent. By the time he had returned to the hotel lobby he had three pages of foolscap paper covered with information. From beginning to end that information, though leading to no definite conclusion, struck him as sinister. . . .

As the lobby clock ticked past the time of his appointment with Benedict, Milden grew restless. Three times he pushed tobacco into his bulldog briar, passed a match over the bowl and sucked it to the heel. Then impulse seized him, and he strode to the desk.

He folded his three sheets of information into an envelope supplied by the clerk and enclosed a brief note to the detective. The note said: "Going out to the roadhouse for a look-see." Then he paced out of the hotel and headed for the adjoining garage.

Fifteen minutes later New Orleans' outskirts was behind him. Behind the wheel of Benedict's roadster he roared down the highway toward Club Satan.

The grinning skull sign at the entrance to the swamp lane was no less sinister in the gray daylight than it had been at night. Milden, shuddering involuntarily at sight of it, ran the car forward a hundred yards, parked it on the shoulder of the highway and strode toward the tavern on foot.

Moments later the ex-lawyer was once again gazing upon the somber facade of the tavern. The place was silent and deserted now. The rain-water dripping from the eaves made the only sound. Even stronger than the night before was the sense of evil that lurked over the building like a material pall. For a moment Milden stood there, staring at the curtained, eyelike windows and the frowning, disproportionate door. Then he turned, slipped into the swamp underbrush and began to circle toward the rear of the structure.

The back wall was a white, blind face brooding under the sullen sky. Each of the four windows had been boarded up. The single door, tilted in decay, was secured by a new inlaid lock.

Milden moved forward for closer examination. Wind swept the rain before him in long, slanting streaks. Water drooled from his hatbrim.

Abruptly he forgot his discomforts and stiffened in his tracks. He had heard the scrape of slow-moving footsteps within. Even as he darted behind the bole of a nearby tree, a key rasped in the lock, and the door grated open. A thick-set Negro face with white, staring eyes peered out.

An instant later Milden pressed his teeth hard into his lips while a wave of horror swept over him. Four men had emerged from the blackness of that doorway—four Negroes in long, black coats. They carried the body of a young woman, a woman tall and slender, clad in a low-cut green silk evening gown.

Her face was contorted into a mask of terror. The eyes, protruding far from the sockets, were white and glassy with the sightless stare of death. The mouth was stretched wide open, and the tongue hung far out as if it had been partially jerked from its roots. Her body at the waist was caved inward, crushed by some terrific pressure. A long, gaping, bloody slash stretched from her throat downward over her exposed breasts.

SLOWLY, and deliberately, the expressionless Negroes paced out into the yard with their burden. They carried her by the loose end of her long hair and by her silver-slippered feet. Milden, stifling his horror, kept himself concealed behind the tree until the procession had marched past. Then, bending low in the ripe grass, he followed.

Fifty yards into the depths of the dripping swamp the Negroes went. Following a beaten path, they emerged in a kind of glade. It was a wide clearing where the underbrush had but recently been removed. In the center, the freshly-turned earth heaped in a pile at the side, was a new grave. And near it lay a white pine box, a wooden coffin.

With horrible abandon the four Negroes dropped the body of the young girl into the box, kicked down the cover and pushed it into the hole. It fell with a harsh thump. Seizing shovels, they began to fill the grave.

Milden's tongue was dry in his mouth as he stood there. His hands opened and closed convulsively. An instant he remained, watching the clods as they fell hollowly on the wooden coffin. Then with a sharp intake of breath he turned and ran.

He reached the clearing that formed the yard, crossed it and sloshed through puddles to the front of the building. Not until he came to the parking space at the end of the swamp lane did he draw up, and then only to regain his breath. Over his shoulder he stared in weird fascination at the somber tavern.

For the space of five seconds the ex-lawyer remained there, gazing behind him. Mechanically his hand drew out his pipe, jammed it unlighted between his teeth.

Then a sound came to his ears, filtering through the heavy air. It began low at first, like the whine of a distant motor. Gradually it mounted in pitch and crescendo. It was the piercing scream of a woman in terror!

With a shudder Milden turned his gaze to the curtained second story windows, listened for a repetition of the sound.

None came. Scowling, he sucked on his cold pipe a moment, then paced slowly across the open space and up the rotted steps to the front door. He tried the latch. It was unlocked.

For a long while he hesitated, weighing the unknown dangers that he knew confronted him. Then he pushed open the door and stepped inside.

Thick blackness, made even more intense by the light from the doorway, met his eyes. He stood there, vainly trying to see ahead. Above, like blood in a slaughter-house, rain gurgled through the roof troughs. The wind whined and beat against the ancient walls.

Milden groped forward. There was a wide doorway ahead of him, he remembered, leading to the central chamber of the tavern. To the right lay the corridor that connected in turn with the staircase leading to the second floor. Benedict and he had passed up that staircase on their futile search the night before. He moved toward it—and stopped, galvanized to attention.

That scream again! Ricocheting through the rotted partitions, wailing higher and higher, it cadenced down from the abandoned upper tiers of the structure like the cry of a lost soul. It was a woman's terror-stricken plea for help. Twice in hideous succession that scream was repeated. Then it ended in a choking gurgle.

With a muttered oath the ex-lawyer raced up the stairs to the second floor. There was no light at all now, and reaching the upper corridor, he moved down it, a step at a time, arms outstretched before him. Then the end wall barred his passage, and he struck a match. Before the feeble glow died, he had a glimpse of the corridor, empty and deserted, continuing to the south end of the house, a line of closed doors on either side.

He strode to the first door, twisted the knob and threw the barrier open wide.

For an instant he saw there only a tiny wavering dot of red like a glowing cigarette end. Then shoes scraped on the floor in the blackness before him. Milden stepped backward—too late. Something swished through the air, and it seemed the whole world had descended on his head. He slumped forward, unconscious.

CHAPTER FIVE

Den of Horror

IT LACKED twenty minutes of four o'clock that afternoon when Stephen Benedict, trench coat dripping, gray felt hat a soggy black, entered the lobby of his downtown hotel and found waiting for him at the desk two envelopes, a white one from Hugh Milden and a yellow one containing a telegram.

The wire was from Louis Clermont in New York City. It said:

STATION WXKY TO BROADCAST RECORD OF ANN'S VOICE AT 3:55 P. M. TODAY.

Benedict nodded, glanced at the clock, and turned his attention to the three pages of information compactly written in his assistant's hand. As he read on, the detective's face hardened. All his suspicions, wild as they were, had been well grounded. Lodge was right.

But when he reached the fourth sheet containing the ex-lawyer's explanation of his whereabouts, Benedict frowned and clamped his teeth hard on the cigar. "The crazy fool!" he muttered. "If I can only head him off before—!"

But first he must find if his hunch were correct. . . . The clock stood at eleven minutes of four now. Benedict crossed the room to the lobby radio, switched on the contact and began to twist the dials. Presently the announcer's voice said:

"You are listening to station WXKY, the Stanson Tobacco Company station. By special request we are about to broadcast a recording of the voice of Ann Clermont, daughter of Louis Clermont, president of the C-L Shipping Yards. Police have as yet been unable to find Miss Clermont, who disappeared almost three weeks ago, and it is hoped that the playing of this record will aid in her discovery. One moment, please."

The record began, with the accompaniment, a piano. The voice was low-pitched and throaty, sung in the popular blues manner with a slow, moaning rhythm. For several minutes it continued while Benedict listened in silence, nodding as if in satisfaction at an expected discovery. When it finally stopped, he clicked off the radio, jammed Milden's papers into his pocket and strode swiftly toward the street door.

Halfway there a bell-hop crossed to his side, touched his shoulder.

"Telephone call for you, sir."

Benedict turned slowly about.

"Which phone?"

"Number three, sir."

Five seconds later when the detective grunted "Hello" into the mouthpiece of the booth instrument, there was only an imperceptible trace of surprise in his voice.

"Stephen Benedict," said the voice at the other end of the wire, "this is Fabre Leveau. Listen very carefully and pay attention to all I have to say. Do you hear me?"

"Yes." Benedict spoke the single word while his eyes narrowed.

"Benedict, there is a train leaving New Orleans for New York City in one hour, at five p. m. You will take that train and forget everything you have seen or learned about Club Satan. You will make no report to the New York police concerning a certain James Lodge, newspaper reporter, who met his unfortunate death last night. Is that perfectly plain?"

A grim, mirthless smile curled the corners of the detevtive's lips. He rubbed the ash of his cigar against the booth wall, said shortly: "And if I don't. . .?"

"If you don't, I'm afraid the future will be most unpleasant for you. You were successful in warding off a little visit we planned for you earlier in the day. The second time we will take greater pains. But beside that, your co-partner—Milden, I believe is his name—happens to be our uninvited guest at the present time. Should you fail to follow these orders, you will never see him again."

The receiver clicked, and Benedict was standing in a silent booth.

VERY quietly he stepped out, strode once again through the lobby to the door. At the sidewalk he paused, relit his cigar and cast a quick glance in either direction. Twenty feet down the curb a black limousine with curtained windows was parked, engine idling.

Benedict flipped away his match, stepped into a cab before the hotel entrance and directed the driver in a loud voice to the depot. He noted with satisfaction that the black limousine geared into traffic and followed directly behind.

Arriving at the station, Benedict purchased a first class ticket to New York and sat stiffly on one of the benches in the waiting room. He waited until the caller announced his train, then rose and passed through the gate.

Five seconds later he had mingled with the incoming crowd of the Dallas-Fort Worth train and was back again in the streets of New Orleans.

And now the detective dropped his quiet attitude and turned into a man of action. He hailed a cab, slipped a bill into the driver's hand, said: "Club Satan. Thirty-two miles out the north highway. Know it?"

The man nodded, the meter clicked, and they swept down the street.

The rain was pouring in torrents when the cab finally screeched to a halt before the tavern lane. Benedict leaped out and hurried down the swamp road on foot. The wind was blowing a gale now, the thunder booming steadily.

He had covered one half the distance when the creak of wheels and the beat of hoofs sounded from behind. The detective darted into the sodden underbrush and crouched down. The creaking grew nearer and a dilapidated farm wagon lurched into view. The driver, a young Negro clad in a dripping poncho, held the reins loosely and drowsed on the high seat, unmindful of the steady downpour.

Waiting until the wagon had lumbered past his hiding spot, Benedict rose to his feet, darted after it and leaped silently into its open back end. The wagon moved steadily forward. The driver did not turn about.

A large mass of old tarpaulins covered the floor of the wagon, were piled high over a long, rectangular object. Careful to make no sound, the detective lifted the canvas and peered underneath. He saw a heavy iron-bound chest made of grainless wood, the top plastered with shipping stickers, railway tickets and insurance stamps. Stenciled deeply in one corner, the address and shipping instructions read:

From: Freetown, Sierra Leone, Africa, West Coast.
To: Fabre Leveau, New Orleans, La., U. S. A.
Routing: (Freetown to England; Liverpool to New York.)
HANDLE WITH EXTREME CARE. DO NOT JAR. KEEP THIS END UP.

Benedict, eyes glittering, bent closer to examine a series of small, round holes bored at regular intervals along the sides of the box. As he did so, his head jerked back with sudden revulsion. A horrible, fetid stench had seared into his nostrils, an animal odor of slime and must! The smell swept over him like a blanket of green mold, sickened him, gagged his throat and larynx.

OVER the driver's shoulder now, Benedict saw the white front of Club Satan coming ahead. Silently the detective dropped off the rear of the wagon and pushed into the swamp grass.

While the wagon rumbled around the right side of the building, Benedict turned to the left. And presently he stood before a small half-size door cut in the damp stones of the foundation, secured with a padlock and a staple. Without hesitation the detective seized a rock, placed his hand under one side of the padlock and dealt the rusted iron a sharp blow.

An instant later he was stumbling into the dark interior. He switched on an electric flash, closed the door behind him, and probed the white beam in a slow circle. He stood on the landing of a staircase, the rotten steps leading downward to the cellar. Clammy silence like the interior of a mausoleum pressed about him.

Drawing his service revolver, Benedict paced slowly down the steps, crossed the cellar until he reached the south wall. Here he moved the flash back and forth, up and down, examining the masonry. He saw nothing but a smooth expanse of stone. Frowning, he dug in his pocket, drew forth Milden's three sheets of information and studied one marked: *Interior decorations.*

A second time he examined the wall, moving the palm of his hand carefully over the surface. And at length he found what he was looking for, a small slot in the stonework with a tiny hard-rubber button. Benedict shot a look over his shoulder, listened, and pressed hard on the button.

There was an instant groan of muffled machinery from somewhere below the floor. With a rasping creak, the entire wall began to slide outward, moving on a concealed pivot. Flash extended before him, Benedict stared in satisfaction.

It was a tunnel, a wide passage almost five feet across and ceiling high. It extended far ahead of him, the floor gradually tilting downward, the walls green with mold and drooling black water.

Benedict advanced, making no sound on the soft mud floor. For thirty yards the tunnel continued. Then abruptly it turned to the right, and a second door barred his progress. He clicked off the flash, twisted the latch and inched the barrier open.

For an instant his eyes were blinded by a glaring light, stabbing through that narrow opening like a yellow flame. Then his pupils narrowed, and he stared open-mouthed at what he saw.

Stretching before him, the proportions immeasurable because of the polished mirror walls, was a huge underground room. Lighted by hundreds of candles and powerful floodlights, the red-painted floor glimmered like a sea of fresh blood. In the center, upraised on a kind of stone kiln, was an enormous iron vat with a roaring fire underneath, a thick black miasma rising from its open top. And gathered about that vat stood some fifty white women and men, clad in evening clothes.

But there was more, and Benedict felt himself growing suddenly sick from the horror of it. On the right side of the room, dangling before their elongated reflections, suspended on a long slack wire that stretched from wall to wall, were the nude corpses of ten young white women! They hung by their hair like butchered swine, eyes protruding like white marbles, tongues lolling stickily over bloated lips, faces colored a hideous purple. Their bodies at the waist were caved in, crushed by some terrific external pressure.

Across the room on a second slack wire twenty rattlesnakes, fastened by their tails, writhed and lashed back and forth in maddened fury. Above, leering down from its hollowed socket in the dirt ceiling, was the same decapitated head that had appeared on a platter in the central chamber of the tavern the night before. That head was black now with the first steps of decay.

Benedict felt himself growing sick at the pit of his stomach. But he forced back the mounting nausea, opened the door wider.

A BREATHLESS hush, a strained silence hung over that underground room. The crowd of fifty, mostly women, a few men, stood there grouped in a semi-circle about the iron vat like mummies in an Egyptian tableau. Their faces were set, expressionless; their hands hung stiffly at their sides. Only the writhing snakes and the gargoyle shadows flung by the lighted candles exhibited any motion.

And then from the room's far end a black curtain was flung aside, and Fabre Leveau stepped forward. Mulatto face gleaming like yellowed parchment, he was clad in a cloak of black silk that hung shapeless from the throat like a monk's cowl. His face was hideously disfigured with streaks of yellow and white paint, and a crown of feathers rested upon his head.

Sweeping both hands above him, Leveau intoned loudly in a deep rolling voice: "It is here. It has come. Danh-gbi! Danh-gbi! Are you in readiness?"

A low muttering like the distant roar of an angry sea issued from the mouths of the fifty persons. It rose louder and louder, climbing the vocal octaves. It pounded through the room, reverberated from wall to wall.

"Danh-gbi! Danh-gbi! Li Grand Zombi! Li Grand Zombi! Aiiiiie!"

Benedict pushed the door open wide, slipped inside, and darted unseen across ten feet of open floor space to a wide wooden pillar that served as one of the supports of the underground roof. Revolver in readiness, he crouched there, well hidden from the occupants of the room.

The cries of the audience diminished to a low muttering again. And simultaneously the black curtain was whipped aside from the doorway at the far end, and a slow-moving procession entered in single file. In the lead came five huge Negroes, stripped to the waist, each carrying a large urnlike jar. Behind them, moving in the same funeral-cortege step, followed five Negro girls likewise bare of clothing to the waist. The girls held crude drums fashioned of old hides, stretched taut over small wooden kegs. They were beating these drums now in a slow rhythmic cadence, a *boom, boom* that thundered heavily down from the earthen ceiling.

And then Benedict abruptly clenched his fists hard around the butt of his revolver. For the figure of Hugh Milden had appeared in the doorway, pacing with that same mechanical step, eyes staring ahead with a hypnotic gaze. The ex-lawyer's hands were manacled with heavy chains in front of him, and a white crucifix was suspended upside down from his throat.

Behind Milden, rolling apparently without motive power, came a wide, flat-topped cart with small gilded wheels and black-draped superstructure. In the middle of the cart lay a large chest. It was the same iron-bound box the detective had seen on the farm wagon, the case with shipping marks from Sierra Leone.

All the while the procession was moving into the room, Fabre Leveau had stood with folded arms beside the iron vat. Only once did he move, that time to draw a small vial from the folds of his robe and pour the liquid contents into the kettle's interior. The liquid fell with a sharp hiss, and a column of steam spiraled upwards.

But now that the black drape again closed the doorway, he raised himself to his full, towering height and clapped his hands for silence. A ringing hush descended over the audience. Then he called loudly:

"Aie! Aie!

"Voodo Magnam!"

As if in response to his words, the smoke and steam pouring from the iron vat abruptly ceased. The fire beneath it dimmed, flickered, and went out. Two Negroes stepped forward, dipped their hands into the vat's interior and slowly lifted something out.

Benedict stared. It couldn't be, what he saw. It was against all logic. And yet there, unharmed apparently by her immersion into the steaming kettle, was the figure of the same girl he had heard singing the night before in the main room of the tavern upstairs! She was clad as before, long black hair streaming down her back, naked save for a sash of scarlet silk.

CHAPTER SIX

The Sacrifice

MOVING like automatons, the two Negroes carried the girl to the wagon, placed her on the platform beside it. With slow-moving hands they undid the lashings of the box, threw open its cover and leaped back.

And then those fifty people in the room went wild. They broke out into a delirious sing-song wail, a hideous, insane threnody —as from the open lid of the box, sliding outward in slow undulating coils, came a fat, yellowish body. To its full loathsome length it emerged, dropped to the floor and stood gazing at the girl with gleaming eyes.

It was a twenty-foot python, a monstrous repulsive snake, body glistening slime, head weaving from side to side. Close to the girl it poised there, gradually awakening from its torpor. Yet the girl did not move.

Once again Leveau uttered his deep-throated scream:

"Aie! Aie!

"Voodoo Magnam!

"The new Priestess of Li Grand Zombi will sacrifice herself to Danh-gbi, the God of the Serpent. She will join the others on the wire."

The crowd roared its approval. Back at the farther wall the drums began their obligatto again, pounded until the room seemed to pulsate with the repercussions. And above the drumming sounded the fanatic roar of fifty maddened throats.

> Eh! Eh! Bomba, hen, hen
> Canga bafio te
> Canga moune de le,
> Canga do ki la
> Canga li!

The python slid nearer. Eyes fixed upon the helpless prey in its path, the snake moved its fat body slowly, deliberately over the crimson floor. The foul mouth was open, slime and saliva drooling from it. A forked tongue lanced the air. Held there by some will other than her own, the girl stood rigid, arms dangling motionless, eyes fixed in space.

The drums swelled louder, faster in their cadence. And then the fifty white persons leaped into motion as a single body! In a wild dance of savage lust and frenzy they ripped the clothing from each other's back, whirled and gyrated, threw themselves screaming upon the floor! The five Negroes, carrying urns, passed among them. One after another the guests seized those urns, tilted them to their lips and drank long and greedily. When they finally looked up, gasping, their mouths were red and sticky, slobbered with fresh blood!

A wave of horror swept over Benedict, left him weak and trembling. He felt like a man who had penerated the last boundary of an abysmal hell.

And now the whites separated into two groups. Half lunged toward one wall, ripped from their wire support the corpses of the ten young women, clasped them to their bosoms and shrieked like animals while they fondled them and held the unspeakable embrace. The other group, laughing, yelling hysterically, darted to the second wire, jerked down the long line of rattlesnakes and twined the writhing reptiles about their necks.

Up front the python was watching the girl, gloating over the moment when it would surge forward and wrap its lubricous coils over her slim white body. To the right and safely out of the reptile's reach, Fabre Leveau stood like a Thibetan monk, watching the drama of his making.

But Benedict had no wish to see more. With a choking cry of horror, he lunged forward, raced through the aisle of screaming humanity and pounded up the steps to the platform. His right arm slipped about the girl, jerked her backward, flung her to the floor. Whirling, he leveled his revolver and pumped three shots at the rearing python. Two of those shots thudded harmlessly into the floor. The third ripped into scaly flesh and drew thick, oozing blood.

THE room was as if electrified. The dancing ceased; the guests stopped, riveted in their tracks. Benedict leaped backward, away from the thrashing serpent and across to Hugh Milden. Sharply he struck the ex-lawyer across the face.

"Milden!" he snapped. "Milden! I need help. Milden, do you hear me? Out of it!"

Again and again he struck the man, pummeled his clothes. Slowly, as one emerging from a heavy dream, the ex-lawyer relaxed. Intelligence returned to his staring eyes. His mouth opened and closed. Then he jerked forward and with his manacled hands thrust the detective to one side.

"Behind you!" he screamed.

A twelve inch cleaver whizzed through the air, missed Benedict's head by a fraction of an inch and buried itself in the red floor. The detective whirled, whipped his revolver forward and sent a single shot crashing into the brain of the huge black who towered over him.

Up on the platform Fabre Leveau was chanting slowly into the silence of the room. "An unbeliever is in our midst. Li Grand Zombi has been defiled. The Queen has been touched by an outsider. Kill him!"

Benedict's right hand slipped into his pocket, came out with a second revolver. Shoving the weapon into Milden's manacled hands, the detective turned, lunged up on the platform and seized the chanting Leveau by the throat.

Instantly he realized that the inaction had been a trick. Fabre Leveau threw himself forward, a long-bladed knife appearing as if by magic in his hand. As he countered with a blow to the jaw and a quick sidestep, Benedict saw the five half-naked Negroes rush toward him as one man. Two reports thundered from Milden's gun, and the foremost pitched on his face with a gurgling scream.

It was open hell then. While Benedict and the club manager lunged and side-stepped, clutched for each other's throat, the blacks, shrieking hideously, sought to cross the intervening space and reach the two intruders. Down by the iron-bound chest Milden stood with manacled hands, firing with calm precision, reloading the weapon like a machine. Powder-smoke rose upward like a fog.

Lashing its wounded body like a whip, the python reared and coiled in maddened fury.

Benedict and Leveau were fighting like crazed tigers now. The club manager had one arm free, strove to break the detective's iron grip on his knife-hand, to release the pressure that was slowly tightening on his windpipe.

They broke apart, stood facing each other. Leveau's lips were gushing blood. One eye was gouged. A bestial sneer twisted his face. With a quick movement he snapped his arm backward, poised it for an instant and hurled the knife with all the strength he could command.

Benedict ducked his head to the split second. The knife, blade foremost, shot by his ear, a glittering streak, and twanged into the floor beyond. One instant the detective waited, seeking an opening. One instant he watched Leveau as the man reeled, lurched for a second attack. Then Benedict hurled himself forward, slammed his right hand to the manager's jaw with a trip-hammer blow.

There was a grinding of bone and muscle. Leveau staggered, screamed and slumped to the floor.

AND now for the first time in those thundering seconds, the detective looked for the girl. She was standing huddled against the wall, eyes wide with terror. Striding to her and lifting her bodily in his arms, the detective paced down off the platform. To the audience he said: "Get out of here, the whole drunken lot of you. Get! You hear me?"

For a moment those fifty whites stood motionless in their tracks, staring blankly. Then with wild cries they turned and charged en masse for the rear door. The black girls and men followed close behind.

Down the length of the shambled room Benedict strode with his burden, picking his way between discarded corpses and squirming rattlesnakes. Over his shoulder he called to Milden. "Coming, old man? These rattlers won't hurt you. Their fangs have been pulled."

Milden followed. They reached the outer door, passed through the tunnel to the tavern's cellar. Through the intervening inky blackness they went, up the rotted staircase and out the half-sized door into the gloom of the yard. But they did not stop there. With Benedict marching stiffly ahead, the girl mute with terror in his arms and Milden scuffling silently behind, they made their way past the front of the building to the entrance of the swamp lane.

An ear-splitting scream of agony sounded from behind them. Whirling, they looked on a horrible sight. Feet braced far apart on the lawn before the entrance to Club Satan, Fabre Leveau stood with face twisted in excruciating pain. His eyes were bulging from their sockets, his mouth wide open. *And draped about his body like a slowly tightening length of yellowish brown rope, was the fat body of the python.*

Five steps forward the club manager staggered, the heavy weight pushing him downward. He clawed his arms wildly about the sinuous, slimy body while his throat belched forth piercing screams.

Then, even as Milden, revolver drawn, moved to his aid, the reptile abruptly jerked its fat folds tighter. Its tail lashed the air, its head shot upward, and Leveau's spine snapped like a broken lath! Thick blood gushed from his mouth. He coughed a death-rattle, and fell forward into the wet grass.

Shuddering, Benedict unclasped the girl's arms from around his neck and laid her gently down.

"Milden," he said, as she moaned and moved her lips tremulously, "Milden, the case is finished. I want you to meet Miss Ann Clermont, the girl we've been searching for these many days."

THE New Orleans to New York train was plunging through the night darkness somewhere in the State of Mississippi, carrying among its passengers three tired individuals. For hours Stephen Benedict had sat by the window, staring outward, taking no part in the conversation Milden was holding with Ann Clermont.

The ship-builder's daughter was attired in a traveling suit of gray broadcloth now, and though her face was still wan and haggard, she seemed trim and gracefully at ease as she looked across at the two men.

Abruptly the detective drew a Rosa Trofero cigar from his vest pocket, jammed it unlighted between his lips and began to speak.

"It was a clear case from beginning to end," he said. "I knew what I was up against the moment I saw that acorn with the feathers and tuft of human hair. It was a voodoo charm, a Negro *gris-gris* with a warning of death. And what we saw afterward, all of it, was voodooism in the vilest form.

"Leveau comes from Sierra Leone, on the West Coast of Africa. He was a witch-doctor in a Benga village on the upper reaches of the Niger, driven from his tribe because of his constant dealings with the white men. Educated in Accra, he smuggled his way into this country, bringing with him all his black beliefs in his snake-worshipping religion and a fanatic zeal to raise himself once again to power. He wasn't a true native, incidentally. His mother was a white hag from the opium quarter of Porto Novo, who found her way inland into the jungle years before.

"That information was given me over long-distance telephone by the New York Federal Immigration authorities. Leveau was arrested last September when he was caught inciting a group of Harlem Negroes. He escaped and disappeared. Wandering down into Louisiana, he must have been pleased to find a distorted remnant of his own native religious cult existing as a secret and suppressed witchcraft, a throw-back from slave-trade days and Obeah beliefs in Haiti.

"Voodooism, of course, was once all-powerful in the South. It was a society that had far-reaching tentacles. The last voodoo Queen was the famous Marie Leveau, who operated around New Orleans. Assuming the same name, Leveau, conceived the idea of Club Satan, a modernized roadhouse where the serpent-worshipping cult could be practiced in secret."

"But Miss Clermont," broke in Milden, "the white guests, those strange songs. . ."

"Miss Clermont was lured into the horror principally because of her voice. Leveau, while in New York, was attracted to her and brought her under his power by hypnotism. By this time he was crazed with his desire to advance the python-adoration cult. It was necessary that he always have a white woman to act as Queen, and the ritual called for the sacrifice of that queen to the serpent. Miss Clermont wasn't the first girl Leveau lured into his trap. The corpses you saw on the wire in the underground room were those of the poor wretches who served as her predecessors. The police told me that they came from New Orleans and vicinity. Each night one of them met her death, crushed to death by the python —Danh-gbi.

"Leveau also threw to the python the poor Negro Lodge had hired, when he caught him prying around the outside of the roadhouse; and one of the women guests, who must have rebelled against his practices and tried to leave. And he intended to do the same with you.

"As the popularity of the club increased, Leveau had shipped from Sierra Leone a second and larger python to amuse his guests. The strange song used as a theme song is an African chant, a death wail that has its origin in the swamp jungles of the Niger. Many of the effects were stage trickeries. During the last ceremony Miss Clermont, still under the effect of hypnotism, was kept in an inner core of that big vat, an inner core which was insulated from the fire.

"Jimmy Lodge, of course, was mur-dered because he discovered the secret of Club Satan. And Leveau tried to scare me off for a similar reason. That monster who attacked me in Lodge's hotel room was a club Negro wearing an African upper Niger witchcraft mask which Leveau had brought to this country."

Benedict removed his cigar and placed it carefully back in his pocket. "But that's enough of that, Milden," he said. "Such things are better forgotten. All that counts now is that we have Miss Clermont safe and sound. You see, even though Leveau disguised her by dyeing her hair and making-up her face, he couldn't disguise her voice. I recognized it from the broadcasted record."

Across from them on the opposite seat, Ann Clermont shuddered once at the memories behind her, then settled back and smiled at the two. The smile was wan, but it was nevertheless a smile.

THE END

—— N E X T M O N T H ——

FOOD FOR THE DEVIL

A Blood--Tingling, Soul-Chilling Mystery-Terror Novelette

by

GEORGE EDSON

A tale of a greedy swamp and a bleak house where horror reigned! Of a hideous, man-eating Thing whose soul belonged to Satan—and the dark terrors that it wrought.

IN THE NOVEMBER ISSUE—OUT SEPTEMBER 25th!

From Out the Shadows

By

Frances Bragg Middleton

It was hard for Shelley Reeves, city-bred, not to fear the musty, super-stitious legends of that bleak bayou land where her husband's people dwelt.

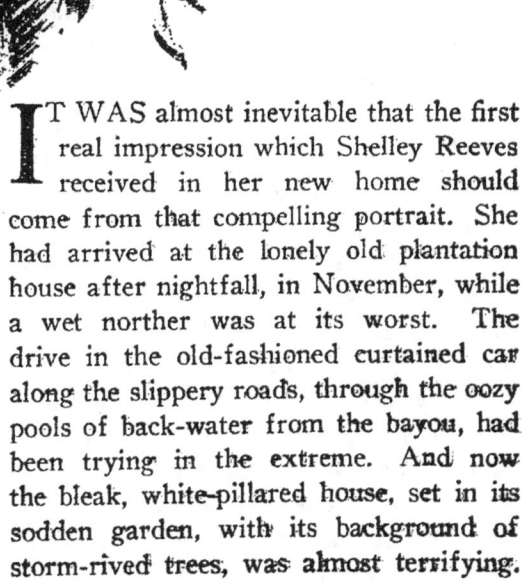

IT WAS almost inevitable that the first real impression which Shelley Reeves received in her new home should come from that compelling portrait. She had arrived at the lonely old plantation house after nightfall, in November, while a wet norther was at its worst. The drive in the old-fashioned curtained car along the slippery roads, through the oozy pools of back-water from the bayou, had been trying in the extreme. And now the bleak, white-pillared house, set in its sodden garden, with its background of storm-rived trees, was almost terrifying.

Her husband of a week, Graham

Reeves, spoke a few words of welcome, shyly, almost stammering, as they waited a few minutes on the deep, wide-boarded gallery. Then the door opened and an old black woman, exactly like somebody from a story book, was courtesying to them. To Shelley it was the last touch of unreality. So great was the change from all the world she knew that her overstrained nerves suddenly gave way. She caught at her husband's arm with a desperate little cry, and, her eyes closed, let him carry her across the room to a chair.

She pulled herself together presently, drank the cordial—it was astonishingly good—which old black Mammy Lou brought to her, and looked about her.

And then, for the first time, she saw Alisande Reeves look down at her.

The portrait—it was life-size—hung above the mantel. Below it a dreary fire of green wood burned sullenly, flaring and sputtering as the rain drops dripped upon it down the chimney. The lamplight made of the big square room an unknown cavern of eerie, moving shadows. Outside, the north wind mourned, the rain came in crazy flurries; an unpruned tree rasped and rubbed against the gable. Upstairs, somewhere, a loose shutter swung and banged unceasingly. But she forgot all that. The eyes of the portrait held her.

" 'Madonna,' " her husband murmured behind her. " 'Madonna—in Bronze.' "

Yes, that would be its name. Must be. The woman in the portrait was bronzed of skin—tanned, one saw, by the merciless summer sun. For though she wore the doeskin dress of an Indian she was white: white by birth, that is. But her eyes told you, unmistakably, that she was all Indian at heart. Wild eyes they were, brooding and rebellious, yet somehow stoical. The eyes of a wild thing imprisoned, knowing escape to be impossible, yet longing for it, plotting for it. And her arms— Shelley noticed them of a sudden—were

held as if they bore a baby. But they were empty.

"Poor thing," Shelley whispered pitifully, "Oh, the poor, poor thing!"

"The baby was born dead," her husband explained. "It never breathed at all. You see, the Indians kidnapped her when she was a very little girl. She married a brave and was recaptured years later by the whites with her two sons. She had forgotten her people, of course. She hated them and the life they lived. But they wouldn't let her go. Seems queer to think of that now, doesn't it? But people used to be like that. Her baby was born dead, as I said. One of the boys—the oldest— was drowned in the bayou. Nobody ever knew whether it was suicide or not. And after a while she died. There wasn't any reason. She just didn't want to live.

"And the other boy?" Shelley's eyes were still on the portrait. Ah, yes, she thought, it was well named "Madonna— in Bronze."

"Oh!" her husband shrugged. "He stayed and carried on. My great, great grandfather. You see, it was all a long time ago."

A long time ago. Yes. A long time. But, Shelley thought, Alisande Reeves still lived. She still sought to hold her still-born baby, though no one could see it but her. She lived. Such eyes as hers could never, never die.

"A masterly portrait-painter that one must have been," her husband murmured. "A Spaniard, I think they said. Took refuge here from a hurricane—"

Shelley wrenched her eyes away. The woman in the portrait knew too much. "Show me the house," she whispered.

SHE tried faithfully to make a home in the big, rambling house during the years that followed. But it was hard to do. The place was so alien, so dour. It stood on a little promontory near the point where

Chenango Bayou met the Gulf. Storm-twisted live-oaks stood about it, shutting out the sun. The Gulf wind mourned in their branches, kept their long gray dangles of Spanish moss in constant dreary motion. The bayou slipped by sullenly, turgidly, never singing. The sea water moaned in on quiet days over the treacherous sand bars, or raged and threatened when the storm winds struck.

And beyond the bayou the endless prairie stretched, bright as a shield of brass in the merciless sunlight, soulless and empty, more lonely even than the crying sea.

Behind the house lay endless cotton fields and the gin; the negro quarters, where plaintive banjos twanged, and negro chants rose, mournfully worshipful, or strident as instruments of brass at camp-meeting time.

To Shelley it was all so new and strange and terrifying. If only she could get away, get back to the life she knew, to brisk city streets, and gayety, and security. But she could not. Her husband loved this house of his ancestors. He was chained to it by a thousand unseen but potent bonds. Cotton was his fetich, as it had been his forefathers'. He was a slave to it. A slave, too, to the traditions of the house and of the family, proud—too proud—of his people's place in local history. He loved to tell Shelley old, heroic tales of fights with Indians—Mexicans—Yankees—all three were in the same class to him. He loved to show her the old, old silver, the gems in their quaint settings that had been buried so many times to save them from marauders. Oh, yes, she could see how he loved the old place, all the more, perhaps, because of things forgotten, secrets about it which he had never known. There was a hidden crypt under the house somewhere, he told her, which he had never found—

It had been November when she came. It was November again when their child was born. Throughout that night of agony the north wind blew, the slow rain dripped and drizzled, the limbs of the live-oaks groaned and ground together. And the room was full of memories of other births, of sufferings, of deaths. Shelley felt them, knew them, though she could not see. And Alisande Reeves lived and moved among the shadows, and watched the night through with her living eyes.

"Madonna—in Bronze!" Shelley could not lose her any more. Always she was conscious of her, yearning in the darkling corners, behind the curtains, lurking outside on the stair. And she caught her small son ever more closely to her heart. She was terrified. Surely Alisande, bereft, longed for a child to fill her empty arms—

ONE day in the summer Shelley laid a little fire of paper and kindlings wet with kerosene in the big fireplace downstairs. She was cold with sweat as she climbed upon a chair and laid both hands on the picture frame. She could not bear it any longer. Perhaps if the painting with its haunting presence went, if those compelling, living eyes no longer followed her—perhaps then she would have the courage to fire the house as well. For if the house were gone, then Graham might—oh, surely, surely, he would take her back to the life she yearned for.

Her hands closed hard upon the picture frame. But she did not move it. Her hands were rigid, cold as ice, and one by one her fingers lost their hold. It was as if another hand had loosed them, another hand that had once been strong with the cunning and the sureness learned in forests long since laid low and burned.

Shelley cried out and fell, lay prone upon the single, huge, white slab of rock which was the hearthstone. It seemed to her dazed and overwrought mind that noiseless feet moved toward her, that slim hands touched her gently. How long she lay there she never knew. But when the stupor left her the paper and the shavings were nothing more than a little heap of cooling ash.

And Alisande Reeves still watched her, unresentful, with her living eyes. The days went by, too quietly. The shadow still loitered in the corners and flitted up and down the creaking stair. And always there was the feeling of something hovering, hovering above the baby's bed upstairs. . . .

Until, one day, when Shelley was quite, quite sure that she had seen the figure in its doeskin dress leaning over the railing of the gallery that overhung the big hall where the stairs went up, her self-control broke suddenly, and she ran up the stairs in pursuit. Her baby was up there, sleeping. Why should Alisande be up there too, unless—unless—

Terror lent wings to her feet, but when she reached the upper hall the shadow had slipped away. Up there was nothing but sunlight, and silence, and the heavy scent of honeysuckle pouring in through the big south windows. But Shelley did not pause. She ran to the door of the room she shared with her husband and her child and stepped inside.

And then she stopped, dead still, staring, her throat tight, the cold sweat starting through her skin. For a snake was coiled by the baby's bed, a rattlesnake, huge as a python to her terrified eyes, its swaying head hardly a foot away from the face of the sleeping child. If he should stir—

But the reptile had heard her coming. Its lidless eyes were on her now, waiting, watching, knowing, she felt sure in her dazed, numbed brain, that the balance of power lay all on its side.

Held in the vise of dread and horror as she was, she had no idea what to do. A child so young could never survive the sting of a rattlesnake, especially now in the full tide of summer, when the rep-

tile's venom had reached the height of its malignant strength. If she cried out, if she moved, if she frightened it in any way—

Yet she did move. One could hardly say of her own volition. Slowly, deliberately, without the rustle of a garment or the tap of a shoe, not knowing what she did, her eyes held by the eyes of the serpent in a hypnotic stare, she moved into the room, along the wall, to the opposite side of the bed. On the table there was the baby's bottle, an inch of milk still in it, set in a saucer as her habit was, to save the fine old mahogany from a stain. And with slow, cold, steady hands, she removed the nipple, poured the milk into the saucer, and moved back toward the door with it.

Never for an instant had the snake's unwinking stare left her. Its head moved as she moved. But when she set the saucer down just beyond the threshold and edged her way back into the room again, its eyes remained on the saucer. Slowly its head went lower. Slowly its coils unwound. It slipped outside and bent its head to the tepid milk in the saucer. And Shelley slammed the door and barred it and began to scream.

She stood there by the bed, shaking, her little son snatched close to her heart, listening to the horrid sounds of slaughter as the negroes stormed up with axes and clubs and hoes. Not until they had assured her that the snake was killed, and its carcass thrown into the bayou would she unbar that door. She might have delayed even longer, had not Mammy Lou insisted that the room must be thoroughly scoured to remove all scent of the serpent and thus keep its mate from following its trail. Then indeed Shelley fled from it with her baby, and could not be persuaded to enter it again for many days.

WHEN her husband came home he tried to reason with her. He was patient. Yet there was in his manner a trace of irritation too. For he was matter of fact and practical, neither imaginative nor over-sensitive, as Shelley was. Yet she felt that she must convince him. She talked as she had never talked before. And all the festering horror of those long months came out.

And then his patience snapped, completely. "But that's plain foolishness, Shelley. You ought to know better than to listen to Mammy Lou's chimney-corner tales. The niggers believe those things. They always have. Witches, 'ha'nts,' 'conjur'—it's all as real as bread and meat to them. If you'd been raised down here you'd know how to take it. I told Mammy Lou not to fill your head with that old poppy-cock. I'm going to get after her, good."

Shelley stared, wide-eyed. So there was something then. . . . It wasn't all her imagination. The blacks believed. *What did they believe?* Somehow she had to find out.

"But Mammy Lou didn't tell me. I— I—saw! And Alisande wants her baby —" Shelley whispered fearfully, "or mine!"

Shelley's husband almost swore. "And I tell you it's all nonsense," he cried fiercely. "You're hysterical, and I don't blame you. That snake was real enough, in all conscience. And you acted like a soldier till the danger was over. God knows, I'm proud of you. It's natural enough for the reaction to hit you hard. But you've got to pull out of it."

"But she sent the snake," Shelley insisted, her lips white and stiff. "How could it have got in if she hadn't? And I saw her—upstairs. She *wants* the baby—"

Graham Reeves drew her closer into his arms.

"Try to be reasonable, Shelley," he pleaded. "In spite of the tales the niggers

tell—and if you'd been raised down here you'd know that, to hear them tell it, any house as old as this has a ghost in every room—Alisande Reeves is dead and gone like the rest of her generation. She can't come back. That's certain. But if she could, why should she want to harm the baby? If you must have a ghost, why not believe she warned you, summoned you to help him?"

Shelley shook her head.

"She was so unhappy," she persisted. "She hated her people for keeping her. Her baby was born dead, and one of her boys was drowned. She envies our happiness, I think—"

"When the baby is her own flesh and blood—as I am?" he snorted explosively. "Get hold of yourself, Shelley!"

It could not be said that either won the argument. When it stopped, it was only because they were both too weary to carry it further. Nor did they ever learn how the snake had entered. Old though it was, the house was in good repair. There were no chinks in the chimneys, no cracks in the floors. The windows and doors were screened. One could only conclude that a screen had been left open. Yet, with Shelley and Mammy Lou waging war on flies as they were, all day long—

There was never any real peace for Shelley any more, though, as the years passed and two more babies came, she grew used to her uneasiness, as pioneer women must have grown accustomed to the constant threat of Indian raids. Gradually, too, she learned a little more of the legend of Alisande, just a bit here and a bit there, for, with the threat of Graham Reeves' anger over their heads, the negroes were afraid to talk to her about it.

BUT Shelley had patience and perseverance, and the plantation days were long. She dug into the files of old letters and papers stored in the cabinets of the dim old library. And she came to know many things of Alisande's ruthless, indomitable spirit. She had not submitted tamely to capture. She had killed one white man in her struggle to get away. And later, in the home of her own people, she had fought—here in this very house, as Shelley remembered with a shiver—for the freedom her wild heart craved.

And more than once Shelley found mention of her by those who had never seen her in the flesh, but who had dwelt in that house long after she had gone, and had themselves long ago followed her and not returned. And those who had set down the words on the old pale-blue letter-paper in fadeless ink had all said the same thing, the thing that the artist had realized when he painted that portrait which hung above the parlor mantel, the thing of which Shelley had always been convinced. "She is hunting for her baby."

There it was, plain to read in that cramped, angular handwriting. She hadn't imagined it. It was written in many places, always in delicate, feminine hands.

And, just once, she prevailed upon Mammy Lou to talk.

It was her oldest boy's interest in Alisande's portrait that brought it about. It had been one of the first things he had ever noticed. He would look at it for many minutes together. And he began to call it "Grandmother" as soon as he could talk.

It worried Shelley inexpressibly, and one day she reproached Mammy Lou for teaching him the word.

Mammy Lou denied it, flatly, vigorously. And young Graham spoke up from his position on the wide white slab of stone that made the hearth. His fascinated eyes were glued to the portrait while he spoke.

"Nobody told me, mother," he asserted serenely. "I always knew."

Shelley hastily sent him out with one of the nurse girls. Young Graham frightened her sometimes, he was so old for his years, so unchildishly fond of playing alone. Was Alisande with him sometimes, when she didn't know?

"I wish that portrait was burned and forgotten," she cried then, out of her uneasiness and her exasperation.

Mammy Lou fairly seemed to shrivel in her chair.

"Don't say dat, Miss Shelley," she begged. "Don' say dat. Don' neber touch dat picture. Some folks, dey tried it once, en'—"

She stopped short then, with a shiver.

It was hard work to draw the rest of the tale from her. Not another word would she say under the compelling gaze of Alisande's painted eyes. But Shelley finally took her upstairs and got the rest of it.

It happened during what has always been known in that section as the War Between the States, along toward the close of it, when Texas, for so long safe from invasion, was being overrun by Union troops. A small party of them had come to the Reeves' place while the men were still away. A malingering party, evidently, for their sole object was loot.

Shelley got the picture, as much from Mammy Lou's gestures and quakings, as from her halting speech. The flight of the women and children before that skulking, uncontrollable fringe of an invading army. The hiding of the few horses and cattle deep in the bottoms, guarded by swamps across which strangers could not find their way. The unsuccessful search for "family silver," and the resulting rage. And then,

"So dey say dey gwine take de picture in de parlor en' den set de house on fiah. So dey went in dar ter do it. En' nobody neber seen 'em no mo'!"

Ice water began to trickle through Shelley's veins. She remembered her own attempt so long ago. She gasped, "Surely you don't mean to say—"

"I don' mean ter say nothin'. Hit jest like I'm a-tellin' you. Dey done went in dar—*an' dey neber come outer dat room!*"

IT WAS in the winter time that the blow struck, that winter when the highways of Texas burned with the speed of bandit cars, when the city police and the sheriffs' men drove warily, machine-guns in their hands and cold terror in their souls. In the winter, on a darkened morning when the wind drove strongly from the northeast, and the rain came with it, rain that lashed the bayou into a lather of foam and sent it roaring down into the shouting breakers of the Gulf.

There was a fire that day, of course, in the great fireplace under the portrait of Alisande. Graham Reeves had gone to town, since the weather had made the day a holiday, and young Graham was upstairs, as he often liked to be, engaged in some curious game of his own. But Shelley sat before the great white hearth-stone with the two younger children, and Mammy Lou, and big, black Mordecai, the blacksmith, who had come to cajole the usual "birthday" for his new-born child. All outside noises were drowned by the ramping wind, so she had no warning of the horror that was on her till the door into the hall burst open, and she saw. An embodied crime wave there, half a dozen thugs chill-eyed, flat-mouthed, driving the terrified house servants into the room before them. Snub-nosed guns they had, as venomous-looking as the men themselves.

Mammy Lou gave one startled gasp. Her face was ashen, but she did not quail. Her old black arms reached out and swept her two small nurselings to her knees. The same savage, defiant courage was in her old black eyes as that which blazes in the eyes of sore-pressed cattle, when, ringed in a horn-tipped phalanx older than Mace-

don's, they meet the onslaught of the hungry wolves.

These, too, were wolves, was the thought in Shelley's mind as, cold and white, and as still inside as marble, she came to her feet and faced them.

The leader snarled at her out of one corner of his thin-lipped mouth.

"The silver, and the jewelry," he demanded stridently. "We know you've got it. We've heard about this place. And that antique stuff's valuable now. Better fork it over, or—"

His mouth shut like a trap. He jerked his gun hand toward the frightened, staring children in a gesture not to be misunderstood.

"Remember the Lindbergh baby!" he added with a grim significance. His eyes were cold and ugly, like a wolf's.

Black Mordecai made a sudden dive toward the back-door, reached it in what seemed to be a single bound of his long legs. Shelley cried to him to come back, but for once he did not obey her voice. It is doubtful if he even heard it. Through the windows they could see him leap the length of the long back-gallery, one of the bandits close upon his heels. They saw the big blacksmith snatch the heavy bar from its rack, bring it down mightily on the iron gong that hung there to call the field hands from the quarters. The resounding clang and the gangster's shot made one thunder crash that rose above the noise of the water and the wind. Black Mordecai lurched forward, stricken. But with almost his last breath his giant-thewed arms swung the iron bar again, and crushed the murderer's skull as if it had been an eggshell.

The bandit leader swore. "Do you want us to kill another one?" he screamed at Shelley, and called her by a name unprintable.

But, mercifully, Shelley never heard him. She was not seeing him. Nor was she looking at the two men lying in their blood outside the long back windows. She was staring, drawn by a fascination she could neither resist nor control, through the door into the hall behind the invaders. In the dim upstairs gallery, near the head of the stairway, five-year-old Graham Reeves stood leaning against the banisters, and behind him—

SHELLEY tried to cry out and could not. Her throat was tight. That awesome presence, compelling, alluring, yet seeming still no more than a shadow among the other darkling shadows of the hall. . . . Those slim brown hands outstretched above the boy's head . . . That look upon the face . . . Oh, not at all the look that the artist had painted long ago. The heartbreak, the yearning tenderness, were lacking. That deeply-bronzed face that showed so eerily through the gloom of the hallway was cold, now, and still, implacable, set in a relentless purpose.

It was Shelley's spellbound gaze that warned the gangsters. Instinctively crowding closer together, they swung about to meet the unknown menace behind them. But before they had caught sight of it, the shadowy face had changed. It smiled.

Shelley still stood there, incapable of movement, still staring. And the wolves of the Texas highway were staring too. They had moved forward, toward that compelling presence, into the big, high-ceilinged hall. For a power lay on that shadowy figure, a glamour, invisible, yet palpable as mist. No wonder, Shelley thought, she had been able to feel that overmastering presence even when she had not seen! It must have been this same power of magnetism, of allure, that the unknown painter had seen and felt so many years ago. The fire of his genius had flared up to meet it, had made it immortal in the canvas above the mantel. No wonder those eyes seemed alive.

"I can show you what you came to find." The child was speaking, but Shelley had never heard that voice before. It wasn't the child's. He was speaking, she thought fearfully, for someone else, but that, of course, the bandits could not know. "My grandmother is old, you would never believe how old, and very, very wise. She knows so much more of this old house, and of its treasures, than anybody else has ever dreamed of. She says our people had dealings with Lafitte!"

The voice of a sleepwalker, Shelley thought, in torment. Would the child ever wake to normal life again? But the mob still stared, like men hypnotized. Their eyes were avid. Tongues licked out greedily over wolfish lips. Pirate treasure! Unhallowed toll from Spanish galleons! No greater allure in all the world than that!

But Shelley, sick and shaking, wondered what they would do when they learned that they had been duped, that there was no pirate treasure? How could she tell them there was no one there? They would not believe her, and they might harm the child—

"She can tell you where to find the treasure," the voice that was not the child's voice went on monotonously. "But you must pay her for it. You must go away and leave us all in peace."

"That's a bargain." The leader's voice was a mere croak in his eagerness. "But if you don't play the game—" His gun-hand jerked. His grin was hideous in its suggestiveness. "There's still you kids, you know!" Shelley's tortured heart was wrung again.

"Ah, but my people were always fair with those who were fair with them!" Again it was the child who spoke, but it was at the shadowy figure of the woman in the doeskin dress that the bandits looked. It was her smile that wrapped them as in a garment, possessed them utterly. Swaying behind the banisters, her slender, brown arms outstretched, she held her audience as in the hollow of one hand. They were lost in that eternal, universal lust of that gold-craze which has maddened so many millions of men.

"The portrait above the mantel," the boy's voice droned on tonelessly. "Lift it down carefully. It will take all of you to handle it. And you will find all the treasure you will ever want in this world behind it."

He ceased, and stared out over their heads with the wide, unseeing eyes of the sleepwalker. And the face above him smiled again, an indescribable, Circe smile.

The gangsters trooped back into the parlor, guns in hand, and the house servants broke and fled before them, pressed far back against the wall. Mammy Lou, her eyeballs rolling, her face ashen, went with them, a baby on each arm. Shelley, still numbed and powerless, watched the bandits converge before the portrait. They would never keep faith, her mind kept telling her. Even if there were an ancient cache of pirate loot in there—and Shelley doubted it—the mob would still plunder the rest of the house, perhaps even take the children with them to hold for ransom. Mordecai had died to summon aid for her. But no aid had come. No aid would come. Perhaps the blacks were afraid. Perhaps the storm outside had smothered the clang of the iron gong. And she herself was helpless, helpless—unable to save the babies downstairs from the human wolves—unable to save her eldest from *what now stood behind him.*

THE bandits had set the piano bench upon the hearth, so close to the fire that the melting varnish stung Shelley's nostrils. Three of them had climbed upon it. The others, below them on the hearth-stone, held their guns on the crowd.

For a reason she could not have named, Shelley's eyes darted from the thugs to the gallery upstairs. The face still loomed above the boy's head, but it had changed again. It was as still, now, as stolid, as an Indian's, and grim with a cold, set purpose. The brown hands were still hovering over the child as the figure stood poised there, motionless, the face a mask of awful triumph.

And suddenly one of the men on the bench gave a grunt of satisfaction. He seemed to have found something, a spring, perhaps. He caught hold of the frame and wrenched at it. It did not budge, but on the instant the hearth stone dropped from beneath the bandits' feet. Their helpless bodies dropped with it, hurtled into the abyss below. And when the stone rose to its place again, none of the awe-struck watchers could tell, by any sign upon it, that it had ever moved. Only, the piano bench was forever gone—

When they looked up to the gallery again, the figure in doeskin garments had already melted soundlessly into the darker shadows of the hall. The blacks, all but Mammy Lou, were huddled in a shuddering heap on the floor. Mammy Lou still stood erect, but she was moaning prayers, her arms still locked around the children as if she still feared to let them go. But Shelley looked up into the brooding eyes of the portrait above the mantel. And for the first time it seemed to her they smiled.

Young Graham Reeves walked down the stairs in his slow, old-fashioned way, and came straight into his mother's trembling arms. His eyes were quite clear as he looked up into her white face.

"I had a funny kind of a dream, mother," he told her soberly. "It wasn't a nice dream at all. But I wasn't a bit afraid."

And neither would she be afraid again, Shelley vowed fiercely to herself, never, never again.

DEATH'S

by
Hugh B. Cave
(Author of "Terror Island")

NORMAN BLAKE, star news-hound of the *Examiner*, squashed a five-dollar bill against the grimy palm of the night watchman and said with a shrug: "Okay, buddy. Thanks for the break." Staring ahead across the darkened

LOVING ARMS

Horror Novelette

Out of some distant jungle land she came—that strange, lustful woman beast, whose marble beauty was lure beyond control; whose loving touch meant screaming death!

no-man's-land of Morton Wharf, he advanced slowly, his mouth hooked into a scowl as he made out the sinister black hulk of the steamer.

The Leavitt expedition had returned at last from its secrecy-wrapped mission to South America's deep jungles. Blake himself had hammered out news and feature copy on that same expedition, upon its departure six months ago: "Professor

Alexander Leavitt, noted scientist-explorer, in company with his attractive 21-year-old daughter Irma, his three learned partners and a crew of fourteen able men, will go where no other white persons have ever dared penetrate. The purpose of their perilous journey has not been made public. . . ."

Well, this dirty black hulk tied up at the wharf's end was the *Research*. And Alexander Leavitt, with his ugly reputation for manhandling newsmen who got too curious, was back. Shadowed human shapes, silhouetted against scattered patches of yellow light, were moving about on the ship's deck in the business of unloading.

Blake moved closer. Ahead of him iron wheels rumbled over wooden planks; heavy boxes squealed down damp runways; men were talking in low tones, moving awkwardly as though unaccustomed to their work. Blake peered closer. No; those dark spider shapes prowling about in the gloom were not regular stevedores. They were members of the ship's crew.

But why unload at night? . . .

And then, as the first roll of thunder of the approaching storm echoed across the dark wharf like a rifle salute fired over a grave—then Blake knew. A drop of rain struck his face, ran like cold blood down his cheek, and he shivered. For the sweating, half-naked men moving eerily outside the glare of light amidships, were carrying coffins! There could be no doubt of it. Three times a dark and sinister box was carried warily around that circle of light, sent overside, loaded into a waiting truck.

But the thing which made Norman Blake oblivious to the increasing rain, which tightened his muscles and set his heart to pounding, was the expression on the faces of the crew. As they circled the midships space instead of taking the direct route across it, their faces were silhouetted against the light. And each face was a mask of terror. The men moved, stumbling with their heavy burdens, keeping their eyes away from the light as if by some superhuman effort of the will—seeming to know that if they failed, they were as doomed as the boxed corpses they carried!

Blake sucked in his breath, clenched his fists. He had an unreasonable desire to turn and run, tell his city editor there was no story. But he moved resolutely forward. What black, malignant doom had taken the lives of three men, turned their companions into stumbling cravens? Somehow the answer to that lay within the yellow glare of light amidships.

And in that light was but one thing: a kind of upright wooden packing-case that had iron bars for a door. Staring intently, Blake made out a moving white shape that seemed to be restlessly pacing back and forth inside the cage.

An animal? Undoubtedly, Leavitt had brought animals back with him from the jungle. But a caged animal could not terrorize.

Blake halted, and stood rigid, eyes wide. On deck, near that particular patch of light, a seaman had trundled a two-wheeled truck and dropped it, let it fall with a thud. The truck itself, too heavily laden, had dragged him near the cage. He threw up his head, looked swiftly to see how close he was . . . and stood staring like a man hypnotized, both hands extended stiffly before him as if warding off some malignant evil!

THE others had not seen. This one took a step forward, and another, moved his feet as if they were weighted with lead. Yellow light flooded his face, exposing sweat-drenched, writhing muscles, bulging eyes, lips working soundlessly. Step by step the man advanced; and the white shape in the cage was now motionless, waiting for him to come within reach.

A cry of warning, warning against some unknown peril, found its way out of Norman Blake's lips. On deck, other men saw and bellowed frenzied words. Then a short stumpy shape that Blake knew to be Professor Leavitt himself, came lurching up from below, hurling harsh clipped syllables at the terrified seaman.

"Get back, you fool! Back! You've been warned a thousand times. . . ."

The warning came too late. In another stride the man reached his objective, came within reach of a pair of leprous-white arms that coiled toward him through the bars of the cage. Locked in the embrace of those gleaming arms, he seemed to go suddenly limp, to yield willingly to their pressure.

Then with equal abruptness he staggered backward, screaming. A mad shriek of agony tocsined from the depths of his soul, filled the night with vibrations that stabbed Norman Blake's eardrums. Writhing in torment, the man reeled across the deck, crashed into the rail and slumped in a contorted, squirming heap. Then he was still.

Not until then did the others go to his assistance, and then it was too late. The limp shape that they raised from the deck and carried silently into darkness was no longer alive; Blake knew that. And he knew with the section of his mind not frozen by the sudden drama, that the man had fought against his fate, helplessly. Now he, Norman Blake, had to go aboard that vessel of mystery and death and get the story—if he could learn what was in that cage, and live.

As the crew carried that lifeless form from beneath the light, Blake saw the terror and agony engraved in the man's face, saw a mass of bloody scratches on his naked chest.

On the deck Leavitt snarled at the crew, "It was his own fault! Now get on with your work—and *stay away from that cage!*"

Blake's long legs felt childishly weak as he slid furtively toward the ship. He reached the dark hulk, slid along the side of it until his groping hands found something to cling to. A moment later, shielded by darkness, he was prowling warily toward the iron-barred box where the seaman had met his death.

Then, staring, he opened his eyes to saucer bigness, and stood stock still.

That naked shape, sprawled in a bed of straw on the floor of the cage, was a human being! A woman! Something about the color and texture of her skin was not normal, but she was unmistakably a woman.

Blake started forward impetuously, then came to a shaking halt, remembering what had happened to the seaman. For two minutes he stood motionless, cursing the dim light that blurred the strange naked shape. Then, remembering his original intent, he turned—and was jerked violently back by a heavy hand that clamped down on his shoulder.

He stared. His own six-feet-two lacked at least three inches of reaching the height of the square-faced, bearded man who held him in a grip of iron.

The big man growled out nasally: "What are you doing here? Who are you?"

"Reporter," Blake said with forced indifference. "Looking for Leavitt."

"How did you get aboard?"

"I walked."

The big man said: "You'll do more walking, right now. You're going below."

A gun came into the fellow's hand and Blake made a face at it. Guns he understood, and though this one was pointed at him it gave him a sense of security after the thought of that strange woman whose power of death was stronger than the iron bars of a cage. With the big man behind him, Blake crossed the deck, descended the companionway and paced along the dimly lighted passage. The gun prodded him through an open door.

FOUR men were there at a cluttered table. And a woman. All stared; Blake stared back, centering his gaze on the gray eyes of Professor Alexander Leavitt.

The big man at Blake's elbow said grimly, "I found this fellow on deck, snooping around. He's a reporter."

The men at the table were silent. They were, Blake realized, the brain-trust of Leavitt's expedition. One of them, Eric Gromalin, was a faculty member of a large Eastern university; one was Dr. Paul Willoughby, of Boston; the good-looking, not-too-old chap in white shirt and white flannel trousers was Mr. Geoffrey Marsden, Leavitt's literary-minded secretary. And the girl, sitting there very quietly like something out of a cigarette advertisement, was the professor's daughter, Irma.

All were waiting for Leavitt to speak. Leavitt stood up, flattened his hands on the table and leaned forward on stiff arms, glaring. That bearded face had a quality of cast iron.

"You are a reporter?"

"Norman Blake of the *Examiner*. The same Blake who gave you a royal send-off in print, six months ago."

That was a mistake. Leavitt's face crimsoned, went from red to white with anger. He opened his mouth to speak, choked on the words and then blurted out: "Get out of here! You and your filthy breed—"

Blake stook a step backward without meaning to. Dr. Paul Willoughby said: "Easy, Professor. The man is only doing his job. He was probably sent here."

"I'll have none of him, or any of them! This is my ship!"

Willoughby shrugged, walked around the table and put a hand on Blake's arm. "You'd better clear out. You came at a most inopportune time."

Inopportune? Blake shuddered at thought of the three coffins, of the seaman who had staggered back in agony from the embrace of the woman in that cage on deck. If these men wouldn't explain he'd break the story, make them clear up the fiendish mystery of this beast woman they had brought from the age-old jungle back to a civilized world. He said softly "You might tell the professor that I've seen enough already to write a whole extra edition." Then he turned and went out.

On deck he stared again at the iron-barred cage at the abnormally white flesh, the sensuous, pantherish pose of the sleeping woman within. He felt the hair on his neck rise as a dog's hackles rise. This woman had killed a man less than half an hour before, yet now she was sleeping quietly as a kitten. Sleeping like a well-fed cat. Fed . . . on the blood of a human being? . . .

He went forward, cautiously. At least Leavitt had not sent a guard along to make certain that he cleared out. That was a break. Using his eyes, he might yet learn something.

There were other cages, smaller than the death-cage and containing dark shapes that filled the night with whimpering sounds, guttural growling noises, occasional soft whines. Sweat-drenched men were unloading the cages to the wharf. . . .

Behind Blake, naked feet made a sudden whispering sound on the deck, ominously close. He whirled, sucked breath and lunged desperately backward.

The lunge came too late. Thick-lipped, ugly features snarled in Blake's face—

features that belonged to no white man but to a lithe, brown-skinned savage, naked save for a filthy breech-clout!

One sinewy arm was viciously descending, powerful fingers locked around an iron marlin-spike solid enough to crush a man's skull. Before Blake could lurch clear, the spike finished its downward swing, made glancing contact with his head.

Limp-legged, Blake slid silently to the deck. . . .

A N UNPLEASANT stench was in his nostrils when he came to. Something cold, wet, moved sluggishly inside his clothes. Above him a haloed streetlamp flickered dismally.

He put out a hand, and the hand dipped into cold water to its wrist. Shivering, he stared around him, groaned dully from the sledge-hammer thumping of his skull. This was a side-street near the docks. And Norman Blake, star newshound for the city's best sheet, had been unceremoniously dumped into a filthy gutter and left there.

Evidently he had been out a long time. Rain-water ran in the gutter; beyond the yellow glare of the street-lamp lay a world of gray gloom.

He stood up, stamped angrily on the curb to drive water out of his shoes. His clothes were soaked; a stink of gutter refuse clung to them.

Men who knew Norman Blake would have backed away from the expression on his face at that moment. Words came out of his throat and blasted the silence.

"Knocked on the head and thrown out! Me, a push-over for an undersized native rat that never even saw a prize-ring. By God, if it's the last thing I ever do. . . ."

They had not carried him far, not more than three streets from the waterfront. It took him five minutes of sullen striding to get back to Morton Wharf.

He was too late. Lights no longer burned on the black hulk of Professor Leavitt's chartered tramp. Men were no longer unloading. The place was deserted, closed up tight.

He left the docks slowly, talked to himself as he strode through side-streets to the curb where he had long ago parked his car. He had plenty to make a story, a big one. He could stop now, not risk his life with that mad group who had brought back from the jungle a strange white and naked woman whose touch meant death—and who drew her victims as a flame draws candle flies. That seaman had fought against her, Blake had seen that. Yet he had been pulled to the woman as surely as if a rope. . . . And yet Blake knew that he had to go. His pride, his profession meant something to him. If he did not go he could never again respect himself. Besides that, by God! he was angry.

Six months ago Norman Blake had visited Alexander Leavitt's private home far outside the city to get copy on the expedition's departure. Now he began again the same perilous journey. And driving he thought of Irma Leavitt. If he could see her again. . . .

He knew where to stop the car, where to get out and begin walking. And ahead of him, after he walked slowly for five minutes, staring involuntarily into the whispering rain on each side—ahead of him loomed his destination.

It was a big house, frowning above a broad expanse of level lawn. Lighted windows watched through the mist. Trucks, emptied now of their loads, loomed gaunt and black beside a rutted driveway, showing how Leavitt and his companions had transported the stuff from the steamer. Beyond, in darkness, squatted a small square building that was Leavitt's workshop.

Somewhere here was a brown savage

who moved with feet of silence, and who struck swiftly, mercilessly. There was a woman who lured her victims, killed, then curled in contented sleep as though death had fed and satisfied her. Blake shrugged the terror from his mind, forced himself forward.

Birches, white in the drizzle, offered shelter as he crept on.

In the grass, just ahead, something dark, inert, loomed out of the drizzle. Blake stopped, stood stiff for ten seconds, but the shape did not move.

He advanced, stood over it and stared down. His eyes widened. Sucking breath, he went abruptly to his knees in the wet grass, reached out a hand and touched the shape cautiously, as if fearful that it might leap up at him.

But that shape would never again move of its own volition. Dead, contorted, sprawled there like a broken spider, it lay in a pool of its own blood, congealed blood that had long ago ceased flowing from jagged gashes in the man's bare chest.

The face that gaped up into Blake's own, bloodless and fixed in a fearful mask of death, belonged to the man who had defended Norman Blake back in the cabin of the *Research*. This—this dead thing on the lawn of Professor Leavitt's isolated home was Dr. Paul Willoughby!

CHAPTER TWO

Marked For Death

AND though Blake had witnessed death before, in many strange forms, he shrank with a violent shudder from Willoughby's mutilated body and found himself unable to close his gaping eyes, upon the horror that confronted them.

Willoughby had helped capture that woman, should have known how to protect himself. And yet savage fingers had ripped the doctor's shirt to shreds, raked the flesh beneath, leaving parallel wounds that were caked now with half-dry blood. And in the dead man's convulsed face lay the same frozen expression of hideous fear that had festered in the face of the unwary seaman on the *Research's* deck.

Blake stood up slowly, stood swaying, aware that his own face had lost color and his own blood was running cold, chilling him. Then he was aware that just ahead, the front door of Leavitt's house was open—had been opened during the past few minutes. And across the lawn, through a pall of gray drizzle that distorted everything within it, came two ill-defined shapes, striding toward him.

He opened his mouth, but no sound came. His chest was a vacuum and the pressure of the wet outside air seemed ready to crush in his ribs.

He stared, and suddenly laughed loudly, wildly with relief. For the faces that loomed out of the mist toward him were familiar faces, both of them. One, comparatively young and undeniably good-looking, powerful with square jaw and prominent cheekbones, belonged to Geoffrey Marsden, Leavitt's secretary. The other belonged to Eric Gromalin. And Gromalin, big and strong as an ox, held a gun, looked straight at Blake's tense face.

The man stared holes in Blake's head, twisted his bearded countenance into a scowl black as night and growled out: "You! Again!"

"Me again," Blake retorted quietly. "Still snooping. This time I found something to snoop at." He aimed a stiff forefinger at the shape in the grass, and leaned forward on the balls of his feet as both Gromalin and Marsden peered down.

Both men gaped. Marsden, stooping, said in a half-whisper: "Good God! It's Willoughby!" Gromalin, forgetting his gun for a fraction of an instant, took a step forward and let a gasping sound spray through his moist lips.

Blake lunged, clamped a hand over the revolver and with a vicious downward thrust tore it from Gromalin's grasp. Rammed by the impact, the big man stumbled, caught one foot in the sprawled body of the dead man and fell with his arms flailing empty air.

When he got up again, sputtering and snarling, Blake stood wide-legged, gripping the gun in stiff fingers. The gun-muzzle covered both of Leavitt's partners.

"Start something," Blake advised them harshly. "There's been so much killing a little more won't matter much.

"You figured on taking me to your lord and master, didn't you? All right, I'm going anyway. But if we meet that—that—" He stopped. What could he call that white and sensuous woman of death —if she was a woman? He swallowed, motioned with the gun, said, "Get inside."

They had no alternative. Gromalin turned, walked slowly, stiffly, in a sort of exaggerated goose-step, toward the house. Marsden, silent and afraid, walked slightly behind him, taking shorter steps.

"Wait a minute," Blake ordered. "Just where *is* Leavitt?"

"He is in his study."

"Alone?"

"His daughter is with him."

"Okay," Blake growled. "Walk me straight to the study, and no detours."

The gun felt good in his hand. But as he followed Leavitt's men, every nerve was alert, so that he felt each separate raindrop which struck him, and the whisper of their feet in the grass sounded like the giant rustling of the wings of death.

THE study contained two occupants. Both snapped to attention as Gromalin tramped slowly over the threshold. Alexander Leavitt was evidently not accustomed to being disturbed, even by his colleagues. His plumpish body went stiff behind the desk that half concealed it; his eyes popped in astonishment. They popped even wider when Blake trailed Gromalin and Goeffrey Marsden into the room and kicked the door shut, reaching behind him to turn a key in the lock. Iron bars had not stopped the caged woman from taking her toll, but a door. . . .

Leavitt gaped at the gun and went white under his flush of anger. Blake looked at him squarely, shifted his gaze and stared at the girl beside the desk.

She had half risen, then slumped back again. She returned Blake's gaze not hostilely, but as if she were bewildered. She was beautiful. Almost she made him forget this was a house of horror. She had all her father's good points, none of his bad ones. She was all woman. But Norman Blake was not particularly interested in women. Not right now.

"Just what," Alexander Leavitt snarled, "does this intrusion mean?"

Blake leaned against the wall, away from the door, fingered the revolver, his watchful eyes going swiftly from one curtained window to another. "That's foolish question number one," he said, forcing his voice to calmness. "Especially after you took such great pains to have me knocked on the head and heaved into a gutter."

"I *what?*"

From somewhere in the depths of the house an animal, or a person, screamed. Blake's gun jerked up, covered the men in the room. His voice, when he spoke, grated.

"Has your death woman rested from her last feeding? Is she drinking blood again?"

Leavitt frowned, said slowly: "What do you mean?"

Licking dry lips, Marsden put in fearfully: "It—Doctor Willoughby . . . dead

. . . the way the others died. The same horrible . . . Good God, if we don't do something soon . . . !"

Leavitt stiffened, opened his clenched hands convulsively. His daughter jerked about in her chair and stared at him with widening eyes.

"No, no! I tell you—" Leavitt caught himself, sucked a deep, noisy breath that swelled his chest and brought color back into his face. He had plenty of self-control, used it all and squared off behind the desk as he glared into Blake's face.

"You are mistaken." Leavitt's words slid gently through slightly parted lips. "There is no woman. If Willoughby is dead, he was killed by one of the jungle beasts that we brought back with us. One of them must have—"

His words were cut off by another scream which echoed dully in the room. And in the death-like silence which descended, Norman Blake acted.

Stiffly, because the terror of the place had made his muscles wooden, Blake used the gun to wave Gromalin and Marsden aside. He reached the desk, slid the phone toward him and called a number. Mouth close to the instrument, he said hoarsely:

"Blake talking. Yeah, Blake of the *Examiner.* Listen. Tell Captain Kenney here's a job for him. Murder, in the home of Professor Alexander Leavitt, on the Waban Road. Got it? And get out here in a hurry, because. . . ."

He let his words trail off. If he explained that here there was a nude woman whose glance meant desire, whose touch meant death, they'd think him drunk.

He forked the phone, walked slowly backward to the door and leaned there.

IT WAS a long wait and a nerve-racking one. Outside there were Leavitt's men, at least one savage, and the beast woman. Inside he was one against four, counting the girl. Wondering about her,

Blake took a long sideways look without letting her know it. She seemed bewildered by the whole business. This whole household, just now, was a place of hideous death, an evil, dangerous, black-bordered domain of hell.

Blake thought about it, kept on thinking about it for an eternity, while the old house creaked in the gusts of windy rain and his stomach coiled sickeningly at the memory of a woman's bloodlust. When at last a doorbell droned somewhere nearby the sound made him jump, caused him to leap to attention.

Footsteps pounded the corridor outside, and a door opened. Blake heard voices, recognized one of them as belonging to Captain Kenney of LaRonge Street Headquarters. Silently he reached behind him, unlocked the study door and, without shifting his gaze from his prisoners, called out: "This way, Kenney."

Kenney came into the room, with men in uniform. One of the men was holding by an arm the brown-skinned native who had done the job on Norman Blake. Kenney stared, hooked his head around to shift his stare to Blake, and said: "Well, speak your piece, mister."

Blake told him, made it short and curt. When he had finished, Kenney rocked on stiff legs, pushed one of his men to the door and growled, "Go out and bring in the stiff." Then, rocking back, he peered at Alexander Leavitt. "It's your turn. What's your story?"

Leavitt said: "This reporter is insane." He spoke the words as if he had been weighing them a long while and memorizing them for the occasion. "It is true that two persons have been killed; but this man's insane talk of coffins and a caged murderess—that is sheer nonsense!"

"Then who killed the two men?"

"One of them," Leavitt declared, "was killed on board the *Research* when he stepped too close to a cage containing a savage ape. We were unable to save him; the beast tore him to pieces. The second man I know nothing about. I have been held prisoner here by this madman."

Kenney nodded slowly, turned to the uniformed men behind him and said without visible emotion: "Go look around. Check up on Blake's 'caged woman,' and report back here."

There was a glint of triumph in the professor's eyes that Norman Blake did not fail to notice. What it meant he was not sure, but he stepped forward, about to question Leavitt.

Abruptly then, he stopped, snapped to attention. Echoes of the sound that had startled him still rolled in jangling clamor through the house. Someone had fired a heavy revolver. Someone not on this level, but downstairs, deep down.

Blake and Kenney exchanged glances; across the room, the brown-skinned native, Cheega, had an expression of animal fear on his ugly face. Blake opened the door, strode across the threshold. Voices drifted up to him from somewhere below.

Footsteps, a moment later, sounded on the same level as the study. Kenney's men, some of them carrying a heavy burden, came slowly along the hall, lugged their burden past Blake and dumped it on the floor inside.

Blake knew suddenly that he had failed. The answer lay in Leavitt's features, where a vague smile still lingered. The thing on the floor, over which Kenney was bent in silent examination, was a huge, dirty brown monkey.

A huge, hairy anthropoid. And one of Kenney's men was saying in a voice that slightly trembled: "The professor here was right, all right. We found a busted cage down in the cellar, and then we ran smack into this thing on our way upstairs again. It come for us with murder in its

mug, and Sellers give it the works from no more'n ten feet. Gawd, don't it look human!"

Kenney straightened. "You inspected the whole house?"

"Every damned inch of it. We didn't find no caged woman nor any woman at all. There's plenty cages in the cellar, but they're full of monkeys and snakes and about fifty other kinds of hamburger on the hoof. No woman."

Kenney shrugged, looked at Blake. "There's your answer, Blake."

LEAVITT was still smiling. So, too, was Eric Gromalin. Marsden and the girl were staring at the monstrous thing on the floor. Blake said, "Maybe this satisfies you, Kenney. Not me, it doesn't."

Again Kenney shrugged. "I guess you're nuts." He lit a cigarette, emptied his smoke-filled nostrils in the professor's direction. "You better make sure none of the rest of your menagerie don't break loose, Leavitt. And make out a signed report on this business, first thing in the morning, and bring it to Headquarters."

"I shall do that." Leavitt turned to Norman Blake, his face grim. "And you, Blake . . . clear out. And be careful what you put in your paper. If you don't forget about animal women you may find them—dangerous."

Blake's mouth was tight, his eyes smouldering. Leavitt was threatening him. Five men had met their deaths at the hands of a nude woman. Now she had vanished . . . perhaps was hidden in the darkness outside.

One thing was certain: she had not had her fill of killing. Under the spiteful gleam of Leavitt's eyes Norman Blake felt as chilled as if an arctic blast had struck him. It took all his courage to toss Gromalin's gun carelessly on the desk, turn to Leavitt.

"All right. I'll scram. But I'll be back, frog-face. I'll hound this story to its roots if it takes the rest of my life."

Leavitt's smile was gone, his face scarlet. And Norman Blake knew instinctively as he left the house that he was marked 'for death. Fear reached out and shook him so that when he found his car he was stumbling, eyes twitching at the rain-drenched darkness, nerves jumping at every sound.

It lacked an hour to murky daylight when he got out of his car in front of his apartment house.

A light was burning in the living-room. Frowning, Blake kicked the hall door shut, walked cat-footed across the living-room. Was the woman of death waiting here for him? He had to know, though it meant his life. He could not spend his days fleeing a memory. Blake stepped into the room.

"What the hell," he demanded, "are you doing here?"

There was a day-bed against the wall, under a window, and on it in a sprawled heap lay a man of about Norman Blake's age, head lolling, arms dangling, legs extended like open scissor-blades. He had a bottle on his stomach, and the bottle had tipped sideways, spilling its contents over him.

He rolled his head now, and peered at Blake through alcoholic eyes. "H'lo, Blake," he said good-naturedly. "How's tricks, huh?"

Blake said: "Casey, of all the helpless drunks, you're it." He shrugged, peeled off his coat and tossed it on a chair, eyeing Casey disgustedly. Bill Casey was night rewrite man for the *Examiner*. A man with a capacity.

"How'd you get in?" Blake demanded.

Casey grinned broadly. "I got sick of workin', so I jus' took the spare key out of your desk and come up here to have a li'l' drink." He sat half up and made

movements with his hands. "It ain't your liquor. I brought it myself."

Blake walked into the bedroom, snorted noisily as he yanked off his clothes and got into pajamas. He was all in, exhausted. And he admitted to himself that, after Leavitt's threat, he was glad of Casey's companionship.

He sprawled into bed and was soon asleep.

CHAPTER THREE

A Woman's Scream

BLAKE awoke with a sensation of having been disturbed by an alien sound somewhere in the room. The window had been closed; now a breeze came from it, cooling his face as he sat up staring. He had not slept long. The room was dark except for a faint light which came from the living-room.

He opened his eyes and gaped, and then suddenly heaved himself off the bed, pushed himself backward on bare feet and flattened hard against the wall.

He was not alone. The window in the far wall was open, and beside it stood something white, something tall and motionless and strangely lovely.

Not so long ago, another man had carelessly approached as close to that same white shape as Norman Blake was standing now. And Alexander Leavitt, rushing from the cabin of the *Research*, had screamed at the man to get back, get back before it was too late.

But the man had been unable to go back. And now Norman Blake, too, found himself unable to move.

He stood rigid, aware of a strange numbing sensation that sped through him, chilling the blood in his veins and speeding the beat of his already thumping heart. His eyes were bulging, so wide open that they hurt. His tongue came out to lick dry lips. With a growing feeling of horror he returned the gaze of the creature before him.

Yet there was nothing horrible, nothing terrible, about the creature herself. Tall and white, she stood there in the faint darkness that merely accentuated the glowing paleness of her naked body. Utterly devoid of clothes, of life, of movement, she confronted him.

Blake shuddered. Women were nothing new; he had seen them before, seen them naked and near-naked. But this one was beauty personified, lovely as no other woman could be lovely. White hair crowned her sensuous face; lips white as fine-grained gypsum were slightly parted, revealing the tip of a white tongue between even teeth. Like an alabaster statue she stood against the wall, arms slightly extended as if waiting patiently, confidently, for Blake to come to her.

Blake's feet clung to the floor; his big body swayed. Something . . . something in the woman's eyes was commanding him to move, to walk forward. Holding him back was a vision of what had happened to the seaman on the deck of the *Research*. Conflicting emotions fought within him, heated the blood in his body, brought a hoarse, violent outcry of fear to his gaping mouth.

"Stop it! For the love of God, leave me alone!"

The woman smiled. For the first time, she moved, reached her arms out until they were level with her smooth shoulders. She was breathing now, breathing perhaps with the desire that consumed her. Her beautifully moulded breasts rose and fell, not swiftly, but with an even rhythmic motion that brought a strange lust to Blake's eyes—a lust that had never before festered there for any woman.

He took a step forward, fought blindly to drag himself back again. But the woman's eyes never blinked, never shifted their commanding gaze. Her lips were curved in a vague smile; she moved her extended arms sideways to expose the secrets of her lovely body. Naked, aluringly exquisite, she stood waiting, while Blake feasted his eyes upon her and caught a quick deep breath of amazement and yearning.

Again his bare feet moved on the floor, and this time his pajama-clad legs failed to stiffen again, failed to stop in their slow advance. Dully he realized what the woman was commanding him to do. But it did not matter. She was lovely . . . lovely and naked and waiting to take him in her outstretched arms.

Words came from his lips, came in what he thought to be a whisper. In reality the words were a shriek, tocsinning through the apartment, eating their shrill way down the corridor.

"Don't—stare at me so! I'm coming!"

Mad words for Norman Blake to be uttering. Yet they came, came violently, hoarsely, flung from his throat in strange delirium. And in the other room, where Bill Casey was sleeping, the day-bed creaked dismally, feet thumped on the floor and a drunken voice spilled out: "Hey, what the hell—"

But Blake continued his mad words, continued his slow advance toward the naked woman who stood awaiting him. Conscious only of her sensuous beauty, he failed to hear the drunken thumping of Casey's staggering body as it came down the hall. And the woman, staring straight into Blake's wide eyes, was concerned only with the man before her, the man who was almost within reach of her half-open hands.

Those hands were moving, opening and closing convulsively. White, tapered fingers, terminating in abnormally long nails, were waiting to make contact. And Blake's own hands were out, yearning to caress naked flesh, to touch those alabaster breasts, those flawlessly smooth hips and thighs. . . .

INTO the room, behind him, stumbled Casey. But Blake did not turn. Drunk, staggering, Casey clawed the sides of the door-frame, rocked there and stared with bleary eyes. His mouth opened, drooled saliva over the front of his crumpled shirt. His eyes widened in amazement, filled suddenly with a glow of delight. He made a face, lurched forward again.

"Well, I'll be g'damned," he blurted. "I'll be g'damned if I won't be g'damned! I'sh a woman!"

Drunkenly he surged forward, mumbling, laughing, striving hard to keep his feet. His arms were outthrust; his hands made contact with Blake's slowly moving body even as those other hands reached out a final inch to fasten themselves in Blake's pajamas.

Casey's lumbering bulk went off balance, fell against Blake and pushed him aside, thrust him clear of the woman's eager grip. Staggering, Casey regained balance, peered groggily at the woman's nakedness and said aloud:

"My goodnesh me! The lady has no clo'es on, she has! Baby, you an' me should oughta get better acquainted immeshately!"

The woman's hands gripped him, fastened like claws in the front of his crumpled shirt and ripped downward, tearing cloth. Blake, rammed back against the foot of the bed, clung there and gaped wide-eyed, striving desperately to remember. He . . . he himself had wanted this woman, this naked, strangely white woman who was clinging to Bill Casey. But he did not want her now. Something had snapped inside him and let go. Those eyes of hers were no longer commanding him.

Yet he could not straighten out his jumbled thoughts, the vague memories in his laboring mind. The woman and Casey —they were locked together, and the woman's hands had torn Casey's shirt, ripped his undershirt and were caressing his bare chest, working slowly upward to his neck, his throat. Casey was in danger, somehow. Bill Casey, drunkenly telling the woman that she was his baby, his special sweetheart . . . drunkenly fondling her nakedness and oblivious to the hungry clutch of her probing fingers. . . . *Casey was in danger!*

The thought drove home, penetrated the fog that enveloped Blake's consciousness. Blindly he swayed erect, bellowed a hoarse warning. Stumbling, he took three steps, stabbed his hands out and caught up a chair that held most of his clothes. The clothes spilled to the floor as he swung the chair shoulder-high and surged forward to free Casey from the woman's savage embrace.

"You damned witch!" he shrieked. "Let him go! Let him go, or by God—"

He was too late. The woman had already thrust Casey aside, hurled his drunken, bleeding body to the floor. Her face had changed expression; it was savage, bestial. Wide-legged, she stood rigid, staring as Blake lunged toward her. The chair went out of Blake's hands, missed its mark by inches as that nude body leaped sideways with the swift gliding ease of a panther.

Off-balance, Blake continued in a headlong lunge, crashed violently into the wall and went down in a heap, legs tangled in the broken wreckage of the chair. But the woman did not attack. Like a ghost, she sped to the open window, slid her naked body in a serpentine glide over the sill. When Blake swayed erect again, stumbled forward, the woman was gone and the room was empty except for the sprawled, unconscious, half-stripped body of Bill Casey.

Unconscious? Cold dread assailed

Blake's brain as he went to his knees and put trembling hands on Casey's shoulders. A shudder went through him. Dully he stared down at the bare chest beneath him: a swollen chest, bloody and inflamed, in which parallel lines of flesh had been gouged out. The same ugly markings that had disfigured the bodies of Dr. Paul Willoughby and the unlucky seaman on board Leavitt's death-ship.

Dead. Bill Casey was dead, as the others were dead. An expression of drunken bewilderment hung in his frozen features; his eyes were wide open, glazed, his tongue lolling between gaping lips. Bewilderment, mingled with the same drunken grin that had wrinkled his face as he attempted to embrace the strange woman of hell, filled his dead countenance.

Never again would Bill Casey get drunk.

But *how?* How in the name of all things unholy had she sapped the life from that rugged, big-boned mass of strength? How, in God's name, had an unarmed, nude woman done murder so swiftly, so surely? Blake stared and shook his head, unable to understand. There were bloody gashes in Casey's exposed chest, and the gashes were deep . . . but not deep enough to bring death. Not even deep enough to cause unconsciousness.

How then, unless Leavitt's woman of hell were in truth a creature of supernatural powers. . . .

Blake swayed erect, made his way slowly to the open window. His head throbbed; something black, heavy, still festered in his brain, a hangover from the fiendish power of the eyes that had bored into him, taken possession of his soul.

Dully, he remembered that the woman had escaped.

Escaped where? He shook his head, shuddered with the thought that she might even now be prowling the streets: a na-ked, sensuous woman walking the night, seeking other unlucky, bewildered wretches who would obey the awful command of those stabbing eyes.

Or would she return to Leavitt's house, to her master? . . . If, in truth, she had a master. . . .

Blake exhaled slowly, put a hand to his throbbing head and groaned with the pain that burned in his brain. The room was no longer totally dark; a gray murk marked the oblong of the window, and in a little while the murk would become daylight.

Stiffly, he paced into the living-room, picked up a telephone and laboriously dialed Police Headquarters. His hand made a damp mark on the wall while he waited.

"Kenney? I want Kenney. Listen . . . Blake talking. Blake again. Come up here to my apartment and I'll show you proof that I wasn't kidding about that woman. My apartment. . . . I'll be waiting."

He forked the phone, lit a cigarette and lowered his aching body into an overstuffed chair. After a while he got up and put a disc on the electric phonograph in the corner, opened the liquor cabinet in the phonograph's false base, and poured himself a stiff drink.

MacLEAN, city editor of the *Examiner*, made a face over the pile of copy Blake had spilled on his desk, and slanted his gaze through rimless eyeglasses into Blake's tired face.

"Where you goin'?"

Blake had a hat on and was tightening the knot of a crumpled necktie. The clock behind him said seven-ten. Seven-ten p.m. A little more than twelve hours ago he had been standing beside the sprawled body of Bill Casey, laboriously explaining to Captain Kenney, of Headquarters, how the thing had happened. Kenney had openly disbelieved him.

"Where you goin'!" MacLean said again.

Blake shrugged, stuffed a cigarette in his mouth. "Home first. Then out to get the rest of that." He stabbed a grimy forefinger at the yellow copy-sheets. "Maybe I'm crazy."

"Yeah, maybe you're crazy. You heard from Kenney?"

"He says I *am* crazy. He's been out to Leavitt's place, took some good men with him and turned the house inside out, but didn't find the woman."

"So you think you can?"

"Bill Casey was my pal," Blake said simply.

He drove home in his own coupe, parked it and let himself into the apartment. Casey's body had been removed by the police, was now in the hands of the medical examiner. In a little while darkness would take the place of daylight. Then it would be safe for Norman Blake to drive to the sinister home of Professor Alexander Leavitt and search for the woman whose body was lust and beauty —and whose touch was death. Blake didn't want to go. He admitted to himself that he was afraid, horribly afraid. What chance did he have against a woman who wasn't human? Then he thought of Bill Casey again, and muscle bulged cold along his jaw.

He poured a drink, gulped it, and was refilling the glass when the phone rang. Scowling, he scooped up the instrument. A girl's voice said anxiously, "Is this Mr. Blake? Is it—"

"Speaking," Blake grunted.

"I've tried to get you a dozen times! Something has happened here. I—don't know what, but something terrible! I need help and—and I can't call the police because I think my own father—"

Blake knew who was talking. That voice, and the face that went with it, had done things to him long ago. It was Irma Leavitt.

"If they knew I was calling you, they would—"

The girl's voice choked off; the phone made a jarring, thudding sound in Blake's ear, as if someone at the other end had seized the instrument from Irma Leavitt's hand and hurled it aside!

Savagely, Blake dropped his own phone, spun on stiff legs and raced from the room.

He drove through city traffic with both hands gripping the wheel, accelerator-foot on the floor-boards. There was cold sweat on his fingers and cold terror in his chest. If anything had happened to Irma Leavitt. . . .

Darkness set in while he drove and it was nearly eight when the car groaned to a stop. Sucking air to straighten his cramped body, Blake pushed himself clear and ran toward the big house that loomed ahead.

The house was a black, bulging pile, towering ominously in darkness. No lights. Beyond it, at the far end of the yard, an ocher oblong glared like a single animal eye, and as Blake pounded forward, a dark shape moved across the source of the light, blotted it out and let it blink on again. That light was a window, a window in the small square building which was Alexander Leavitt's laboratory.

Gravel crunched under Blake's feet. Again the light blurred, went bright again as a dark shape moved past it.

And then, from the bowels of the building came a sound that chilled the sweat on Blake's forehead, a shrill scream of terror from the same lips that had spoken to him over the phone!

CHAPTER FOUR

The Beast Feeds

THE scream jerked Blake to a halt, stopped the labored beating of his heart while fear crowded his lungs into stillness. Irma Leavitt was in danger. And she would still be in danger if Blake blundered headlong into a baited trap.

He catfooted forward through the darkness, eyes jerking from side to side, fingers stiff. The laboratory door was closed, not locked. The knob turned in Blake's hand; the door groaned open, let him in. His silent feet found a corridor that swung sharply to the left, toward the end of the building where that oblong window had glowed yellow. Slowly he toed forward over smooth cement, past side-doors where no lights gleamed.

At the corridor's end a door hung ajar; ocher light streaked the threshold, made a fantastic pattern on the wall of the passage. Inside that room, a deep voice was intoning words, words mingled with throaty, triumphant laughter. And a girl was sobbing.

Blake's hands pawed the smooth wall as he slid forward, reached the opening. Then he stopped, opened his eyes wide and stood stiff as a big-bodied figure in a wax museum. Horror clogged his throat, stopped his breath.

This was Alexander Leavitt's workroom, and Leavitt himself was one of the chamber's occupants. But it was not the professor who commanded Blake's gaze; it was another figure, pacing slowly, dramatically back and forth in front of a row of steel-barred cages, his back toward the doorway that framed Blake's stiff body.

Those cages contained animals, jungle beasts, some of them asleep, others pacing as relentlessly as the strange figure before them.

Staring at that figure, Blake licked dry lips, felt suddenly as if he had invaded a subterranean torture vault in some ancient den of iniquity. A black hood concealed the man's features, masking all but a pair of glittering, beady eyes that shone like animal orbs through oblong slits in the cloth. And the hood itself was part of an ominous black robe that hung in loose folds, whispering on the floor as its wearer paced unceasingly to and fro.

Rigid in the narrow doorway, Blake stared at the two bound figures and saw fear in both faces. Alexander Leavitt's plump body was jammed hard against the back of a chair, striving desperately to retreat from the glare of those twin eye-slits. A tangle of ropes encircled the man's arms and legs, binding him in a position of torment.

Beyond him, near the wall, another helpless shape stared fearfully up from the stone floor. Near-naked, roped securely, viciously, to the leg of a table, Irma Leavitt watched the robed figure as a hypnotized bird might have watched the every movement of a snake. Helpless to move, her slender body exposed to the fiendish glare of those eyes, she cringed in terror, sobbed with the pain of the ropes that cut the satin-smooth flesh of her breasts and choked the breath in her slender throat.

Words . . . rumbling in rising crescendo from the monster's throat:

"Yes, it was I who arranged to have several of our company die on shipboard, and it was I who staged the death of Doctor Willoughby."

A lean forefinger stabbed out, pointed into Leavitt's chalk-colored face. "You thought I did not know; you and the others planned to leave me out of it, forcing me to remain here while you made a return trip to the jungles. And you thought to keep it from me; but from the very beginning I have known. *Gold!*

Waiting there to be carried out! And you thought I did not know!"

Laughter rumbled from the monster's throat. Slowly the man advanced, stood above Leavitt's bound body.

"You see, I intend to have *all* the gold, Professor. I had intended to take Irma, but she has learned too much. She dies as you die, as the others died. Are you quite ready, Professor? And—" He swung about to peer at the near-naked girl —"are *you?*"

Norman Blake waited for no more. Slowly he inched his feet over the threshhold, toed his way forward. He had ceased to breathe and his muscles were cold and quivering. If he failed now it meant his life, and Irma's. It meant torture. . . .

The black fiend would be armed. If Blake's feet made a whisper of sound on the stone floor, the man would hear. Blake cursed himself silently for having rushed off without a gun.

Slowly, very slowly, he crept forward, hands open and extended. The robed figure did not turn. If Alexander Leavitt and his daughter were aware of Blake's presence, they gave no indication. Leavitt was squirming helplessly at the ropes that held him; the girl was shuddering as the robed monster stared down at her nakedness.

Then, seemingly from out of nowhere, a naked arm whipped around Blake's throat, coiled there like a constricting snake. An upthrust knee ground into the small of his back, jarring the breath from his body. With a hoarse gurgling cry twisting his lips, he went over backwards, hurled to the floor by a brown-skinned panther-shape that had leaped upon him from the shadows of the doorway.

The arms that encircled him were powerful as steel chains. But Blake had no chance even to fight them. The stone floor made sudden grinding contact with his head; blackness surged over him, blurring the triumphant face of Leavitt's native servant, Cheega. . . .

BLAKE was not unconscious long. When the blackness left him and his throbbing eyes focused again on the occupants of Leavitt's strange workshop, the creature in the black robe was again standing motionless before Leavitt's bound figure, and words were once more rumbling from beneath that dark mask.

"Think, Professor, of a day, quite some time ago, when you and Doctor Willoughby came out of a deep-jungle village with a strange witch-woman, an *obi* woman who had the instincts of an animal. It amazed you to find such a creature in the jungle. You determined to bring her back. And *I* determined to use her in ridding the world of persons who stood in my way.

"Those eyes of hers—you have looked into them and realized their power. Not a strange power, not more mysterious than other forms of hypnotism . . . but she is remarkably gifted that way. I think you mentioned once that very many native witch-women are gifted that way. And this one is particularly dangerous, because she is half animal; her prime instinct is to destroy, to kill. And with those eyes of hers she is able to lure her victims. . . ."

A throaty chuckle accompanied the fiend's words. "You see, Professor, with Cheega's help I have been able to make excellent use of the woman. Those eyes of hers do not annoy Cheega at all; you knew that a long time ago. And when he became attached to me, I found him invaluable.

"Only last night, for instance, he aided me in transporting the woman to the apartment of this meddling reporter." He turned, glared at Blake. "Something went wrong with my plans, but Cheega was not at fault. And again, when this same interfering idiot summoned the police here, it was Cheega who released one of the apes, to supply an explanation of Doctor Willoughby's death."

Slowly the man turned, stared at the native who stood near him. "Bring the woman here!" he snapped. Then he turned again, feasted his eyes on Irma Leavitt's nakedness as Cheega paced silently to the door.

Norman Blake felt horror crawl like a spider along his spine. In another minute the woman would be here. Her eyes would call him, force him to her. And the touch of her fingers would bring writhing, agonized death. He could feel even before he saw her the terrible magnetism of her eyes, drawing him against his will, making him powerless to fight. Yet the robed fiend had so far paid him no attention, evidently believed him to be still unconscious.

Footsteps grated on the stone threshold behind him, and into the room, pacing slowly, inexorably forward, came the native, Cheega, dragging behind him the same portable prison which had stood on the deck of the *Research*. Rubber-tired wheels made a sucking sound on stone as the huge cage came to a stop in the center of the room. Then, without visible emotion, Cheega unlocked the iron-barred door in the front of the box and allowed the imprisoned woman to step forth.

The black-robed figure stepped suddenly backward as the woman was liberated. Swiftly, but not so swiftly that Blake failed to catch the move, he reached up with both hands and did something to his eyes. Some protection, no doubt, against the hypnotic power of the naked creature who came slowly out of the cage.

The woman stepped forward, stared around her as a suddenly liberated animal might have stared curiously to determine the nature of its new surroundings. Stark naked, white as alabaster in the glow of the overhead light, she held her savagely beautiful body rigid, turned her head from side to side, peering.

Then she drew a deep breath, raised her hands to stroke her own sensuous body. And Blake saw that those hands, both of them, were wrapped now in tightly wound strips of white cloth, bound at the wrists.

And Gromalin—if that black monster were in truth Gromalin—was saying: "Perhaps you have wondered, Professor, how this creature of yours—of mine, rather—is able to kill her victims so swiftly. It is no mystery. Look at those hands. For safety's sake, I keep them bound, but beneath the bindings are strong white fingers, each one tipped with a sharpened nail.

"She is a tigress, this sweetheart of mine. Her every instinct is to claw and scratch and destroy. Aconitine, Professor, blended with cyanide of potassium and other gentle ingredients, then caked beneath those lovely nails so that the least scratch. . . ."

Norman Blake fought his muscles to stillness. He couldn't let them know he was conscious. He had to wait, wait until there was some chance. He could feel desire to look at the woman struggling in him and his teeth clenched in his lips as he kept his gaze averted.

The monster turned slowly, took a step toward Irma Leavitt and made a snarling sound in his masked throat. "It will be a pleasure to watch you die, my dear. Once I thought that by winning you I could win your father's confidence and so share in the spoils. But evidently you did not care to be loved my way."

He swayed backward, chuckled evilly as he gazed at Cheega. "We have waited long enough, Cheega. Talk to the woman. Tell her that here is something for her to play with. Here—" His outthrust hand stabbed toward Irma. "Tell her!"

WORDS came from Cheega's thick lips as he led the naked woman forward. Very carefully, as he continued speaking in a tongue that Norman Blake did not understand, he unwound the strips of cloth that covered those deadly hands. Very, very carefully, lest those poisoned fingers come in contact with his own!

Then he stepped back, left the nude woman to her own devices. And she, in obedience to the commands that had come gutturally from his lips, advanced slowly, in a snakelike glide, toward the defenseless girl who was bound to the table-leg.

With folded arms the robed creature watched, waited. Cheega, beside him, was grinning with savage anticipation. Blake found himself unable to move, watching terrified. Alexander Leavitt licked dry lips, strained frantically at his bonds and screamed luridly:

"Stop her! In the name of God, don't let her do it! My daughter has never harmed you—"

The robed monster laughed softly, made no move to interfere. Slowly, relentlessly, the beast-woman advanced, staring straight into the terror-filled eyes of her intended victim. Her hands were outstretched; those death-tipped fingers gleamed like polished ivory as they neared the girl's throat.

Irma Leavitt did not scream, no longer fought to escape. Wide-eyed, she returned the beast-woman's hypnotic gaze, watched the woman's every move and even leaned forward in her bonds as if possessed with a strange desire to be embraced by those outstretched hands.

Inches more, and the death-dealing nails would make contact, draw blood from that lovely throat. . . .

But Norman Blake moved first.

With a sucking intake of breath, he surged up from the floor, hurled himself forward. Fists clenched, mouth fuming, with a roar that rocked the chamber with its mad reverberations, he threw his six-foot-two bulk across the stone floor.

The beast-woman whirled, leaped away from him with lips curled back over gleaming teeth, hissing sounds issuing from her throat. She leaped out with poisoned hands. But Blake's body failed to strike those sharpened nails. Pivoting, he buried a knotted fist in the face of the brown-skinned native who leaped to drag him down. The fist ground into Chega's mouth; jagged teeth made raw meat of Blake's knuckles.

Cheega rocked backward, staggered blindly with both hands flailing empty air. Like a broken spider he clawed the wall, crumpled in a writhing heap.

But Blake did not see. Shoulders hunched, big body bent into a human question-mark, he lunged toward the black-gowned monster who stood in front of the row of cages.

Frantically the man clawed the folds of his black robe, thrust a hand inside. The hand leaped out again, fingers fumbling with the safety-catch of a blunt-nosed automatic. But Blake was there first.

His stabbing fist made contact, slammed the fiend backward. The gun flew from paralyzed fingers, skidded grotesquely across the floor. In blind fury, Blake drove blow after savage blow, struck with such pile-driver force that the fiend's black head-covering became a sodden rag of crimson.

Flung back against the table by Blake's fists, he caromed in a screaming heap, staggered sideways. Blake's fingers caught the head-covering. With a staccato tearing sound, the mask came loose.

And the battered, bloody face beneath it—the face that went reeling backward across the floor, screaming in agony—was the face of Geoffrey Marsden!

But it was not over. In a direct line with Marsden's stumbling body was another shape, a staring, hungry shape that stood with arms outstretched, teeth bared. Blindly, Marsden pitched backward, away from Blake's relentless attack. Too late he tried to regain balance and throw himself clear of the thing that awaited him.

The woman's hands made contact. Savagely, viciously they raked downward, tearing flesh from Marsden's face and throat. Death-tipped fingers drew blood. And the shriek that welled from the killer's lips, as he sought to free himself from that deadly embrace, was a shriek of utter terror, a wail of stark, hideous fear. Like the death-cry of a tortured child it filled the chamber, endured for an eternity before it died.

Then it ended, and the woman stepped backward, letting the contorted, bloody body of her victim slump to the floor.

She turned then, eyes blazing, strange animal sounds spilling from her mouth. When she turned, Norman Blake was standing very stiff, facing her, holding in one hand the automatic that Marsden had dropped. For an instant Blake hesitated, returned the perilous stare of those unholy eyes. In that moment the fury went from him to be replaced by a wild desire for the woman, to hold that white body in his arms. His breath husked in his nostrils. He took one step forward.

Behind him, the cracked voice of Alexander Leavitt screamed out, "Shoot her! For God's sake don't wait, or—"

The cry snapped Blake's eyes from the woman's. His finger tightened on the trigger. The gun belched once, filling the room with sudden thunder. The beast-woman stopped in her tracks, reached jerkily upward with both hands. Then she fell, with crimson blood oozing between her spread fingers and trickling slowly down the hollow between her breasts.

Dully, Blake turned, pocketed the gun and released Leavitt's bonds. Then, gently, he released Irma, covered her nakedness as he gathered her in his arms. Exhaling slowly, he said to Leavitt:

"I—I could use a good shot of raw whisky. Let's get out of here."

A N HOUR later, Blake stood beside Irma Leavitt on the front veranda of the big house, and made a bluff at listening to what she was saying while he studied the soft lines of her throat.

"When I phoned you this evening," she faltered, "I was terribly afraid. Father had just confessed to me that the beast-woman had been stolen from him. Then I found Eric Gromalin dead in the front hall, and father had disappeared. Then Geoffrey Marsden came into my room while I was phoning you, and—"

Blake nodded. "There's just one thing more, before I have enough to do my story. This beast-woman that your father brought home. Why all the secrecy?"

"Father didn't want people to know. To him, she was just a very rare specimen, to be studied. That's why he resented your snooping around."

Blake said: "Thanks, Miss Leavitt. Thanks a lot."

"What did you call me?"

He stared at her, grinned, and glanced at the watch on his wrist. "I'm a working man, young lady. Got a job to do. What's your phone number—Irma?"

"Speaking professionally?" she demanded.

"Personally," Blake said softly. "Very personally. . . ."

THE END

Another Great Hugh B. Cove Story in the Next Issue!

THE LAUGHING CORPSE

When the reeking corpse stood over them in the dining saloon of the ADEN, the passengers knew fear. But not till darkness came and they saw faceless men die laughing—did they know utter, gibbering terror!

SILENCE burst like a bombshell over the dining saloon of the *Aden*. Up and down the two long tables, the score or more of passengers sat frozen, their eyes jerking around toward the open door.

Nancy Summers had the feeling that death itself, invisible and horrible, was floating inward on the breath of the baking, fetid air from the steamer's deck.

The mangy little coaster, with its miscellaneous load of freight and travelers, had jerked up its mud-hook and steamed out of the white-hot inferno of Dhambara harbor some four hours before. It was just getting dark when the steward's gong boomed for the first meal on board. The passengers had barely settled themselves

by
James A.
Goldthwaite

Novelette
of Ghastly Dread

in their allotted places when this had happened.

The thing that was coming in through the doorway, that had caused this frozen silence, seemed to reach out invisible, ghastly talons that clutched the passengers by the throats. Yet it was nothing that anyone could see. It was a smell. The smell of putrefaction. The strangling, soul-retching aroma of rotting flesh. . . .

Then, close-following that smell, footsteps came scuffling down the deck. A figure paused in the doorway of the saloon.

The man who stood there was dressed in the long, black robes of a priest. But the face that rose above the billowing jet garments was the face of a corpse! High forehead and hard, square-cut jaw, set in the wax-hued matrix of death. The lack-luster black eyes bulged fixed and sightless. The green-yellow lips showed the white teeth in a frozen, sardonic grin.

And from the corpse that stood there on its own two feet there reeked that nauseating, unspeakable stench of sloughing flesh.

For an instant longer, a hush of horrified silence gripped the room. Over across the table, a short, purple-faced fat man with bulging eyes had turned the color of raw dough.

"Great God! It's Phillips!" he gasped. "Don't let him come in here! Take him away—"

The big, tallow-faced man with the green chip-diamond eyes who sat at his side, muttered something under his breath and gripped his elbow savagely below the table-edge.

Slowly the corpse was walking into the dining-room. Around both tables, the passengers sat rigid and white, spoons and forks frozen in their hands. Terror sagged their faces. The two yellow-skinned waiters yelped out howls of fear and bolted, their eyes staring white over their shoulders.

The corpse crossed the floor toward a chair standing vacant at one of the tables. He reached out a hand and grasped its back. The veins stood out like swollen blue threads on the waxy white, putty-like skin of the hand.

But the walking dead man did not sit down. Standing behind the chair, he fastened his mummy-like gaze on three men in turn—the short, fat one who had gasped out the cry, the tall, gray-faced one with the shifty yellow eyes who sat on his left, and the tallow-faced giant on the other side. Slowly, sardonically, the lifeless head inclined in a mocking bow.

A woman screamed. Two men jumped up to their feet, their chairs clattering over backward.

The other passengers still sat as though turned to stone. The corpse swung around. Slowly, contemptuous in its mocking deliberation, it strode the length of the saloon and out through the open door.

The next instant, a babel of voices and a scuffing of feet burst out as the passengers swarmed up from the tables. Some of the boldest of them made a rush for the door. The others flocked after them.

OUTSIDE, on the deck, there was no sign of the walking corpse. The pas-sengers scattered a little and then stood around in nervous, chattering knots.

"It looked like a dead man, but it couldn't have been, of course," the shrill voice of a fluffy-haired blonde school-teacher on vacation chattered out. "It must have been that cocktail I was drink-ing." Her China-blue eyes were sticking out of their sockets and her skin was paper white around the splashes of rouge on her flabby cheeks.

"So you don't think he was dead, huh? You ought to have been sitting where I was, and—*smelled* him," the woman next to her grunted back. She shivered. She scratched a match and lit a cigarette with long, feverish puffs. "I'm from N'Yawk, sister, and I seen a few, but I never lamped anything like that before—not even after ten cocktails."

All over the deck, the passengers were talking in tense, amazed voices. As they talked, they darted white-eyed, shudder-ing glances into the blots of blue shadow that coiled like dragons over the planking. Something horrible seemed to be hovering there, just out of sight. . . .

Nancy Summers looked up to see the big, yellow-haired and blue-eyed young man who had sat next to her at the table standing by her side. His name was Paul Nelson.

"What was it, anyway?" she mur-mured up to him.

Nelson shook his head. His face was pale and grimly set.

"It's got me," he muttered back.

Then abruptly he gripped the girl's arm.

"Look ahead up there," he whispered.

Ten yards up the deck, a vague shape was moving in the shadows of the life-boats. Streamers of billowing black robes like wreaths of smoke. . . .

"There it is again!" somebody yelled.

Half a dozen of the men passengers made a rush toward the shape. But even as they moved the thing dissolved into the gloom like a vanishing shadow.

A couple of minutes passed. The passengers stood about, nervous and white-faced, waiting for they knew not what.

Abruptly a woman grabbed her husband's arm and gasped out a scream. From up the deck in the direction where the robed thing had been, another figure came into sight.

The creature was half running, half staggering down the deck. Only his uniform of white drill told that he was Connors, the boatswain. Only his uniform told that—for he had no face! Flesh and blood, eyes, nose and lips, had been stripped clean from the bones as if by the raking of a tiger's claws.

"Great God, look at him!" a voice broke out. "He's laughing!"

It was the truth. Connor's lipless fleshless jaws were wrenched apart in a hideous grin. Through the gory, red-dripping skull, he was roaring peal after peal of agony-strained merriment. The sardonic, jeering laughter of a damned soul contemplating its own image in the fiery pit.

Chalk-faced, the pasengers tumbled backward, running away as the thing advanced.

"Stop him! Stop him!" a woman screamed. "He's coming after us!"

Connors was laughing louder. Burst after burst of diabolical, mad glee racked his body. In the glare of the deck lights, his face was a raspberry-tinted skeleton skull of naked bones.

Abruptly, then, he pitched forward onto the deck. He was writhing in convulsions now while the peals of horrible laughter still poured from his throat.

For a minute or two longer he lay with arms and legs thrashing into knots. He shuddered once more and lay motionless.

His cheeks ashy gray and glistening with sweat under the deck lights, Captain

McTighe stumbled across the deck and stooped over the dead man. He reached down a finger and touched the gory face.

"Flesh all ripped off—like a leopard's claws had raked him," he muttered. His voice clicked hoarse with horrified amazement. "Nothing left but the bones. And with the face torn off him by the roots, he was laughing. He laughed himself to death. . . ."

Slowly, McTighe straightened up. Horror dragged at his eyes. He stood with his jaws dropping, his gaze fascinated by the bloody thing at his feet.

Step by step, the pasengers were shrinking away, moving still further backward. They talked in tense, horrified whispers, and looked backward over their shoulders, as though they expected to see black-robed specters stalking behind them.

"Great God, what did it?" a man muttered. "What kind of a thing out of hell have we got here on board, to strip a man's face off and then make him laugh himself to death? A dead man couldn't have done that. . . ."

The captain spoke again.

"For their own safety, I am asking all the passengers to go back into the dining room and stay there for the present," he said. "Mr. Sampson, take some men and search the ship. Find a walking dead man and put him in irons—and be damned careful of yourself while you're doing it. . . ."

MOMENTS later, Captain McTighe stood facing the group of white-faced men and women in the dining saloon. His eyes bored into the little purple-faced fat man.

"You, Mr. Bronson," he said, "called out the name of Phillips when that thing came in here. Who was Phillips? What did you know about him, and where?"

Bronson cleared his throat. His twitching blue eyes darted to North, the tallow-faced giant.

"Why, Phillips—he was a man I happened to run into a few weeks ago up at Campabur," he muttered back. He wet his lips. "North, Waters and I had gone up there to look into the chances of buying those new rubber developments. We —er—ran into Phillips at the hotel. All Americans in a strange country, you know—natural that we should get to talking. We heard afterwards that he had gone up into the hills and been ambushed by natives. I really don't know a thing about him, other than that."

McTighe grunted sardonically. For a moment, his hawk-gray eyes locked with Bronson's. Without a word, he swung on his heel and stalked out of the room.

There was silence in the little dining saloon for a minute after he had gone. Little by little, the other passengers drew away from Bronson, Waters and North. Heads close together, the trio were talking in tense whispers behind the smoke-screen of their cigars. Their faces had a curious green-gray tinge. Talons of sickening fear dragged at their eyes.

"Suppose those three did know Phillips —knew him well," a man muttered to Nelson. "Suppose the three of them butchered him—"

"And suppose he hopped up out of his grave and staged a comeback right here to haunt them?" Nelson grunted dryly. "All right—if you can make yourself believe in ghosts."

"Just a moment, my friends."

Nancy and Neslon turned at the sound of the voice behind them.

A tall, thin man with olive-tinted complexion had spoken. He had the deep, oily black eyes and suave, purring gutteral accents of a Levantine. Nelson happened to remember that his name was Mastrides.

"If, as you have suggested, the motive of Phillips in causing his corpse to come on board this ship is to revenge himself on those who may have been the instruments of his death, does it not seem strange that his first victim was not one of them but a member of the crew, a man who could not possibly have harmed him?"

"That would put quite a different angle on it, wouldn't it?" Nelson admitted thoughtfully.

"He killed a man just for nothing," a woman screamed out. "He will kill others." She was on the verge of hysterics. In the sweltering heat she shivered as with a chill. "Maybe I'll be the next one."

Suddenly a man jumped out of his chair. He ran over to the sliding door that opened out onto the deck and slammed it shut. He was mopping beads of cold sweat off his forehead as he swung around.

"Something might come in before we could stop it," he muttered hoarsely.

Over acros the room, a woman gasped and held up her hand.

"Hark!" she cried.

There was an instant of frozen silence. The woman laughed shakily and dropped the hand.

"I just thought I heard—somebody laughing," she stammered.

Nobody moved for an instant. Then Mastrides, the Greek, unfolded his slender, elegant figure from the depths of his chair, crossed the saloon, opened the sliding door and stepped out on deck.

Paul Nelson touched Nancy's arm. "Look—"

Over in a corner of the room, Wang T'Sai Liang, the Chinese traveling salesman who had sat at their table, was curled up like a fat Buddha in a big chair, smoking a cigarette in a foot-long green holder. His round, chipped agate eyes stared owlishly after Mastrides. Abruptly he slid his feet down to the floor, jumped up, glided across to the door, pushed it open and vanished outside.

Somebody rang for cocktails. The stewards came in with trays of glasses.

The men and women talked in tense whispers as they sipped the drinks. Any one of them would have been brave enough if he or she had been up against a danger that they could understand. But here on the little *Aden*, they were face to face with the impossible. They were locked in a cage with the walking, killing monster of life-in-death.

They were looking at one another and listening. Listening for the sound of diabolical laughter. And sniffing. Sniffing for the soul-sickening aroma of rotting flesh. . . .

NANCY SUMMERS looked up at Nelson, and sighed a little breath of relief. With things of this sort happening, it was a comfort to find a man like him beside her.

The two young people had met for the first time a few hours before, on the deck of the *Aden* as it steamed away from the dock. Nancy knew little or nothing about the clean-limbed, freckle-faced and blue-eyed young giant save that he was a sailor, had been the captain of a small vessel, and was now going back to America without a command. From the way in which he had spoken and the fine lines of suffering stenciled across his lean, sun-bronzed face, she guessed that he had been involved in some kind of trouble.

Nancy—slender, gray-eyed, golden-haired, and pretty as she was competent—had told him her own story in a very few words. She had traveled out from San Francisco as companion nurse to a fussy old lady with globe-trotter's mania, still going strong at eighty-three. The old lady had died over-night from a stroke, leaving Nancy to get back home as best

she could—with two months' wages still unpaid.

"Wonder what's happened to the mate?" Nelson said suddenly. "He started out to search the ship."

Nelson's words died on his lips. There was an instant of deathly silence.

Abruptly, all the lights in the saloon had gone out! A copper-green haze of moonlight shining in through a port-hole was all that thinned the pitch darkness.

Then a woman screamed.

"It's coming again! I'm afraid. Put on the lights. . . ."

Nelson could smell it now—the strangling, soul-sickening reek of death and musty tombs. It was wafting in through a port-hole.

In the pitch darkness back in a corner, a chair clattered to the deck. There was a rush of feet toward the door.

"I've got to get out of here!" a voice screamed. "I'm afraid!"

Nelson sprinted the half dozen steps to the door.

"Stop," he ordered curtly. "You're safer in here than out there on deck."

Behind him, he could hear the room in an uproar of voices and clattering feet. Panic was boiling hot in the green darkness.

Nelson shoved the door open and peered outside. His face went gray.

Sampson, the mate, was coming down the deck. Nelson recognized him by the bars on the sleeves of his white uniform. Otherwise he would not have known—for all that was left of his face were shards of flesh dangling here and there from gory skeleton bones! Horror-crazed, his eyes glared out over the blood-dripping death's mask.

Sampson was making for the dining-room door. By now the passengers clustered there had glimpsed the horror over Nelson's shoulder. Women screaming, men cursing, they tumbled back into the room again.

For an instant there was a hubbub of breathless voices. Then silence fell.

Sampson was knocking on the door that someone had closed. He was pounding against the panels with both fists. The long, whistling gasps of his breathing shrilled up over the hollow sound of the hammering.

"Don't let him in!" a woman shrieked. "Lock the door. . . ."

Nobody moved. In the green-orange darkness of the little saloon, the passengers stood paralyzed with horror, their jaws agape as they listened.

Now Sampson was fumbling for the knob. His fingers scraped and gritted over the wood. The latch clicked as they fell on it.

He had commenced to laugh. His voice was gurgling up in a diabolical chuckle of glee as he finally threw the door open.

For an instant, he halted on the threshold, holding himself up with his two hands gripping the jambs. He was trying to say something. Over the choking, belly-bursts of laughter, he was striving frantically to pronounce a name through the ribboned flesh where his lips had been.

Now the laughter was mounting in screaming shouts, strangling the word. Step by step, Sampson staggered into the room. Half a dozen yards inside, his legs and arms commenced a crazy twisting.

Then, abruptly he pitched down to the floor. For a minute there was the demoniac laughter of a raging beast. One last screaming shout of ribald merriment . . . and the thing that lay on the floor was writhing and thrashing like a gigantic, blood-bathed crab. . . .

Back in the darkness, away from the halo of light around the door, a man gritted a curse and a woman sobbed out a moaning scream of horror. One by one, their faces pasty blue in the moonlight, the passengers sidled around the thing on the floor and fled through the open door onto the deck.

CHAPTER TWO

Men Without Faces

OUT here was pitch darkness also, save where the hot tropic moonlight poured down between the black hulks of the deck-houses. Over by the rail, where the moonlight was brightest, the passengers flocked together and stood huddled like terrified sheep.

"He did it again," a man muttered. "McTighe sent the mate out after him, and he got him, too. In God's name, what is it?"

"If we only had some light, it wouldn't be so bad," another voice jerked out. The man it belonged to was shivering so that his teeth chattered. "I can't stand it. I can't stand this hellish dark—"

"He was dead, and he killed him!" a woman's voice wailed up. "A dead man tore his face off and made him laugh!"

The woman sobbed long shuddering gasps of terror. Then her voice shrilled up into wild, hysterical laughter. Peal after peal, it jangled through the night.

"For God's sake, make her stop!" somebody yelled. "Make her stop laughing!"

Two of the men passengers took the woman by the arms and shook her. Gradually her hysterics died away in whispering moans.

"Look! Look out there," a man suddenly shouted. "He's coming again! Anyone got a gun?"

Everyone whirled the way his arm pointed. There was nothing there but the eddying shifting blots of blue-black shadows between the deck-houses.

A moment later, feet scuffed on the planking. It was the captain. He had been into the saloon and come out again. In the moonlight, his face had a look as if the fingers of death had blighted it.

"Ladies and gentlemen, this is a terrible thing." McTighe's voice clicked through his dry, twitching lips. "Who did it or how he did it, I have no idea. And that isn't all. Somebody who knew his business has got at the dynamos. All three of them have been short-circuited and ruined. There will be no light on the ship for the balance of the run."

"That means he isn't done yet," the man next to Paul Nelson muttered. "He's got more jobs to do, and he wants a dark ship for them."

"You passengers will have to get inside somewhere," the captain went on. "Under the circumstances, with this thing around, I won't be responsible for your safety if you stay out here. Better go into the smoking saloon. I'll be right with you."

Without a word, the passengers wheeled around and started back down the deck.

Halfway to the door of the lounge, they halted abruptly and stood listening.

"What's that?" one of them muttered.

A sound like the wailing of a company of lost souls was wafting down the breeze from the forward part of the ship. Singly, in twos and threes and then in a chorus, voices were crooning unearthly howlings.

"The Malays up in the forecastle," Paul Nelson said, as he started along. "They're scared to death. Those beggars are psychic. Any time that they start taking on like this, it's a sure sign there's going to be plenty wrong. . . . Well let's go. . . ."

IT WAS deathly hot in the little smoking room, with the electric fans stilled. Stewards, yellow-faced with terror, were bringing lighted candles and setting them around. The orange flames threw weird shadows of orange and black across the tense, drawn faces of the women and men who stood waiting for the captain to speak.

"Ladies and gentlemen, what we've got loose on this ship is worse than a maniac killer. He's a ghost or a ghoul or something—God only knows what," McTighe blurted out at last. He wet his lips and crushed an unlighted cigar to pulp in his powerful white fingers. "I've sailed the seas for thirty years, and this is beyond me. . . . Now, outside of you passengers here, there are just four white men left alive on board—myself, Mr. Norcross, the second mate, McTavish the engineer and Butler, the purser. The four of us officers alone cannot do very much toward covering the whole ship. And of course the Malays are no good in a jam like this. . . . Now, what I am going to do is to ask the men here to help patrol the deck. If enough of us go out and do as I'll tell you, we stand a good chance of grabbing this fiend the next time he starts to do anything. . . . Well, gentlemen, how about it? Are you with me?"

Paul Nelson was the first to step forward and offer his services. Mastrides, Wang T'Sai Liang, Bronson and North came next. In rapid succession, all the men present save three white-haired and rather feeble old gentlemen silently followed him.

McTighe nodded.

"Good. Now, I haven't got any firearms on board, except my own pistol. But that doesn't mean that you will have to go unarmed. Mr. Norcross, take some of these men and go down to the engineroom. Get Mr. McTavish to give you anything big and long and hard that he's got there—wrenches and furnace bars and belaying pins—the like of that."

In another five minutes, Norcross and his squad of grim-faced men had made the trip down into the bowels of the ship and back again. They carried an assortment of ugly-looking tools, any one of which was capable of braining a man at a single blow.

McTighe led the file of volunteers out on deck. One after another, he posted them in blots of shadow in the corners of the deck-houses, and against the packing cases amidships.

"Stay where you are and keep quiet," he whispered to each man as he left him. "Don't try to walk around. Let him come to you. Don't move unless you see the thing near enough to get him with the first swing. And if you swing at him, be sure you *do* get him."

McTighe had directed the women to stay in the smoking-room, and detailed three of the men to stay there and guard them. But in the confusion, Nancy slipped out onto the deck. Frightened though she was, some inward compulsion had driven her to leave behind the terror-stricken, cowering women, to join with the men in watching for the horror that lurked here amid the hulking black shadows and weird yellow moonlight of the Indian Ocean.

Nancy paused for an instant, looking about her. Nobody was in sight. A few yards away the shadows lay close and blue-black in an angle of the deck-house. She glided over and squeezed herself back into the corner.

FOR ten minutes or so, nothing happened. Then Nancy felt her flesh tingle.

Something was coming down the deck. It was creeping down on her like a dun, eddying wall of fog. It had neither sound nor substance—only smell. The ghostly reek of rotting flesh. It sickened her at her stomach, made her knees water-weak.

As though turned to stone, Nancy stood jammed in the corner between the walls. Now something else was coming. So close that she could have reached out and touched it, a form came stealing around the angle of the deck-house.

There was just light enough for Nancy to recognize the tall, slender figure with the sallow skin and gleaming white teeth. It was Mastrides, the Greek. The moonlight glinted on the gray steel fang of a knife-blade gripped in his hand.

Mastrides floated past and disappeared in the darkness.

Another fifteen seconds passed. Now still other footsteps. . . . The wheeze of tense breathing. . . .

This time it was Bronson, the purple-jowled fat man with the terrified eyes who had blurted out the name of Phillips at sight of the ghost.

Bronson's face shone livid as he passed through a patch of moonlight. His jaw sagged open. A wicked-looking automatic was frozen in his pudgy fat fingers.

Bronson went on down the deck. Under cover of ventilators and the big packing cases of the deck load that was piled amidships, he was creeping after Mastrides. The next instant, he disappeared in the shadows.

The deck was empty now. All around Nancy, silence of solitude and orange moonlight. . . . Silence save for the unearthly crooning singsong of the Malays up in the forecastle.

Suddenly, Nancy heard another step at her side. She looked around swiftly, her heart in her mouth.

It was Paul Nelson. She put out her hand and touched his arm.

Nelson jumped and whirled.

"You're crazy to be out here," he muttered as he recognized her.

"I'm scared stiff," Nancy confessed with a shiver. "But it's terribly exciting. Mastrides and Bronson just went past here. They were headed up forward. Let's try and find them."

Nelson squeezed her hand.

"I ought not to let you," he muttered. "But keep close to me and keep quiet."

They started on. In a moment they came to the corner of the pile of packing cases stacked up amidships. They paused to peer around it. Nobody was in sight. All up and down the deck, the moonlight splashed jagged yellow pools between the hulking black shadow blots.

Suddenly, Nancy felt Nelson's fingers gripping her hand. Somewhere, a voice had started to laugh. The sound was coming from a distance, softened and muted by intervening walls.

Louder and louder it rang through the dark. It was the wild, mocking glee of a damned soul watching itself be crucified with unspeakable horror.

Now it shrilled up into convulsions of frenzied agony. A moment and it fell away in choked, strangled croakings. The coughing gasps of a dying dog. . . .

Little by little the coughing faded away into whispers. And then silence. Silence of yellow moonglow and black shadows.

NANCY was trembling as she clung to Nelson.

"He—it—has killed somebody else," she whispered through chattering teeth. "Down below in the ship—"

Nelson nodded in the dark. "And that makes three," he muttered grimly.

Half an hour or more dragged past without anything happening. Some of the patrols went inside to investigate the laughter, but Nelson and Nancy stayed out on deck. They were back in the corner where Nancy had posted herself at first.

Up ahead, in the forecastle, the terrified yammering of the crew had died away. Solitude of moonlight and shadows and creeping death reigned on the *Aden*.

Abruptly, Nelson squeezed Nancy's arm. Something was coming up the deck. A man. Crouched low, silent as a cat, he dodged from shadow to shadow. It was too dark to see his face. There was just a vague, ghostly eddying among the shadows, and he was gone

"That was Wang, the Chinese," Nancy whispered to Paul "I remember that perfume he had on—"

"Shh!" Nelson hissed in the girl's ear.

Fifteen or twenty feet across toward the rail, something was floating across the face of the setting moon. Formless, cloudlike billowings of black—wavering smoke streamers drifting through the murk. Above the shoulders, the grinning head of a corpse was photographed like a cameo of death against the moon's disc.

A gust of wind blew from him, bringing the stench of carrion.

Paul heard the click of steel. Suddenly he realized that two figures had come up and stopped at his elbow. In the darkness, they had not spotted him or Nancy. One of the men standing there had a gun.

Paul saw the glint of light on the barrel as he threw it up. But before he could fire, the trailing black cerements melted out of sight into the gloom.

Soundlessly, the two figures glided after them.

"That was Waters and North," Nelson whispered to Nancy. "They were following Wang. I wonder if he could be the killer. . . ?"

For an instant, the two young people stood listening. There was not a sound to be heard, yet the air hummed with tension. The darkness seemed peopled with slinking, murderous forms. . . .

Nelson stiffened. "What was that?" he muttered.

The next minute, he knew. It was the laughter again! Not on deck, but somewhere deep in the ship, as before, it was screaming up in another wild paroxysm of devilish glee.

Nancy was trembling so that she could hardly stand. She clung to Nelson, sobbing through her chattering teeth.

"Please take me back to the cabin?" she whispered.

Ten minutes later, the men on the deck patrol were all back in the smoking-room. McTighe had called them out of their places and taken them with him to search the ship.

They had found Butler, the purser, frothing mad laughter through his lipless jaws and tieing himself into knots down in his office.

"He knew we were laying for him outside, so he went to work down below." One of the deck patrol drained a highball in a gulp and shivered in the sweltering heat. "And that makes three."

"And Bronson will be four," Nelson said. "Miss Summers and I heard him laughing—somewhere. He hasn't been seen since."

Silence fell. In little white-faced groups, the passengers stood and sat about, doing nothing. They were all waiting. Waiting for they knew not what—for something too horrible for words. For a ghostly figure of death-in-life to come gliding among them again, reaching out its wax-like, taloned hands to snatch a victim, laughing the wild glee of madness, back into eternity with him. . . .

CHAPTER THREE

Clutching Hands

A DECK chair stood in a sheltered corner just outside the door of the dining saloon. A human crab was taking a sun bath in the chair. . . .

It was early the next morning. Nothing further had happened during the night. The passengers had finished out the long hours dozing or sitting bolt erect in the smoking-room. None of them, not even the bravest, cared to face the solitude of his unlighted cabin alone.

Now, at sunrise, they unlocked the door and came trickling out on deck.

North and Waters, first to come out, lighted cigarettes and strolled around the corner of the deck-house, headed aft. Mastrides, the Greek, fell into step beside them. He was talking low and earnestly.

Abruptly he froze in his tracks, his cigarette dropping from his sagging jaws.

His eyes had just lighted on the thing lying in the deck chair in the sunlight.

Once the crab, with his frozen, tangled legs and arms, had been a short, fat little man in a blue serge suit. Now he had no face. Nose, lips, cheeks and chin had been ripped clean off the skull by the scraping of great claws. The red, blood-caked bones, still with shards of flesh sticking here and there, were turned up into the morning sunshine in a jeering, sardonic grin.

"Great God, it's Bronson!"

It was Waters, the horse-faced man, who gasped out the cry.

Nancy and Paul Nelson had come running around the corner of the deck-house. Nancy saw Waters' glance lock with North's and then jerk away. The man's face was pasty blue. Ragged jet furrows carved his cheeks. His eyes were flat and lack-luster like the eyes of a dead fish.

All over the deck, the silence of horror clapped down again. The passengers stood frozen, speechless and motionless, wherever they had happened to be when Waters had blurted out Bronson's name. Without coming to see, they knew what was in the deck chair.

"They've found Bronson," somebody muttered. "The thing killed him somewhere below last night and then hugged him up and dumped him there in the dark—"

Nelson took Nancy's arm and pulled her away. . . .

The day dragged on. The *Aden* floated in a sea of molten brass. A haze of heat rose from the water. The sky pressed down with a terrific weight, cruel and torturing as a furnace dome. Voices were hushed. Under the tide of dazzling light, the only sounds on the ship were the wailings of the terrified Malays and the muffled throb of the engines.

Most of the passengers went to their cabins and locked themselves in hoping to make up some of the sleep they had lost. After a few hours they came out, pale-faced and hollow-eyed. Nobody had slept. They sat around under the awnings, drinking highballs, talking in tense, lowered voices.

During the afternoon, McTighe and a picked squad of the men searched every inch of the ship again from truck to bilge. They turned up nothing save flocks of squealing rats and regiments of cockroaches.

"How about those boxes there?" North jerked his great tallow-faced head at the pile of packing cases on the deck. "A man—or a ghost—or anything else—could hide in one of them and jump out whenever he wanted to."

"I thought of that," McTighe said. "We went all over them. Nailed up tight as drums—every last one."

"If it was a stowaway, he'd have to hide somewhere. So it isn't that," a man muttered. "It's something that doesn't have to hide. . . ."

"And so what?" a passenger named Burns barked out. His voice was ragged and jerking with tension. "What do we care who did it or why he did it? All we want is to get off this damned floating chamber of horrors before the rest of us begin laughing ourselves to death. We're not very far out at sea yet. You can find

some place and put us ashore before dark, Captain."

McTighe shook his head.

"If that had been possible, you would not have had to suggest it, Mr. Burns," he said tartly. "We are about two-thirds of the way from Dhambara to Bombay. Keeping on to Bombay will take us but one more night, whereas putting back to Dhambara would take two."

"And there's no other place we could land? No island or anything?" Burns growled.

"I've told you," McTighe retorted. His voice was saw-edged. "We've got to stick it out here till morning."

DINNER was served that night in the little smoking-room. Nobody on the ship would step a foot inside the saloon where Sampson had died. The meal was served before dark. Not one of the Malay stewards would have shown his face out of the forecastle after sundown.

Most of the passengers pushed their food away untasted.

"We're in for another night of it," a man burst out. He mopped beads of sweat from his face. "If we were on land, there'd be a chance to get away. But here we're like rats in a trap. All he's got to do is reach out and grab the one he wants."

"It seems like that," Nelson said. "But we've got to remember that sooner or later, anyone playing such a game as this killer's, no matter whether he is crazy or sane, always overreaches himself and gets careless. We are dead sure to nail him sometime, if he keeps on. I think we ought to get volunteers to go out and patrol the deck again. I'm offering as number one."

For an instant there was dead silence.

"That might go if he was a human being," a man muttered back. "But he isn't. He's a dead man—a ghost. We'll never get him."

"Bronson took a chance last night. He went out on the damn patrol, and he got the works," somebody else said. "If we all stay in here and keep the door locked, maybe we'll get by."

Waters and North had been talking in whispers in a corner. Now they got up and started for the door.

"We're going out, but we're going alone," North growled. "We've got our own ideas on this business. The rest of you can come too, or stay inside, and be damned to you."

The two big men scuffed out, slamming the door shut behind them. A buzz of whispering ran around the room.

"Those two ought to be watched," a man spoke up. "They know who's doing this."

"They know, all right. And they intend to get him themselves," somebody else answered.

Nancy got up and went over to stand beside Nelson.

"I'm volunteering as number two," she said.

"I could not allow a lady to outdo me," Mastrides smiled, as he got up and stepped across the room.

Wang, the Chinese, and several more of the men finally joined the group.

Nelson stood looking around the room. It was deathly still. Tension hummed like a taut wire. The faces that looked back at him were white masks of dread in the candlelight.

"Well, if nobody else is coming, let's go," he said at last. "It's dark enough outside now so that we can hide in the shadows."

* * *

Two hours passed. The moon was not yet up. Out on the deck was pitch blackness. Jammed back in their corner, Paul and Nancy could see nothing save the jagged black rectangles of the deck-houses and the pile of packing cases amidships.

There was no breeze, and now the smell was everywhere. Squads of drifting black specters seemed to ooze out of the darkness and wave back and forth, mowing and bowing, mocking and jeering. Silence and solitude gripped the *Aden*. Silence of terror and death. Billowing, stinking, whispering death. Malignant, horrible, intangible as smoke. . . .

Up ahead in the forecastle, the Malays were crooning their unearthly singsongs of panic into the night. . . .

Another half hour dragged away. Over the bow, the horizon commenced to show a sullen yellow glow where the moon was about to appear.

The Malays at last had stopped their howling. But now another sound quavered up through the wet silence.

The laughter again! Somewhere not far away, down the deck it seemed, a voice had burst out in wild, strangled peals of manical glee. An instant more and another one joined it! Over the swishing of the water against the bow of the *Aden*, the two voices were screaming a grisly duet of heart-stopping horror.

Nelson wiped cold sweat off his face.

"He's fooled us again," he muttered. "When we're outside, he goes inside—"

Nancy gripped his arm.

"Look! There he is!" she whispered. "You can get him now. . . ."

Nelson strained his eyes into the dark where the girl pointed. Something was drifting past them, headed up forward. Vaguely it was outlined against the yellow glow of the sky. The black, billowing shape of flowing robes. . . .

Paul gripped Nancy's arm.

"You stay here. I'm going after him," he whispered. His nerves were jumping and his voice was thick. "Don't worry about me—I've got my club. . . ."

Nancy pressed his hand. Swiftly, Paul stooped and slipped off his shoes. In his stocking-feet he oozed out of the corner and crept the ten or fifteen yards to the corner of the deck load.

He stopped and peered around. The shape was gone. But in that instant he had seen a face spot-lighted for a split second in the first orange rays of the rising moon.

It was the face of Mastrides, the Greek. The eyes bulged to the whites. The lips jerked back in a wolfish snarl.

Now Mastrides had disappeared. Paul slid ahead, hugging the shadows.

He came to the spot where the Greek had been. Nobody was there now. . . .

Soundlessly, Paul whirled in his tracks. There was something behind him. The faintest possible whisper of stirring air. . . .

He lashed out with his belaying pin. The blow fanned air. The same split second, a pair of arms like steel cables whipped around him from behind!

Bending at the middle, Paul lunged backward, striving to break the hold. The gripping arms were too quick. Swift as a striking snake, one of them whipped up from his waist to his face.

Paul felt the gashing of razor-sharp talons. The claws had struck in at the roots of his hair. They were starting to rip down his forehead.

For an instant, the fangs clung there without moving. Now Paul got the smell. The stench of tombs and rotting flesh strangled him, made his stomach turn over with nausea.

With the claws of the thing hovering over his eyes, Paul did not dare to move. He was bracing himself for the surge of agony when the talons would finish the stroke and rip his face off in dangling shreds. He was seeing himself staggering down the deck, roaring with laughter. . . .

THE thing that was holding Paul snarled. It loosed its grip on him and whirled.

For an instant, Paul stood frozen, cracking his eyes into the gloom. Here in the shadows, it was so dark that he could not even see the outlines of the lifeboats above the rail, twenty feet away. Feet had gritted on the deck as the thing hurled him off. Against the stars he could just make out the slim, wiry figure of Mastrides.

He was fighting with something. He was fighting with shadows. With a formless, fluttering coil of streaming, smoke-like black robes. . . . And out of the stench of carrion came hot gaspings and a guttural voice snarling oaths.

Then abruptly, where the two figures had been was only one. Back behind, feet were pounding up the deck on the run. A flashlight drilled a white finger through the gloom.

The dazzling ray picked up a tall, suavely elegant figure standing a dozen feet away. It was Mastrides. The Greek's face was white as wax. A long, ugly gash down one side of his head was trickling crimson. One shirt-sleeve was ripped from shoulder to wrist. Blood trickled from the ends of his fingers.

McTighe and the others of the deck patrol came up in a rush. Paul told them what had happened.

"I thought I was gone," he finished, "when Mastrides jumped him from behind and he let me go."

"I hit him once with my knife, and he ran," Mastrides said. "He may be a dead man, but he can bleed." He held up the dripping knife-point.

For an instant, nobody said a word. The faces of the little knot of men were white cameo masks in the gloom. They were darting swift, sidelong glances into the darkness. And listening.

The duet of mad laughter that had

started up half a minute before was rising into shrieks of gibbering glee. It was coming from some of the cabins amidships.

McTighe wet his lips.

"He was back there—just coming out after he did for them when you saw him," he muttered to Nelson.

"He's right around here now," a man chattered through his clenched teeth. "If we only had some lights. Some lights and some guns. We haven't got a chance in this bloody dark. . . ."

McTighe was starting down the deck toward the noise of the laughter. The others trailed after him.

Before them two of the doors in the block of cabins swung open. The full moon was just pushing up over the horizon. The long copper-colored beams threw lurid spot-lightings on the pair of figures that came stumbling around the corner of the deck-house.

It was Waters and North. They were laughing as they came half staggering, half running up the deck. Screaming mad torrents of frenzy through heads that did not have any faces on them. The hot orange rays of the moon etched their skeleton skulls in red-cameo masks of naked bone.

Now they were going into the convulsions. Abruptly their legs caved under them.

The two dying men came down in an open space where the slanting orange rays of the moon still lighted them. Legs and arms tangled together, they were writhing and twisting into knots like a pair of faceless wrestlers inventing new contortions of grapevine holds. And all the while as they clinched and gripped their jerking bodies together, they roared with laughter like a pair of tumbling clowns.

AFT down the deck, the smoking-room door banged open. In scattered knots of two and three, the other passengers came trickling out onto the deck. At last, curiosity had proved stronger than horror. . . .

Some of them carried lighted candles held high over their heads. Some of them gripped the clubs they had carried as deck guards the night before. In the eerie orange light, their faces were pasty-hued as old parchment. Slowly, hesitatingly, half paralyzed with horror, they flocked down the deck.

Halfway to the place where the pair of faceless men lay roaring laughter as they locked arms and legs in their weird wrestling bout, the passengers froze in their tracks. A croaking sort of cry, half gasp, half scream, shuddered over them. A man cursed. A woman whimpered a wail of strangling terror.

"It's coming again! Over there! It's going to kill us all! Let's get out of here! Lower the boats—"

"Lower the boats! Lower the boats!"

The cry of panic swept like wildfire over the *Aden*. Cursing and screaming, the men and women from the cabin started to stampede over toward the rail where two of the big lifeboats hung from the davits.

Nelson looked around for Nancy. He had seen her just a moment before, as the smoking-room door opened. She was pushing her way toward him through the uproar. He gripped her arm.

"This is going to be nasty," he shouted down to her. "Don't let go of me—"

Nancy grabbed his hand. She whirled, looking the other way up the deck.

In the last half minute, a new sound had started to add itself to the hubbub. Down in the forecastle, the Malays were howling, shouting, screaming, beating on pans. Rapidly the uproar had swelled to a bedlam of tumult.

And now the thing that Nelson had

been fearing for the last twenty-four hours had happened—the top blew off.

Out of the mouth of the companionway leading down to the crew's quarters a surge of dusky-skinned, white-saronged forms came boiling up onto the deck.

The Malays had gone berserk with terror. Knives glinted against their yellow skins as they whirled down the deck. Yelling like fiends, they were charging toward the same boats that the passengers had started for.

Captain McTighe yanked out his revolver and jumped in between the passengers and the flood of crazed yellow men. He fired twice. A pair of yelling forms went down. Then the mob was on top of him. Knives flashed up and down and then up again, dripping brown in the moonlight. . . .

Screaming, the passengers were stampeding away from the knives, down the deck toward the cabin. Nelson's voice shouted over the uproar.

"Over this way! We'll take the boats on the other side. They won't hurt you if you don't get in front of them. . . ."

One by one, the passengers halted in their rush for safety. Following Nelson they swung across to the other rail of the ship.

The *Aden* was well provided with lifeboats. Three more roomy craft swung above the rail from their cables, on this side of the steamer.

"Women first!" Nelson yelled. "Some of you men there, go back to the cabin and see if there are any more."

The Malays over at the other rail were too crazed with panic to pay further attention to the passengers. Jabbering like parrots, they swarmed up over the rail and into the boats.

On the other side, the passengers worked in tense, white-faced silence—as though any second an unearthly visitor in billowing black robes might stretch out its hand and snatch another one of them into laughing death.

At the last minute, McTavish, the Scotch engineer, and Norcross, the second mate, ran up to climb aboard with the passengers.

The part of the deck where the passengers' boats were loading lay in the deep black shadows of the deck-houses. Nelson pushed back out of the thick of the hubbub and stood looking around. He had lost sight of Nancy. In the thickness of the gloom, it was almost impossible to make out a face.

"Nancy!" he yelled. "Nancy Summers!"

A hand gripped his arm. He whirled. Nancy stood there, her face white and horror-stark in the thin light.

"Paul!" she cried. "I've found him! I know where he's hiding—"

Nelson blurted an oath between his teeth, crashed his shoulder into a fat woman who had come elbowing between him and Nancy and driven them apart.

For midway of what Nancy had started to tell him, her voice had broken off in a gasp! Her white little face had jerked back, out of sight into the dark, as though something unseen had gripped her and yanked her away.

Nelson was like a wild man as he crashed and elbowed his way through the crowd, shouting Nancy's name.

His cries were fruitless. No one answered. Nancy was gone.

CHAPTER FOUR

Phillips Comes

HORROR sucked away Nancy's strength. Her arms and legs were limp as water. Long fluttering streamers of cloth wound about her face. The sickening reek of carrion swirled in her brain and made her sick at her stomach.

But the arms that held her crushed tighly were hard-muscled and tense with power.

Dimly she realized that she was being carried swiftly through the dark. Where she was going, she could not tell.

A door opened and closed. The thing that was carrying her dropped her down into a chair.

In a moment she forced herself to open her eyes and look about her. A haze of light streamed in through a port-hole. It showed her coils of rope, tools and boxes scattered about. She was in one of the ship's storerooms, somewhere below deck.

The sound of shouts and creaking pulleys came down, muffled through iron plating. Feet pounded swiftly across the deck.

Then silence. The engines had stopped. Empty, abandoned, the *Aden* floated a sepulcher of horror in the moonlight.

Nancy turned her head and looked into the opposite corner. The black-robed thing stood there, motionless. It was Phillips, the dead man. He was watching her out of the frozen, glassy eyes of a corpse.

Step by step, he walked across the floor toward her. Now he was bending over her. She could hear the rustle of the black draperies. The streamers flicked across her face.

Half fainting with horror, Nancy shut her eyes.

His hands were reaching out. They touched her shoulders. Now they were on her face. Razor sharp talons, pricking her skin. . . .

The pricking stopped. The hands were moving over her again. They were gliding over her shoulders, her arms. The hot hungry breath that reeked down on her was the stench of rotting meat.

Like a bird charmed by a snake, Nancy could neither scream nor move. All she could think of was the hideous, faceless things that she had seen writhing in con-

vulsions as they laughed themselves to death.

In a minute now, she would feel her face being ripped off. And then she would begin to laugh. . . .

Abruptly the thing jerked its hand off her and whirled around. Behind him, the door of the storeroom had squeaked as it swung open.

Nancy opened her eyes. For an instant she sat with her heart pounding in her throat so that she could not breathe.

A short, stocky man stood in the doorway. He was a man she had never seen before. And yet she had seen him, too.

She had seen his face. She had seen it on the corpse who had walked into the dining-room. She had seen it on the black-robed monster as it flitted across the moonlighted deck. She was looking at it now, as the black-robed thing stood there, half turned toward the newcomer.

It was the face of Phillips, the man who had been killed in Campabur by natives ten days before!

For a long instant the two figures stood staring at one another. Phillips the live man in the doorway, Phillips the specter in the flowing black robes. Save that one was living and the other dead, two identical faces. . . . A man face to face with his own ghost. . . .

Slowly Phillips walked forward. Nancy saw now that he had a big monkey wrench in his hand.

Then the black-robed thing jumped. In one terrific leap he bounded into the air. A gray knife fang leaped out as he crashed down on Phillips.

Whirling up the two-foot monkey wrench, Phillips jumped in to meet him.

The ghost ducked the whizzing swing of the wrench. Inside Phillips' guard, the knife-blade spat through the air.

Phillips gasped as the fang sank out of sight in his chest. The blade whipped back into sight again. Once more it plunged downward.

Phillips' legs caved under him. He crashed down on his back, pulling the ghost half over with him.

The robed thing pushed free and jerked himself back to his feet. He stood an instant looking down at Phillips. He grunted, stirred the limp body with his toe, and turned back to Nancy.

For the first time, the ghost spoke. A drawling, mocking voice came rumbling out from under the folds of the robe.

"And now, my dear, I think I have accomplished what I set out to do. It was a devilish hard job, but it is going to be worth it. You and I are alone on the ship—"

The ghost whirled. Again a step had sounded behind him.

Paul Nelson stood in the doorway.

PAUL wasted no time in swinging the six-foot steel furnace bar in his hand to smash with it. Instead, he dropped his head and rushed, jabbing the bar in front of him like a spear.

The sharpened end caught the ghost in the middle. There was a sodden thud of ripping flesh. The thing in the black robe screamed like a wounded beast as he crashed backward to the floor. The end of the bar was dripping blood when Paul pulled it back.

The shape on the floor was shrieking in whistling moans as Paul stooped over him. Paul gripped the streamers of black cloth and pulled.

Head and shoulders, the whole upper part of the robed figure's body seemed to come away as Paul tugged at the cloth! He yanked it clear and tossed it into a corner. The head landed with a hollow thud and lay grinning like the face of a carved fiend up out of the folds of the cloth.

The man who lay on the floor had an-other head and face now. He was blowing raspberry-tinted bubbles in the foam that churned back and forth through his lips. His long, slender brown fingers were fumbling at the ragged hole in his stomach where a little rivulet of blood was welling up.

Nancy staggered up to her feet.

"It's Mastrides!" she cried. "But I thought—"

She broke off. Mastrides had begun to laugh. Slobbering through the bloody froth, peal after peal of the mad, maniac laughter. . . .

Now he was beginning to writhe in convulsions. His arms and legs knotted in tangles. A ghastly human crab, he twisted and squirmed and tied himself into hideous contortions. And all the while the shrieks of jeering laughter slobbered through the bloody foam. . . .

In a moment he lay still. . . .

Paul drew a long breath and put his arm around Nancy.

"I don't understand this any more than you do," he muttered. "Let's get out—"

"Just a minute before you go," a voice spoke up from the corner where Phillips lay. "I'm not quite gone yet. I can explain some of this. And I think I owe you that much before I check out, considering all the trouble I've made. Come over here, you two. . . ."

Phillips' voice was faint and half choked with blood. But his eyes were keen and his pain-drawn lips had a grimly mocking twist as Paul and Nancy hurried over and knelt at his side.

"No, you can't do anything for me," he muttered, as Nancy tried to staunch the bleeding from his chest with her handkerchief. "I've got five minutes, perhaps. So just listen. . . .

"Waters, North, Bronson and I were all on the same errand. We were headed up into Jackapor to buy rubies. One of those two-for-a-cent native princes had gone broke and advertised to sell off the family jewels. North, Waters and Bronson were together, I was on my own. I had run into them first in Cambapur. After that, it was any man's race the two hundred miles up to Jackapor. I beat them to it, had the best of the sparklers all contracted for—but not paid for— when they landed in the place. So they hired a bunch of natives to cut my throat.

"I saw the fellows before they got to me and I paid them twice as much to let me alone and go back and tell North—he was at the bottom of it all—that they'd cut off my head. It worked. I disappeared and made my way back to Cambapur and then to Dhambara without being seen. North and the others bought the rubies and came back to Dhambara too. They shipped passage on the *Aden* and so did I."

"So did you!" Paul exclaimed. "We never saw you. Where did you hide?"

THE man on the floor spat blood and chuckled sardonically.

"I've always been a practical joker. I have my own ways of squaring up with people who cross me. I knew these little steamers quite often carry a deck load. I had a packing case made so that it looked solidly nailed, but with one side hinged to swing out. It could be locked on the inside. No one examining it from the outside could possibly think that it wasn't what it seemed to be. But I could open it, and go out and slip back inside again in a second whenever I wanted to.

"I had told North and his gang once that if they pulled any rough stuff with me, I'd come back and haunt them. So I went to one of those little shops on a back street in Dhambara where there was an old Chinese workman who could make anything under the sun. It took him two days to make a paper and wax head and face so like mine that if it hadn't represented a dead man, I couldn't have told myself from it in a mirror. Also he made these black robes and put them on a framework of some kind of composition.

"The framework was moulded in the shape of my shoulders. I put it on over my head and strapped it around my waist. I'm rather short, and that brought the head up to about where a man's head would ordinarily be. There were a couple of eye-holes in the front that I could look through. And the same Chinese gave me a bottle of the vile smelling stuff that I used to supply the ten-days-dead odor.

"I shipped my packing case under another name, got into it at night and half a dozen coolies trundled me on board the next morning. I'm no angel. My plan was first of all to scare the bloody daylights out of those thugs who had figured they'd killed me, then stick a knife into North and screw the others into handing over the rubies—they had parked them in the purser's safe. But—"

"But Mastrides stole the show, didn't he?" Paul interrupted. "He was on board with a wilder game than yours to play. You had just made your first appearance in the dining saloon and gone out on deck, when Mastrides started in by grabbing Connors in the confusion and doing some thing to him so that he laughed himself to death—after his face had been torn off."

Phillips swabbed the bloody froth from his lips.

"Mastrides was trying to do something that I've never heard of before. He was a lone wolf pirate. He was trying to capture the ship single-handed. He knew the rubies were on board and he intended to get them. It was out of the question for him to kill everyone on the ship. His idea was to kill half a dozen or so in such a horrible way that the others would get panic-stricken and skip out. Then he'd take his time about cracking the safe, and make it to land in a couple of days in one of the boats that were left behind.

"His way of killing was plenty terrible. Back among the native sorcerers in the bush, I've heard about a drug that will send a man into spasms of terrific laughter and then kill him in convulsions.

"Mastrides' game was to take a time when several of the passengers were out on deck at once. He would prowl around in the dark till he caught some one alone. ... He caught Waters and North in their cabins.... He would grab his victim with one arm around his neck to keep him from yelling while he jabbed the drug into him with a hypodermic needle. It took effect almost instantly. It looks as if he fell on his own needle when he went down just now, and got a dose of it himself. ...

"After he had jabbed his man and before he let him go, he ripped his face off with steel claws that he strapped on over his hands. That didn't make the victims die any faster, but it sure helped out the horror.

PHILLIPS choked, went on with an effort: "Of course my being around with the corpse effect worked in with him plenty. Everyone naturally took it for granted that the black-robed thing was doing the killing. That time when it looked as though I had almost got you and Mastrides rushes in to rescue you, it was just the other way. Mastrides was right on top of you, and I ran in to help you out. Mastrides realized that he was under suspicion and gave himself a rake with his claws for an alibi."

"So that was it," Paul put in as Phillips' voice faded out. "I'd suspected Mastrides myself till that happened. "So it was he that killed the purser after trying to torture him into opening the safe.

... And Mastrides put the dynamos out of commission and—"

"How he happened to have my regalia on—" Phillips broke in—"after Bronson, Waters and North had been killed, I decided to throw in with the passengers and see if I couldn't put this fiend out of business. I could get around and fight better without the robe, so I took it off and threw it in a corner. Mastrides must have —found it and put it on. It was just— what he wanted to make—his disguise perfect. ..."

Phillips' voice had been growing steadily weaker. Now it faded out in mumbling whispers. The man's lips moved twice more and then were still.

"He's gone," he said. "There's nothing we can do. ..."

Nancy slipped her hand into Paul's.

"Let's go back on deck," she whispered.

Paul led the girl back up the flights of narrow stairs and out under the stars. They stood motionless, drawing in deep breaths of the fresh night air.

"What are we going to do now?" Nancy said at last. "Have we got to stay here, alone on the ship?"

"Only till morning," Paul told her. "There's an extra life-boat over there on the davits. I'll fit a mast and sail in her, and we can make Bombay in twelve hours or so. We'll tell the authorities what happened. They'll send a gunboat to find the *Aden* and bring her in."

"Yes ..." said the girl.

"Yes," said Paul. "And after that, I'll take you to lunch, and then we'll see if we can get passage on a ship for home —together." Paul smiled down at her. "Will that be all right?"

Nancy crept closer inside the curve of his arm. "I can't think of anything nicer," she whispered.

THE END

THE BLACK CHAPEL

TERROR stimulates! If you don't believe that, think back a little. Think back to your childhood, when a thousand nameless fears came out of the night to menace you—all the more fearful because they were for the most part of unknown things, of misty horrors that reached out for you with clutching fingers, yet never quite seized you for their own.

Perhaps you never had a childhood experience such as Mark Twain somewhere relates, of awakening in a cabin where he had crept to spend the night, awakening to find the light from the newly-risen moon etching the outlines of a murdered corpse upon the floor; but you have nevertheless felt terror. Remember that night when, left alone in your home by your family, you awoke to the sound of footsteps pacing overhead—footsteps where no living person could possibly be? With half-opened eyes you stared about the darkened room; fear beaded sweat on your forehead and paralyzed you; you knew you must move, must leap from your bed and race from the house, away from this ghastly Thing—yet you could not summon courage to raise yourself an inch from the bed. And then the footsteps crossed the hallway, and step by slow step descended the stairs. . . .

Though before you had turned into a shrieking madman you became aware that there was really nothing to fear, that those footsteps actually were caused by your father or mother, who had entered the house quietly that they might not awaken you—still you had known in that awful moment the stimulus of fear. You had felt your heartbeats quicken, felt your nerve-centers draw together as if prepared to leap. And when it was over, you *liked what you had felt!*

Terror does stimulate, as any man of science will admit. And because it does, we all seek it, consciously or unconsciously, from the most staid of us to the most adventurous. It is the primitive courage in us—demanding a proof of our valor. It prods us continually to nerve-testing daring—The spirit of manhood and adventure.

And it was because these things are true that TERROR TALES was born. It was designed to bring to you the stimulus that in these prosaic days you want and need.

We have given you nerve-shocking fare, and there is more of it to come. In the next issue we have prepared for you such spine-tingling dishes as *The Flame People,* by Hugh B. Cave, *River of Pain,* by Wyatt Blassingame, and *Food For the Devil,* by George Edson. Every story, in fact, is guaranteed to send shivers of dread along your spine and chill the very blood in your veins!

Are you ready for it?

The New, *Different* Western Magazine—

LONGRIDERS OF THE WEST
MAVERICKS

Dedicated and devoted to those grimly colorful, oft-times tragic figures who rode the secret, twisting trails of wanted men—from the stark Missouri River Badlands to the sandy, sun-baked reaches of the Mexican Border country. Mavericks all, wanderers beyond the law, lacking home or brand or permanent friend, yet those men stood true to their individual courage code by which men judge other men the world over. Wanderers along those winding, little-known trails where the owl hoots often and the price of negligence is often a long rope and a short prayer, or an unmarked lonely grave in the malpai . . . .

MESQUITE MANHUNTERS
by Kent Thorn

A gripping, full-length 40,000 word novel of those five reckless and lovable longriders, Lance Clayton, Doc Grimson, Charlie Parr, Flint Maddox and the lethargic Lockjaw Johnson, who was "slow thinkin' but almighty fast with his guns." Men to ride the river with—men who are bound together by the high flame of their courage and loyalty—the unforgettable Bunch who have been called "The Five Musketeers of the Range."

—*Also*—

3 Memorable Action Novelettes by 3 Famous Western Writers

The Wild Bunch Rides On
by Walt Coburn

Another thrilling fictionized adventure of the Wild Bunch and its immortal leader —Butch Cassidy!

Sleeper Pays a Debt
by Max Brand

Sleeper, most quixotic of outlaws, squares accounts with a bounty-hunting posse.

Guns of the Owlhoot Pack
by Ray Nafziger

Billy the Kid rides again along the mesquite shadows.

All in the great October Issue—Watch for it at your newsstand!
On Sale August 24th!